The Line

K J SOUTHWORTH

ISBN: 1548001813
ISBN 13: 9781548001810
Library of Congress Control Number: 2017909358
CreateSpace Independent Publishing Platform
North Charleston, South Carolina

To Kelsey Miller, who has stuck with me through
this *ostensibly* maddening journey;
and,
to Christine Southworth, who reads everything
with unabashed enthusiasm.

ACKNOWLEDGEMENTS

Christine Southworth, Kelsey Miller, Karolina Kowalski, Maya Jarvis, Heather Smith, Ali Cook, Andrew Roth, Farrah Khan-Mousawi, Donna C. Swogger, Annaliese Plowright, Alan Reed, Andrej Culen, Jesse Melnyck, Julie-Ann Miller, Evan Miller, Ashley Grayson, Gerry Jarvis, Kassidy Duncan, Alex Rushmer, Teresa Roth, Michael Rains, Pat and Tom Hjorleifson, Sunny Go-Byers, Lisa Nadj, Daniel Ufuoma, Nate_L, Jacklyn Reynolds, Mac Southworth, John Langdon, Brookie and Owen Brown, the serving staff of the Royal Alexandra Hospital; and all the people who didn't know me, but took time to read this book.

1

The desert's mid-day heat plays mind-games—dead things start to move if you stare at them too long. For over an hour I've been watching the City, a monstrous tomb of sand and metal, and it's starting to writhe against the horizon.

Thick walls encircle this last hint of human civilization; millions of people call it home. They grumble and complain about their lives—the walls within that divide the City into sectors, preventing freedom of travel and communication—but no one publicly questions the system. With nowhere else to go, most of them are afraid of what's outside of its towering walls.

In all honesty, I don't blame them. Only the desperate or the crazy come out here.

I'm not sure which category I fall under. Maybe both. Not that it matters. For now, I just need to remember a few simple facts. I am a Criminal: twenty-eight years old, more bite than bark, and addicted to the rush.

That's why I'm out here. I've been testing out my newly acquired hover-board. Purring contentedly as it soaks in the sun's energy, the sturdy machine's scratched, dust-covered outer shock shell tells of a morning spent amongst the bright red rocks of the Desert Mountains. These are the most dangerous roads for riding. Not only do they twist and turn, making it nearly impossible to perform the simplest tricks, an eight hundred foot drop on one side and an unforgiving rock wall on the other make most mistakes fatal. Amateurs' charred remains are scraped off the rock wall regularly. Those riders who disappear...well, everybody knows they chose to fly instead of burn.

Flying isn't an option for me. I've had bad experiences with heights. Going quick in the crash suits me way better than the agonizing eternity it would take to fall. Whenever I come out here I strap a glider to my back, just in case. Other riders used to give me shit for it. A couple of times I took the glider off, just to shut them up, and they weren't wrong. The juice surges when your life is on the line, taking you higher than you ever thought possible. I rode that high for days afterwards. Today, however, I'm only partly here for the rush. I chose these roads because they're well out of Cop range. Unless they're doing a sweep, I should have complete privacy.

After two years in lock-up, you'd think that the last thing I'd want is to be alone. It's the exact opposite. I crave solitude. Seeing people I knew before...it's too disorienting. There were a few times I sought them out, watched them from a distance, even took a few steps forward. For a glorious moment, I would feel myself resurfacing. My heart lifted, my feet flew and that *place*—the Prison—faded from memory. It was like I had never been there.

But I faltered every time. The fear would invade again, roaring at me that I was a Hack, someone who had survived the Prison but would never find a way back. I was terrified of seeing the horror on their faces, of being a stranger to the people who were once my family.

Something within me has changed, forever, and I don't fit the way I once did.

I gave myself three months of hiding, three months of keeping to my building and my street, three months of living like a citizen. Did I say living? It was more like sleepwalking. Roll out of bed, piss, eat a nutrient bar, stare out my window, convince myself that I wouldn't be arrested for stepping outside, take a walk, avoid eye contact, go back home, piss again, get back in bed, try to sleep. Truth is, when you're broken, routine saves your life.

But then, one day—today, actually—three months was up. I wasn't dreading the moment I had to keep the bargain I'd made with myself. In fact, I'd almost forgotten I'd made it. It turns out that, little by little, the years in the Prison had just become another part of me. How I knew it would take me three months to filter that shit is beyond me. Just another happy coincidence, I suppose. When I woke up this morning I was consumed with the desire to get back on a hover-board. Stealing the ride came naturally. Suddenly, I was ready to feel alive, ready to ride the hardest roads, ready to burn with the rush.

I *feel* Jules approach rather than hear her. Ever since childhood I've had the ability to sense where people are before I see them. It's a rare gift, but the freaks in K Sector have proven it exists. Maury in Y Sector can tell you your future, step by step; pay him enough and he'll tell you how to avoid disaster. I'm an amateur in comparison, but my psychic talent has never failed me. Over the years, I've developed the ability to tell when others are lying. With a little concentration, I can even look through walls.

Without turning around, I close my eyes and watch Jules come up the road behind me. When she's a few metres away, she brings her board to a slow stop.

She's wearing her red leather suit with the black stripe down the side. The black helmet with the visor down hides her face, but I have no interest in seeing her expression. Her presence tells me more than her bright amber gaze ever could.

Being out here with a group of riders is one thing, being out here alone is quite another. No sane person rides these roads without a buddy. We're out of Cop range, miles from the safety checks. Normally, if someone's vehicle dies, they can get to the check and pay a Cop to take them back to the City. But there's no chance of making it to one from here. Night will fall well before you get close; darkness brings the Deadeyes, blind predators who will tear you to shreds in seconds.

It makes perfect sense for me to be here. I survived two years of torture, humiliation and horror—I'm a crazy, desperate Hack stripped of all ability to make rational decisions. Jules, however, is still the Criminal who's never had to earn her keep. Sure, I haven't seen her since before I went into lock-up, but there are some things that can't be hidden. It's in the way she looks down her nose at my ride, the scuff marks from years of use and the bulky, out-dated design. I bristle with anger as she shakes her head in disapproval.

Jules' board is painted the same colour as her suit, complete with a black stripe, and it gleams in the sun. Even the dust can't mar its gorgeous outer shock shell. It's a striking model that can't be found outside of F Sector. Also known as the Court, F Sector is the hardest sector to break into. Populated with the rich and useless, the Court is heavily guarded and only one crew has the ability to get in and out. Naturally, they charge exorbitant prices for the items that they *acquire*. Jules' mother, a highly respected and wealthy Criminal, must have paid a fortune for that board.

I already know Jules isn't crazy. That can mean only one thing—she's desperate. The question is, do I care?

Not even a little bit. I didn't care for her before I went into lock-up and I don't care for her now. There's no denying she's a flawless rider, which wins her my grudging respect, but she lives off her mother's reputation. She's never had to bleed for a job or fight for survival. That makes her soft in my eyes. And it's always the softies who manage to get other people killed.

As I get to my feet and face her I don't bother taking off my helmet. I'm sending a clear message that I'm indifferent to her presence. In fact, I'm pissed that she's interrupted my solitude.

The tall cliff behind us casts a long shadow over us. Standing in my worn and faded brown leather suit, I power down the sunglass feature in my visor so she can see my uncaring expression. She does the same and I see her startling beauty perfectly. Meeting my gaze with her familiar defiance, she hides her inadequacies behind flimsy bravado. Suddenly, she drops her eyes, points to her board and then to mine; she wants a road battle.

My psychic talent immediately starts to scream at me that something isn't right. There's something beyond her challenge, something counterfeit that I need to consider before accepting.

Maybe she's here to murder me.

I laugh outright at the thought. Of the few things that Jules is good at, killing isn't one of them. Besides, if someone wanted me dead they'd send someone that they knew could take me down, like Jace Locket.

Thinking about him makes me shiver with dread. Locket is an assassin, a different breed of Criminal than Jules and me. People who kill for credits are cold and inhuman, part of a world that I've only glanced at a couple of times. Locket is one of the best. He knows the City backwards and forwards, upside-down and right side up. No one can hide from him. And he doesn't discriminate. Old or young, male or female, sick or healthy…everyone is equal in his eyes.

The first time I saw him he killed a friend of mine.

Ivana and I were twelve at the time, orphans who lived on the streets together, and we'd just started working as Criminals. She was the closest thing I had to family. As we were celebrating our latest payday, Locket walked up and casually broke her neck. Death wasn't new to me back then but I was too shocked to move, too terrified to make a sound. I'll never forget the way his icy blue eyes swept over me as her lifeless body slumped to the ground. My heart stopped beating. I met his gaze, my horrified expression asking him if I was next. But he brushed by me without a word.

I found out later that Ivana had stolen from our last employer. She never could resist anything that glittered.

This all happened before Locket was well known. Years later, he became that whispered name that could turn most Criminals a ghastly shade of white. I don't claim to be in the same league as him, not even close, but before the Prison I was a warrior. No one would send a novice to kill me.

Despite my prejudice, Jules can be fierce when she wants to be. I wouldn't underestimate her in a fight. Still, there are those who can kill without conscience and there are those who carry it forever. It would be written all over her face if she were here to take me down.

Jules is still waiting for my answer. I've proven that I'm a Hack by not accepting right away. A challenge is more of a status check than anything else. If you decline, you're deferring to their superior skills, if you accept, you think you can give them a good run. Two years ago I would have jumped onto my board without hesitation. Those days are over. A road battle next to these cliffs is a recipe for death for me right now. I don't know why Jules has challenged me and I'm not sure I care about her motives.

Stepping onto my board, I consider turning my back on her and returning to the City. Then I remember that there isn't much waiting for me back there.

Fuck it.

Heart pounding with adrenaline, I fire on my engine. I point towards the twists and turns of the road ahead and Jules nods her agreement. As always, we carefully check each other's boards for loose wires and any other disasters waiting to happen. There's no glory in winning from a board malfunction. Besides, the smallest problem with either of our rides can send either of us careening to our dooms. In a worst-case scenario we take the other rider with us. There's definitely no glory if we both die.

When we confirm that the boards have no obvious defects, Jules points to the glider on my back. To my annoyance she makes a cutting motion across her throat. She wants me to disconnect what she's always called my *training wheels*. It's a fair demand. With this kind of safety strapped to my back I've got the advantage.

Grumbling under my breath, I grudgingly honour her request. To my surprise, she leans down and powers down her boards computerized auto-adjustments. She's going to be riding rough. There aren't many who can handle a road battle without leaning on their board's computer for support. I should be outraged at the condescending gesture: she's saying that I have no chance if she rides straight. But it really isn't my place to be angry. Even in the old days, she would have been absolutely right.

We both crouch over our boards, waiting for my ride to complete it's power up.

I'm always at my most tranquil before a battle begins. It's my chance to study the road ahead, consider my opponent, and devise a strategy. If we were in a race, the winner would be who gets to the finish line the quickest, but a battle is about forcing your opponent to admit defeat.

We'll be trying to outride each other.

There's no denying that Jules is the better boarder but that doesn't guarantee her the win. If I outperform her with a trick she isn't willing to top, she has to stop. If she loses control of her board, she has to stop. If she can't see, she definitely has to stop. I already know that I won't be out-riding Jules. She's too good. My only option is to lead her into a trap. All I have to do distract her long enough to ensnare her. Jules is great on the reflex but horrible at strategy. At a certain turn in the road, the sun will deliver my victory.

Before then, however, I have to consider the tricks that neither of us will be performing. With the twists and turns ahead there won't be any flips. Flips are disorienting enough on a straight stretch of road. Trying them out here would be suicide. There might be enough room for spins and slips; a rise and fall would be the easiest but even I have *some* pride.

My engine beeps—it's ready to play.

We both take off. I curse my faulty reflexes when I realize that Jules is a fraction of a moment ahead of me. She'll be choosing which part of the road she wants. Knowing how much I hate heights, she hugs the sheer rock wall. A moment later she fires on the hover and shoots into a rise, blowing dust into my visor. Guts churning, I quickly dodge out of the way, missing the worst of the rocky spray. But I've moved too close to the cliff's edge. The steep drop is yawning up at me, making my head spin with vertigo. Desperate to stay calm, I keep my eyes on Jules' board. As my panic slowly recedes I inwardly applaud her boldness.

At these speeds, performing a rise that isn't quickly followed by a fall will alert the level adjustment that the board is too high for the rider's safety. It would power down the board immediately. But Jules is riding rough. There's nothing to knock out so she can perform crazy moves like that. Her years of training and raw talent are keeping her board from going into an out of control spin, which is a death sentence no matter where you're riding. Awed yet nauseated by her flawless technique, I finally admit how horribly out-classed I really am.

When Jules finally comes back down she shrugs her shoulders in a gesture of boredom. It's time for my retaliation.

I don't have much to choose from. My primary concern is getting as far away from the cliff as possible. A slip will give me that comfort and keep my opponent busy. Pumping my break, I slip behind her board. The small engine shoots clear emissions straight up my leg and over my helmet. Gagging, I use my control pad on my jacket sleeve to tell my helmet to filter the air. When the order kicks in I concentrate on Jules' movements.

Travelling straight behind her I don't have to cut through the air. My ride is a lot smoother that way. Also, she has to crane her neck to get a good look at me. In a road battle, on a winding stretch, she has to have one eye on the road or risk crashing. If I get a chance to nudge her hard enough towards the drop or the wall she'll be forced to stop and I'll win. Unfortunately, while she's riding rough, I can't exploit her board's adjustments. I would have to grab her around the waist and heave her towards one side. She knows that too, but not being able to see me is already driving her insane.

She moves frantically to the right and left, up and down, trying to shake me. I stay on her tail. Moving with her I never give her the chance to get a good look at me. A slip into a shadow is a delicate move. My instincts have to be perfect. But with me so close to her tail it will be impossible for her to perform another trick. If I can keep on her she'll have to give me the win.

It isn't until she brakes, spins around twice, the tip of her board fractions of a centimetre from hitting the rock wall, and ends up behind me that I know how good she really is. One millisecond hesitation in her brake and I would have ploughed straight into her. We'd have been a heap of twisted metal and burning flesh. There's no way I can top that.

The moment I know that I'm beat a familiar composure enters my mind. It's the stillness that I found in the Prison, a state of mind that made two years of torment go by in the blink of an eye. It made the last three months of recovery bearable. When I feel like this, all my decisions are made with absolute clarity. The cliff's edge and the rock wall fade away. In between heartbeats, I choose my path.

I push my board into a rise, jerk the board over my head, and turn off the engine. The flip is perfectly timed. As I sail over Jules' head, I grab her shoulders to help direct my descent. I want to land beside her. Twisting my body, I place myself in between her and the rock wall then turn my engine back on at exactly the right moment. I fall to one knee when I land, lowering my center of gravity to keep my balance. The rock wall is rushing by my face but I barely notice how close it is.

I just completed a half-twist flip on the most dangerous road! My mind's stillness washes away as I yell out in triumph. There's no way Jules can top that. Still kneeling on my ride, I perform a congratulatory 360. The edge of my board pushes her to the side. Not enough to put her over, just enough to remind her of the steep drop.

Catching her balance, Jules cocks her head to one side. She has to admit defeat.

Heart pounding, head reeling from the rush, I wait for her to glide to a stop. But Jules is still watching me, trying to figure out how I completed that trick. Even I'm shaking my head in disbelief at my own daring and stupidity. I should have crashed into the wall or sailed over the edge, but I survived.

Jules suddenly accelerates. Confused, I watch as she looks back at me, gauging the distance between our boards, the cliff's edge and the rock wall. My elation crumbles to dust when I realize she's going to retaliate. She's waiting for a part of the road that doesn't twist so much, a place where she'll feel safe enough to perform whatever stunt is buzzing through her head.

Sweet sky! She's going to kill herself to win.

When did she get this reckless? I should turn off my board and end the battle...but I really deserve this victory. Luckily for her, my original plan is about to come to fruition. The next tight curve will take us into a near 180. Easing into it, I offer her a mock salute as I turn on my helmet's sunglass feature.

The harsh morning sun shines directly into her eyes. Blinded, she jerks to the left. The wrenching movement sends her dangerously close to the cliff's edge. Terrified she's going to go over, I try to grab her as I race by. My hands slip past her and I lose my balance. Immediately sensing my uncertain footing, my board decelerates. Praying that Jules is still on the road, I bring it to a stop and quickly turn around.

Twenty feet back, the front of her board hanging over the edge, she's tearing off her helmet and swearing. Her long brown hair falls down her back, gold highlights glittering in the morning sun; her amber eyes sparkle with excitement.

"Daryl, you fucker!"

Sighing in relief, I put one foot back on solid ground. My synapses are buzzing from the rush, making it difficult to focus, but she seems to have enjoyed her brush with death. I take off my helmet to get a better look at her. "Are you all right?"

"It was a road battle!" Jules laughs at my concern, feigning casualness as she coasts up to me. "I should have remembered how the sun works with that curve. Besides, I'm too experienced to fly."

"You're sure? It would have been a long drop."

"Give over. I'm okay." She can't quite meet my gaze so she pretends to check her board for scratches. "Remember what you always used to say? 'Live near death or walk dead in life'. According to you, there's no in between."

"I used to say a lot of things." I'm still worried about her so I don't bother telling her I was quoting a song that I'd heard in H Sector.

"Then what are you doing next to the cliffs?" Her challenge echoes with nervous energy. "What was with that flip? You aren't here for the view."

My concern is quickly replaced with irritation. Leave it to Jules to use insight to deflect from her own fear. It's time to change the subject. "Where'd you get the board?"

"The Court," she replies. Crossing her arms triumphantly over her chest she waits for my astonished reaction. "It's the newest model. After the crew's last heist Wulff painted it for me."

My stomach flips when I hear that name.

Wulff is a member of Heathcliff Jackson's crew, the only people what have a line to the Court. Before I went into lock-up I was part of that operation. Jules just talked about him as though they were working together and it suddenly occurs to me that I've been replaced.

Shocked, I openly stare at Jules. She must have finally proven herself. Jack wouldn't recruit anyone that he didn't trust to get the job done.

Catching my expression, Jules' bravado falters. "Shit. I'm such an idiot."

"That's highly unlikely if Jack is working with you." Trying to hide my displeasure, I turn my gaze towards the horizon. I knew they'd have to replace me but I never thought that Sabine Jules would be on their list. Considering how I feel about her, I'm somewhat insulted. "Congrats. They're a great team."

"The best," Jules agrees.

I could ask how Jack's crew is doing, but the question sticks in my craw. That life is over; I shouldn't prolong the death throws. Opening a small pack on my hip, I pull out a nutrient bar and offer my replacement a bite.

"Are you kidding?" She takes a small block of chocolate from a cooling bag in her back sack.

Mouth watering, I stare at the chocolate's dark splendour. Being part of the only crew with a line to the Court has more than just financial advantages. It's the only place you can find chocolate. The crew makes half of its credit from stealing the dark, creamy candy.

Jules breaks off a piece and throws it to me. I catch it reverently. Biting into the bittersweet paradise, I savour the hypnotizing flavour. It melts in my mouth, coating my tongue and making my taste-buds hum. In the Prison, if you were fed at all, everything tasted like paste. Nutrient bars aren't much of a step up. I don't want to swallow but my reflexes take over; the rich decadence slides down my throat.

I never knew the meaning of the word satisfaction until this moment.

Jules is studying me compassionately. She has no idea how uncomfortable her sympathy is making me, but she's never been one to hide how she feels. Trying to ignore her, I sit down on my board. She follows my lead and we silently sweat away in the hot desert sun.

It's plain as day that my appearance is scaring the shit out of Jules. The Prison has a reputation. Nobody comes back unscathed, nobody gets out whole, no Criminal gets back in the game. I'm not physically scarred, like some Hack's, but anyone can see that I'm half-dead.

"You're not looking good, Daryl," Jules says. Sipping water from her canteen she offers me a swig..

I wave it off, gesturing to my own. "Surprised to see me on the roads?" I ask, wiping sweat off my face.

"I'm surprised to see you anywhere," she admits. Something like shame passes over her face but she quickly covers it with a half-hearted smile. Knowing full well that I stole my ride from an unsuspecting citizen, she shoots my board a significant look. Stealing a board isn't considered real action, but its more than half-deads should be able to do. "You just got out."

"I'm just a Hack taking a ride."

"That's not what people are saying." She's suddenly agitated, chewing her hair and fidgeting with her canteen. "You need to know that."

Made wary by her sudden change in demeanour, I give her my full attention. "What does it matter what people are saying?"

"It matters what Madman thinks," Jules replies, suddenly jumping to her feet and moving away from me. "He's got people looking for you…and he's offering big rewards."

Madman. That's a name I wasn't expecting to hear. A familiar voice of dread whispers in the back of my head.

Madman isn't one person. He's an organization, a business if you will. Generations before I was born the first Madman, Tobias Hansen, died and left a giant vacuum in the Criminal power system. Those who worked for him had to make a new niche for themselves. Some didn't like the idea of starting from scratch and decided to keep the idea of Madman alive. It took some doing but they found a new leader, one who was known by Hansen's associates, and he took over the business.

It's been like that ever since. One leader dies and the four higher-ups, the Generals, choose a new one. Gordon Harcourt assumed the throne about six years ago. Before I went into lock-up his administration had grown to include nearly a third of the Criminals in the City. They give up their freedom to live under Madman's protection. It's probably the most comfortable cage the Criminal world has to offer.

I can't imagine what Madman wants with me and I don't want to know. I used to be an *independent*, talent for hire. Independents steer clear of organizations. We value our freedom above everything else. I've never had anything to do with Madman and I've never wanted anything to do with him. But if he's hungry enough to offer payment to bring me in, it won't be long before someone tries to take me down.

Jules sink into an offensive stance. Unconcerned, I study her anxious yet determined expression. She's going to try and bring me in. Like I said, you're either crazy or desperate when you come out here alone. It looks like I was wrong about her—she's both.

"Big rewards," I echo, amused. I don't bother getting up. "One wrong step, softy, and I'll kill you."

My nonchalance has the desired effect. Uncertainty plays across her face as she reconsiders my ability to defend myself. The problem with desperate people, however, is that they'll rush into suicidal battles.

It's *hope* that will make her do it. Hope that Luck will be on her side, hope that she'll catch me off guard, hope that the two years in lock-up have weakened my fighting skills.

Staring at each other across the thick silence, we wait for someone to make the first move—this only ends with one of us dead.

A tour bus carrying citizens comes around the curve. Our little moment has ended...for now. Gesturing angrily and honking his horn, the driver yells at us through the bus' thick glass. We're right in the middle of the narrow road and he won't be able to continue unless we move. As Jules slowly relaxes, I get to my feet. Our little drama can wait.

Just as we get out boards out of the way, a silent helicopter turns its siren on above us. A fucking sweep.

<Everyone off the bus,> a nasal voice orders over an intercom.

Jules growls angrily when she realizes the Cops are here. "Stupid tourists on their way to the Springs. Desert-humpers always trail them."

I grunt my agreement and suddenly Jules and I are companions. Even Criminals who despise each other feel a sense of camaraderie when a Cop is around. We'll finish our *discussion* later.

Bleary-eyed people in casual civilian clothes trickle off the bus. They're black fingernails identify them as C Sector citizens—the Moles. They work in the underbellies of the system, keeping the sewage running and the water clean. A plague ran rampant a decade ago, killing a quarter of their population, so they have to work all hours. Most have the pasty-faced, bewildered look of people who haven't seen the sun for days, maybe weeks. I know how that feels.

<Line up against the wall>, the nasal voice commands.

Jules and I put our backs against the cliff wall and wait for the desert-humpers to jump out of the carrier. As expected, black ropes are thrown out of the copter onto the dusty road. Four Cops repel down dramatically, but Jules and I aren't impressed. Displays like this are for the citizens. When they land they start herding the Moles around, pushing them roughly against the rock wall. Jules folds her hand into a fist.

Smiling, I consider letting her hang herself, but I wouldn't respect myself if I did. "Don't give them an excuse."

"What...me?" She bats her long eyelashes innocently. "Are you suggesting that I have a history of violence?"

The Cops wear their standard black body armour and black helmets with mirrored visors. The black is more for effect than practicality. It's supposed to inspire fear and respect. To most people they all look the same; it takes a trained eye to see the differences in their uniforms.

Glancing over at one, I notice that this Cop, taller than the others, has a sleeker look. His armour and helmet are higher quality; his equipment is made for hunting in the City, not the burn of the Desert; his stance betrays a restless need for the chase. There's no way this Cop makes a living as a desert-humper, exploiting tourists out here in the sand and heat.

My limbs go numb with terror. I'm staring at a full-fledged bounty hunter.

He's a rare sight out here in the Desert and the last thing I wanted to come up against. Incredible fighters, equipped for taking down the hardest Criminals, bounty hunters are eminent Cops.

The last time I saw one he was throwing me into the Prison.

One of the desert-humpers is studying Jules and me: we obviously didn't come off the tour bus. Hailing the other Cops, she points us out to her comrades. Jules begins her best 'daddy-doesn't-know-I-took-the-board-out' act. I marvel at her acting talents as she rolls her eyes and sighs. The spoiled brat shtick has gotten her out of more than one scrape in the past. I, however, am a terrible actor. Nervously running a hand over my face, I do my best not to stare at the hunter.

The Cops are arguing amongst themselves. None of them want trouble with any Court citizens, which is exactly what Jules looks like in her red suit. But the hunter's presence is making them bold. Finally, two of the desert-humpers walk to the other side of the line.

"They probably think we're playing hooky from a Court training session. You're lucky you look so young."

Jules is teasing me, but I'm too anxious to respond. My silence gives her reason to study my worried expression. She shoots me a look of concern.

<750 credits,> a bored voice says through a helmet mike.

Tourists make easy targets so they're asking for a toll. It's typical of desert-humpers to harass citizens who are probably on their first vacation in years. Standard practice but hard on the credit.

"Bloody Cops always manage to get a part of my pay," Jules grumbles, pulling out her balance. "I should make them panic and tell them my father is a judge."

The fact that they're looking for credits helps me relax. Whether or not they think we're Court citizens they'll still want their payment, which is good. I can authorize the credit transfer and get out of here.

Reaching into my leg pack for my credit balance, I search for the familiar metal disk, but somehow it eludes me. The pouch is small; I shouldn't have trouble finding the balance. Doing my best not to panic, I start pulling everything out. Once it's empty, I realize with mounting anxiety that my credit balance in missing. I could turn all my other packs inside out, but my psychic talent is letting me know that it isn't with me.

For a moment, I wonder if Jules stole it. It would be an easy way to get rid of me. Cops will throw you in for anything, even if they think you're from the Court. Necessity makes them cutthroats and mercenaries. They get paid for every offender they deliver to the Prison; the higher the charge against the offender the higher the pay. Not having my credit balance isn't a huge crime, but it's enough. It's unlikely, however, that Jules would pull something dirty. In my haste to get out here, I probably left the bloody thing next to my bed.

Warily watching the hunter pacing back and forth, I decide that I only have one option.

"I'm not going back to the Prison," I whisper to Jules.

She cocks her head to one side. "Daryl, what's going on?"

"I can't find my credit balance."

"They think we're from the Court," she says. "They'll let you go."

"Wishful thinking," I reply. Hoping not to draw any attention, I casually turn my glider back on. It will take a few moments to confirm it's operational, but I don't know if I can wait for the reassuring beep. "You know how it works."

"You can't run from a toll in the desert." Jules is suddenly alert. "Besides, they're desert-humpers. They're not going to have anything that can bind you for long."

"There's a bounty hunter."

"Where...?" Jules looks them all over but she can't tell the difference. Shaking her head violently, she puts a hand on my arm. "If you're right we'll figure it out."

"The hunter is on the far right, hanging back a little...watch him when I break."

"Break...? Daryl, you can't do this!"

I fix her with a desperate, stony glare. There's no way someone who's never been in lock-up can understand. That place guts you, turns you inside out, and scrapes out the carcass. I'd rather fall to my death than go back.

I glance down the line of Mole tourists. One desert-humper is making sure no one makes a false move while the other two place credit balances in transfer machines. The small, black boxes make annoying blipping noises and a green light flashes to signal that the credits have gone through. Ten more people until they reach me. The bounty hunter watches the process, obviously bored out of his mind.

It's now or never.

I'm terrified but I have to run. If I don't, I'm done for. Staring hard at the red dust on my boots, that familiar stillness creeps through my mind and body again. I feel distant, like I'm made of stone instead of flesh. Detached, dull, remote...

Staring intently at the vast expanse of the Desert, I put on my helmet and race for the cliff's edge.

The Cops shout at me to stop. They weren't ready for a chase. A part of my mind tells me that the bounty hunter is on my tail, breathing down my neck, but my psychic talent tells me he was just as surprised as the rest of the Cops. He isn't anywhere near me. In a few seconds, I reach the edge of the cliff.

There's no time to hesitate. I launch myself over the side.

Free-falling down the side of an eight hundred foot cliff, guts churning and eyes watering, I close my eyes and listen to the voice that isn't scared of anything.

No panicking, it tells me. *Just wait for the beep and press the button on your control pad. It's there on your right forearm, stitched into your suit, remember? You're a southpaw, so they had to make this suit up special. You ordered it and then you stole it. What were you, eighteen? Had this suit that long, have you? It's time for a new one.*

Following its instructions, I wait for the beep. My helmet is tuned in to my gear, so I'll be able to hear it despite the overwhelming sound of the air rushing past my body. The ground still seems like it's eons away, but I can't help but think of bones breaking and the crunch of impact. It feels like days since I jumped. Sweet sky! Where is the beep?

Fuck it!

I reach over to the control pad and press the button. The familiar hiss announces that the glider is deploying quickly and without complaint. A small engine bursts to life. I keep my eyes closed until I feel the pull of the wind under the glider's silk wings. Taking deep breaths, sinking deeper into the stillness, I refuse to let my fear take control. I'm okay...I'm all right...I'm safe. All I can do now is hope that the bounty hunter isn't on my tail.

Once I am gliding through the air, I risk looking back at the cliffs. The copter continues to hover over the tourists; no one is giving chase. Desert-humpers are never well organized. They'll argue amongst themselves for hours before they make a decision. Sighing in relief, careful not to look down, I turn the glider towards my destination.

The City is sprawled out over the horizon. The small engine strapped to my back isn't made for long trips, but it should get me close enough to walk back. Flying low enough so that my terror doesn't take over, I plot my route on autopilot. The low-grade guidance system gurgles angrily before accepting my instructions. I glide silently along, eager to get back to my bed and fall asleep for a year.

2

I land about a quarter mile away from the City wall. The small glider folds neatly back into its pack. Heart still racing from my escape, I have to take deep breaths to stop my body from shaking. The ground doesn't feel like it's under my feet. A couple of times I almost collapse, but I hold on to myself.

It isn't much further. I should be back in bed before nightfall. For the next few weeks I'll lay low, rest up until I'm ready to get back out here. No sense in rushing.

The sun is ready to bake me where I stand. Using my control-pad, I set the bio-conditions in my suit. The controls complain and the suit starts to whine. A high-pitched squeal, like air escaping a tiny hole, invades my ears. Grimacing in pain, I open the pad and take a look at its guts: a wire is hanging loosely from its plug. I set it straight, jam the pad shut and press the buttons again. The air in the suit kicks in and I sigh in relief.

By now the Cops will have my image buzzing over every frequency. My original plan to ride back in through a legitimate doorway, all of which are monitored by Cops, will definitely get me bound and gagged.

Lucky for me, there are more illegal doorways than there are legal ones. Without my balance, however, I can't pay to get back in. Most Criminals will ask for a favour if you're low on credits, but no one will deal with me.

I'm a Hack. There's no way for me to deliver. As far as I know, my old friend Radcliff is the only one who will let me in without payment. I don't want to see him, but Luck has taken away every other option. It almost feels like I was funnelled here.

Radcliff's doorway is located near an unusual rock formation, skinny stones jutting out of the dust like gnarled fingers. They're easy to spot but they're also a popular place for patrols to stop for a rest. Taking out a small pair of binoculars, I nervously check for desert-humpers. When I don't see anything I check again, and then once more—I'm not taking any chances.

Racing towards the wall, I'm not fooled by it's seemingly smooth, grey surface. Somewhere around here is Radcliff's doorway. It wouldn't be much good if it was easy to find. Rocks about the size of my fist lie nearby. Squatting down, I pick the nearest one up. No response. I continue my search until one makes a sound. There's a small microphone embedded in the rock.

Putting it next to my mouth, I hope that Radcliff in a generous mood. "You wouldn't let an old friend fry out here, would you?"

A half a moment later, a human-sized circle slides back and to the side. Radcliff Ivan, pasty faced from lack of sun, puts up a hand to block his eyes against the harsh light. He spent six months in the Prison. Three years later and he still looks just as wrecked as the day he got out. Like all Hacks he never went back into action and never will.

If I could have gotten him out of that place I would have, but there's no rescuing anyone from the Prison. You don't come out until it spits you out. I guess that's pretty much how I feel—like somebody's been chewing on me for the last two years.

It didn't occur to me until now how much I don't want to be here. Just looking into his faded gaze scares me to death.

Those are my eyes; that half-dead stare is seeping through the cracks of my shaky control. But I could have sworn, on the Desert Roads, in that glorious moment of triumph, that I'd finally outrun my own reflection. There was no past there—no pain or fear or trauma. There was no Prison.

Why can't I hold onto that?

Staring at me with an expression of open concern, Radcliff gapes at my sudden reappearance on the Criminal grid. He raises his hand in greeting while his tired half-smile brightens his haggard features. A broken gaze, aglow with friendship, welcomes me home.

"It's good to see you," he says, blinking hard in the sun. It sounds like he hasn't used his voice in weeks. He gently takes in my worn-out appearance. "You look a little like I feel." Stepping aside, he grants me access to his small hideout. "I thought I recognized your suit on the frequency but I didn't believe it was you until now. The Cops have got pictures of you jumping off a cliff and sailing towards the City. They'll all be looking for you."

That was the last thing I needed to hear. As far as I'm concerned my little excursion was a terrible mistake.

Exhausted and miserable, I step into his hideout and study the small, square room. Rocks of all different shapes, colours and sizes fill every available nook except for the bed. Ever since the Prison, Radcliff has collected them. They're his only love now.

"Too bad you had to run from the desert-humpers," he says, following me like a puppy. The doorway slides closed, locking us into his small space. "When you're fresh out of lock-up it's hard to be face to face with the Cops. Three months was probably too early." Biting his already destroyed nails, he sucks at the bleeding soars on the tips of his fingers. "You should have waited before going out there again, right? I didn't go anywhere for six months. You guys couldn't drag me out or I'd start screaming. I don't really remember screaming, but you told me that's what I'd do, so that must have been what I was doing. Friends don't make shit like that up."

My silence is getting him all worked up. He blinks rapidly and huffs a few times. Still chewing on the tips of his fingers, he spits a large chunk of his own flesh onto the ground. I don't want to watch but I'm too sickened to turn away. It's too close—what he's saying, what he's doing—I can feel it trembling under my skin. My arms are covered with fine scars, the only evidence I have of episodes that I don't remember. But I know when they're coming. Watching Radcliff is triggering one.

I shoot him a hostile glare that stops him in his tracks. In my mind, I'm screaming at him to shut up and fuck off. If I didn't know any better, I'd say he could hear every word. But Radcliff has no psychic talent. Still, the light in his eyes dies and his chest caves in. Head down, empty gaze lowered and shoulders hunched, he does his best to disappear from the room. I've seen him do this countless times, but this is the first time that it's been because of me. Ashamed of my weakness, I have to turn away.

Radcliff doesn't owe me anything, but he let me in out of loyalty and friendship. Something tells me it's time to rethink my repayment strategy.

"I've got something for you," I say, too loudly. Reaching into my small ankle pack, I withdraw a blue, glittering rock. I was going to keep it for myself, but ass-holes shouldn't give themselves gifts. "I found it before I started my ride."

Radcliff's eyes light up again. Without raising his head, he carefully reaches out and I place it in his palm. He mumbles a short thank you but doesn't risk any other movement.

"It's all right, Radcliff. You can go."

I'm trying to be gentle, but there's still a worn edge in my voice. Radcliff turns away before daring to look at the small gift. Delicately, lovingly, he blows faint traces of dust off of the stone's surface. Mumbling to himself, he goes over to a desk and produces a small polishing kit out of a drawer. He lays down a soft cloth and places the rock in its centre.

Still hating myself for hurting him, I unzip a long pocket down the front of my suit and remove my citizen clothes. Shaking, I pull on my pants and shirt. I was fooling myself when I thought I could handle going outside of my routine. I know that now. It's time to get out of here.

I fold my suit into a neat pile then press a button on its control pad. The suit compresses, turning into a leather bag. Shoving in my helmet and the five packs I was carrying, I slide into my light jacket and rush for the door.

"Daryl," Radcliff calls quietly, "things have changed out there. Be careful."

He's still too scared to look me in the eyes. That's probably a good thing: I'm too fragile to be gentle. I mumble a short *thank you* before making a hasty retreat.

3

Just outside Radcliff's hideout, a dimly lit hall leads to a ladder that climbs to a hatch. I already know what's waiting for me on the other side. Radcliff lives under the streets of B Sector, where the Fix-its live. They keep technology running and have unlimited access to most sectors. They can't get into A and F, though. Those sectors have special Fix-its, the gifted ones, who disappear inside and are never heard from again.

I hesitate before opening the hatch. B is chaotic, the easiest place to disappear if you need to hide, but the hatch doesn't lead straight onto the streets. It leads into a restaurant...a popular little diner named Heidi's. Before lock-up, it was my favourite haunt. There are too many people on the other side of the hatch who know me. But if Luck is on my side I might be able to sneak past them.

Taking a deep breath, I open the hatch and hop out into a dark utility closet.

At first, the noxious cleaners only affect my eyes. Annoyed, I rub them to neutralize the burning, but then I make the mistake of breathing. The chemicals ruthlessly enter my lungs. I gasp at the scorching sensation. Hacking uncontrollably, I collapse against the wall, knocking a mop and broom over. The ruckus makes me cringe. This whole stealth strategy isn't going according to plan.

The utility closet's door swings open.

"Radcliff...?"

My old friend, Lily, squints into the darkness. On reflex I swallow my coughs, press my back against the far wall, and freeze. It's a stupid reaction. There's no hiding in this small space.

She peers at me curiously. Stunned by her sudden appearance, I voraciously study her familiar face, her soft eyes and long hair. A terrible yearning reaches into my heart and I start to tremble. Yanking pitilessly at my insides, it wails mournfully—*you're safe with her, you can rest now.*

But I can't rest. Safety is an illusion, a worthless fable fed to the blinkered masses. Although my heart is begging me to step forward, to call her name and collapse into her arms, I cower miserably behind a bucket full of poisonous chemicals.

Searching my frightened gaze, Lily struggles to recognize me. She boldly steps forward, reaches out and brushes my sweat-matted hair away from my face. I jerk when her soft hand gently caresses my forehead. Sweet, aching warmth travels down my spine, making it easier to breathe. It's been so long since I've been touched; but I can't let myself feel it.

Mercilessly pulling myself together, I push away from the wall and stand at my full height. Masked in stony apathy, I finally meet her curious gaze.

"Oh, my Sweet Sky..." she whispers. A look of horror passes over her face. It's the first time she's seen me in over two years and it's obvious that the life has been sucked out of me. "Daryl!"

I try to answer, but my lungs have held the chemicals for too long. Hacking coughs swallow my words.

I wish I could quietly slip out the back way, but there's no chance of that now that Lily has seen me. She isn't a Criminal, she doesn't fully understand how our world works. Even with the initial horror, her untameable enthusiasm is building under the surface. Eyes, at first fearful, are now filled with elation; lips, once agape with astonishment, are now turned up in a fierce grin. Any second now, her boundless energy will burst forth, swooping us both off of our feet and careening us towards the unknown. A spark of excitement ignites in my chest.

Suddenly energized, I brace myself for impact.

"Lenny!" Grabbing my shoulders Lily shoves me into the kitchen. "Sweet Sky, Lenny! Look what I dug out of the utility closet!"

Her younger brother, Lenny, the restaurant's cook, looks up from the carrots he's chopping. When he sees me, the knife drops out of his hands.

"Can't you put it back?" His joke is accompanied with a lop-sided grin. Jumping towards me, he engulfs me in a giant bear hug. "It's a damn miracle!"

Squealing happily, Lily launches herself into the hug and holds us both in her arms. With her at my back and Lenny at my front, I am completely enveloped. With a gargantuan effort, I suck back my excitement and happiness, my sorrow and relief, until I am neatly tucked behind the face of the nonchalant. Carefully holding my emotions in check, I let them have their happy reunion.

When Lenny finally lets me go tears of joy stream down his face. He searches my half-dead gaze, his own horror flickering then dying quickly.

"Man-oh-man, Daryl." He jumps into action. "You need a real meal. Gotta keep your strength up. No nutrient bars for my pal!"

On the stove a giant pot is nearly boiling over. Pulling out a bowl, he sticks a huge ladle into the rolling stew. Lenny is the best chef around. It's a wonder he doesn't put in for a transfer to a better sector.

My stomach growls as he slops the food into the bowl. Lily grabs me a spoon and pushes me towards a small worktable at one side of the kitchen. Lucky me! Chocolate and Lenny's famous beef stew all in one day. Lenny places the bowl in front of me. Thankful for real food, I dig in.

"Hyde is going to die when he sees you!" Lily cries, rushing out of the kitchen.

I put a hand out to stop her, but she's already gone. Hyde and I were only passing friends before I went into lock-up. He's what's known as a roller; he gets contraband past sector wall security for the right price. As far as I know he doesn't work for Madman, but that doesn't mean he won't want the reward. Credits are credits for a Criminal.

A tall and lanky, yellow-haired man walks into the kitchen. Lily is pushing on his back to make him move faster, but Hyde still moves like he has lead weights sewn into his clothes.

I anxiously meet his cool gaze, wondering if he's looking to make a quick fortune. When he offers me an idle, predatory smile, all my questions are answered.

Fear quickly sharpens my senses. Hyde sits down next to me and carefully brushes a piece of lint off of his black suit. It looks like new material…swanky. Most people wear recycled clothes. The Collectors in Q Sector sell discarded fabrics to anyone willing to sew them into a wearable anything. Some of us can afford tailors; most of us learn how to sew at a young age.

"There are more customers coming in. We have to get back to work!" Lily calls to us as she rushes back through the door: "I'll be right back."

"Duty calls!" Lenny whistles happily as he returns to his orders.

The kitchen is suddenly way too hot. I am slowly being dragged into something that is way beyond my psychological faculties. Nervously massaging my hands, I let my head fall back and crack my neck. My nerves are screaming at me to run.

Hyde casually leans back in his chair. We both know I could make a break for it, try to lose him in the streets, but it's a foolish impulse. My instincts are telling me that Hyde would take me down in an instant. The smart thing to do is to offer my surrender and ask for a cut of the reward. In fact, it's my only choice.

Gathering my courage I finally acknowledge that Madman is about to get what he wants. I greet the roller with a slight nod of my head. "Hyde."

"The returning champion." He lets out a long, deep yawn. "I'm guessing you know that Madman is looking for you."

"I may have heard something about it." I rest my elbows on the table and take a deep, steadying breath. "I bet you can tell me what he wants."

"He's looking for you to make good on a favour."

"Favour…?" I snort indignantly. "I've never done business with Harcourt."

"I'm sure Harcourt's corpse would confirm that if anyone knew where it was."

My heart skips a beat. Harcourt is dead… there's a new Madman. *Dare I ask…?*

"Lyons Emmett," Hyde obliges. That name makes me jump. My nervous expression is all the confirmation he needs. "I wasn't sure if I was hearing right. People thought you were clean with everybody. I guess we all have our pasts. If his claim is legit, you may as well face the monster."

Squeezing my eyes shut, I force my fear deep inside and prepare for battle. Fuck…of all the times for this to bite me in the ass.

"Fifty-fifty," Hyde says, surprising me with his generosity. "Lily would kill me if I took more, and I don't like upsetting her. She told me about what you did for her and Lenny, getting them in touch with that T Sector Baron, Beatrice-what's-her-name…?"

He's waiting for me to fill in the blank, but I don't have anything to say. T Sector is the Homestead. Every morsel of food in the City is grown there. A dozen powerful families run it and one of the matriarchs, Anna Beatrice, is someone I've known since childhood.

Fixing Hyde with an inquisitive stare, I finally reply. "Putting them in touch with her was easier than spitting. Are they still insisting on acting like I gave up a kidney?"

"It may have been easy for you, but it was a miracle to them."

Motioning towards the restaurant's back entrance, he waits for me to move first. I shove my bag under the small table and call to Lenny, letting him know I'll be back for it. I'm almost outside before I hear Lily's shriek of protest.

"Where are you two sneaking off to?"

"Braggs Bar," Hyde answers. "Business."

"You're not going anywhere without me," she cries, putting down her tray and pulling on her jacket. "Jane just got here and said she'd cover for me."

"Suit yourself." Hyde shrugs and holds the door open for her.

Lily pins me with a suspicious look, waiting for me to argue, but I put my hands up in a gesture of surrender. She can take care of herself. Besides, it's not her that I fear for.

4

B Sector was my home. I wasn't born here, but I lived as an orphan on these streets. It was here that I got my first Criminal job, where I learned how to survive and prosper, where I lived with Heathcliff Jackson's crew. Seeing it all again, so familiar yet so foreign, I have no choice but to retreat within. I'm walking in foggy memories with a distant soul.

Lily points out everything that's changed, her excitement building with every corner that we turn. This family moved, that guy disappeared, that woman was ordered to procreate. I listen to her passionate descriptions, smiling despite how disconnected I feel. Lily is an anomaly in the City—an adult who's experienced first hand the bleakness of this place yet refuses to stop seeing the bright side. If nothing else, I'm happy she hasn't lost that. There are times I rely on it to get through.

"Alex smashed it two nights ago," Lily says, pointing at a broken window. "Enid had to ask Hyde to help calm him down."

"Alex is an angry drunk," Hyde replies.

"Enid hasn't left that jack-ass yet?" I'm trying to be engaging, but I don't really believe that I'm here. "What's she waiting for?"

I feel it before it happens. There's always a slight pressure at the back of my skull before anything violent begins. It's never enough time to prevent anything—just a light warning to prepare myself for a fight. When the wall to my left explodes, I've already retreated into that silent world. It's a reflex now. I don't have control over it. Violence has always had this strange, numbing effect on me. Something beyond me takes over, giving me a chance to catch my breath before the real battle begins.

Through a dusty haze, I register Lily's scream as Hyde protectively steps in front of her. Chunks of brick and drywall fall all over us, but I don't move. I'm frozen in my eerie calmness. People are scrambling around an exposed room. A short man, desperately shoving small boxes into a bag, tries to escape through the damaged wall. Three Cops pounce before he even reaches the hole. From what I can see of their uniforms, two of them are bounty hunters. One hunter takes the screaming man by the hair while the other two disappear into the building. The remaining Cop places a small metal box, a motion inhibitor, on the side of his captive's head. The small man stops struggling: sound waves are rushing through his head at an intense frequency. His brain can't send information to his major muscle groups.

Cocking my head to the side, I watch indifferently as spit runs down the hapless captive's chin.

The bounty hunter takes out a small remote control and presses a few buttons. A hover bike blasts off a nearby roof and sets down next to them. Carefully, the Cop heaves his prize onto its backseat and straps him down with energy cords. When he's sure the little man is secure, the Cop takes off, leaving the other two to root out what they can.

Normally, I would walk away before the Cops notice me, but my psychic talents senses a motion detector. Bounty hunters always leave them outside before they move into a building. Technically, being so close to a raid is illegal. Sure, we didn't know about it, but that doesn't matter to Cops. The motion detector will spray us with a pheromone that they'll be able to trace from anywhere in the City. It only neutralizes if you wash with an expensive soap that most people can't afford. We may very well be fucked.

I spot the motion detector sitting on the wall just outside the hole. It will spray out thirty meters, coating us all in a seemingly odourless mist.

"Don't move," I whisper to Hyde. Motioning towards the technology, I remain perfectly still. He nods, holding Lily close and whispering into her ear.

The second bounty hunter comes out of the building dragging a limp body behind her. Ignoring us completely, she grabs her motion detector and calls her ride. The bike sets down and she takes off with her loot. I'm about to motion that we should get out of here when the third Cop, a patroller, steps back out onto the street. Patrollers work one sector their entire lives. They don't have the same training as hunters, but they have all the same power.

He steps towards us, studying us one by one. When he gets to Lily he motions at her with his charge rod. That weapon can shoot a bolt of electricity that will knock a large man off his feet.

<Come with me,> he commands.

Ignoring a Cop's direct order is illegal. Shaking with fear, Lily gets to her feet as he takes out a set of handcuffs.

"I can pay you for her." Hyde doesn't sound anxious but his desperation is obvious to me. "A thousand credits."

The Cop hesitates as he studies the lanky man's beautiful suit. Pushing Lily into Hyde's arms, he produces his transfer machine. Carefully, Hyde takes his credit balance out of his pocket. Sliding in through the black box, he presses his thumbprint onto a small square to authorize the transaction. When the green light flashes, the Cop puts the machine away and turns towards me. My cold expression is reflected back to me in the Cop's shiny visor.

Grabbing me by the arm, he pulls me roughly to my feet and has me put my hands together in front of my body. The cuffs click into place around my wrists. The sound is distant; the cold metal against my skin doesn't feel real.

Hyde and Lily start to protest but they're quickly silenced when the Cop points his charge rod at them.

<You two are free to go.>

The Cop shoves me towards the gaping hole in the wall. I risk a look back at my companions. Hyde shakes his head in apology while Lily quakes with fear and rage; both are powerless to help me. Still swathed in numbness, I step into the ruined building.

Following closely, the patroller orders me down a long corridor. I'm guessing this place is a Criminal hideout. A sturdy, metal door stands between the Cop and his payday. The door must be rigged with a trap. When I open it, I die, but the patroller collects.

My veil of indifference quickly dissolves. This fucker was going to use Lily to shield him from certain death. I love Lily and her brother fiercely. They were my shelter when I had nowhere left to go. Glancing at the patroller over my shoulder, an immense pocket of seething anger builds inside of me. It's a welcome change from terror, and I intend to use it.

This Cop doesn't know me. He doesn't know what I'm capable of, and he definitely doesn't know that I'm a psychic.

I shut my eyes and place my cuffed hands over the doorknob. Clearing my mind, I see the other side of the door. A woman is desperately trying to open a window…there's a wire running from the doorknob to a sharp projectile attached to the ceiling. When I open the door, the wire pulls the pin, and the weapon is released. I'll have less than a second before the trap is set off. The adrenaline pumping through my veins neutralizes any and all panic. Turning the handle, I pull the door open, and jump to the side.

The weapon passes by me entirely and breaks through the Cop's visor. I roll onto my back, grimacing as he falls over. Blood is pouring out of his helmet. Still twitching, he struggles for breath inside his shattered helmet.

It's not a pretty sight.

"What are you going to do with that thousand now?" I ask as I get to my feet.

I raise my boot to stomp him on his stomach, but decide it's a waste of valuable time. Anger still pulsing through my body, I examine the cuffs and pull a small pin out of the flesh of my wrist. It only stings for a moment, which is exactly how long it takes me to pick the lock of the restraints. I drop them on the patroller as I step over him. His buddies will be back for him when he doesn't check in. We've got to get out of here.

5

Packed to the rafters and roaring with fights, Braggs Bar is a popular Criminal haunt. Everything is like I remember it: holes in the walls, blood stains on the floors, decaying chairs and tables, and rough people looking for trouble. Heavy dread, thick and stifling, has me hesitating on the bar's threshold. I hadn't planned on ever coming here again.

Suck it up, my inner voice chides, *you owe. This is unavoidable. Get it over with and don't draw attention to yourself. You're not going to lose it now. These next hours are about survival…nothing else.*

I nod my agreement. Determined to make good my debt to Lyons Emmett, I step into the thunderous main room.

Making my way through the rough and tumble crowd, I am hyper-aware that I am an easy target. Anyone who cares that I'm out—anyone holding a grudge—will want to exploit my weaknesses. Flexing my hands, I gaze unhappily into the heart of the Criminal underworld.

The bar is crammed tonight. There's barely any breathing room. I do as my inner voice instructed—keep my head down, only move when there's room to, and never look anyone in the eye.

Two men smash bottles over each other's heads and roar with exhilaration, making me jump. Stumbling away from them, careful not to touch anyone, I right myself without making a sound. My heart races wildly.

Shaking with anticipation, I carefully study one man's beer covered face. He suddenly throws an arm around his friend and salutes their bizarre ritual with a new bottle. I watch blood trickle down their faces, study their ruined smiles, and caress the thin scars on my arms with a renewed sense of excitement.

Something within—long dormant—is slowly awakening.

Lily knows better than to ask if I'm okay, and Hyde isn't paying much attention. Why would he? All he cares about is keeping his clothes from being damaged. All power to him on that mission, it really is a beautiful suit.

"*Lily!*" A familiar voice reaches my ears over the noise. A small, striking woman elbows her way through the crowd. "Lily! What are you doing here? I haven't seen you in ages."

"Theo," Lily identifies, catching her friend in her arms, "I came with Daryl!"

Theodora's jaw drops once she recognizes me. Tossing her mane of thick hair, she strikes an alluring pose. Men and women alike turn around to admire her figure and she sneaks a glance to see how many. Theodora is one of Madman's high-class prostitutes and one of the most captivating women in the City. I'm not exaggerating. No matter where she goes, no matter what she wears, people can't help but watch and want her. It's how her body curves and how her eyes flash, how every movement lets everyone know how desirable she is. With a small, derisive snort she takes in my disheveled appearance. I'm getting the distinct impression that she isn't happy to see me and I don't have the energy for her disapproval.

My best bet it to keep the conversation focused on her. Knowing Theo, that won't be too hard. "You're looking good."

She coolly runs her eyes over me before replying. "I'm moving up in the world. Gift status all the way."

I don't know how to reply. Her announcement is supposed to impress me. In the world of prostitution *gift status* means that Madman sends her as a reward to an employee or partner. She's a possession, someone whose told what to do and how to do it. Theo and I were good friends, once upon a time, and I didn't approve of her hooking up with Madman. The streets are a hard place, but she could have made her own way. The organization gave her security but, in return, took her freedom. After she made her decision we couldn't be close anymore—oil and vinegar, after all.

She's looking at me expectantly. I manage a small nod. "Congratulations. A couple of years and you'll be running the operation."

My flattery makes her laugh. The sweet, tinkling sound draws more attention our way. Amused at the lustful gazes aimed at Theo's ripe body, and the teasing gazes she flashes back, I allow myself a mordant smile.

"What are you doing here, Theo?" Lily asks. "I thought you didn't have to come here after you got your promotion."

"I'm chasing after a man," the luscious prostitute admits, biting her lower lip seductively. "I'm going to bump into him unexpectedly."

Now *that* is interesting. Since when has Theo had to lift a finger to get a man that she desires? He's either not into women or impotent.

Flicking her hair, Theo casually motions towards her prey. I follow her gaze and see a tall, muscular, and ruggedly handsome man sitting at the bar. He's cut his hair since I last saw him, but I recognize the scar running down his neck. (I happen to know that it runs right down his chest, but that's another story.) Choking on my own spit, I watch Theo's dark eyes ardently worship Jace Locket.

Lily scans Locket's body appreciatively. "He likes Lenny's three egg omelet, but I don't think he's very friendly."

"That's a huge understatement," I mutter under my breath.

"Ladies," Theo brushes her hands over her hair, "that man knows what he's doing between the sheets."

Ugh. Locket is an attractive man, but I prefer not to think of him having sex with anyone.

Theo, somehow missing my bewilderment, leans in excitedly. "Madman sent me to his box when he was promoted to General. I was only paid for an hour but I decided to stay the entire night."

She gushes on about his sexual prowess but I'm still stuck on the word *promoted*.

General? Locket used to be a die-hard independent. Since when does someone like him join an organization? Radcliff was right, things have changed up here.

Locket must have started working for Madman after I went into the Prison. That means he rose quickly through the ranks, which isn't surprising. I watch Theo run her tongue over her lips as she devours him with her gaze. It looks like she might run over and tear off his clothes in front of everyone. The object of her lust is listening intently to a small, stocky man. A moment later, he throws back his head and laughs. I've never seen him smile before; I didn't even know he could laugh.

His friend notices the women looking their way and nods at us. Locket's blue eyes flick over Theo and Lily with idle interest. There's always a distance in his gaze when he looks at people, as though any one of them could be his next payday. His contented expression immediately hardens when he sees me. My stomach cramps with anxiety, but I still fall easily into our old pattern. Squaring my shoulders, I return his cold stare.

"He knows I'm here." Theo squeals as she begins to preen. Evidently, she missed Locket's change of attitude when he saw me. "That scar runs right down his chest, you know."

"I know," I say, before I can stop myself.

Both Theo and Lily let out little gasps and stare at me in shock. Stupid, stupid, stupid! Maybe they'll let it slide. What am I talking about? Theo is ready to strangle me with her perfectly manicured hands. Hyde's face lights up in anticipation.

"How exactly do *you* know?" Theo's eyes flash dangerously as she crosses her arms over her chest.

I ignore the question.

"Daryl," Lily cries as she grabs my arm. "I didn't know you had a *past* with Locket."

"It's not that kind of past."

Theo is staring daggers at me. "What kind is it then?"

"Give it a rest." Hyde is obviously disappointed that he didn't get to watch two women tearing at each other. "She knows about his scar, who cares?"

"*Fine*, then!" Theo turns away haughtily, adjusting her outfit and smoothing her eyebrows. Flashing me a nasty smile, she tosses her luxurious hair over her shoulder. "I'll just go bump into Jace and escort him back to my place."

"Don't pay any attention to her," Lily says, trying to soften Theo's arrogant display. "She's been talking about this guy for months. Even though she won't admit it, he obviously doesn't care about her. Being so beautiful and all, it's really hard on her ego."

"And she's been really full of herself since she became a *gift*," Hyde pipes in. "I'll be right back."

He disappears into the crowd. Lily says she's going to find a booth until our business is over and then we can go out. "I want you to tell me all about your history with Locket!"

"Lily, *seriously*, it wasn't like that!"

She beams and then winks, her eyes aglow with romantic notions. Fighting her imagination is like trying to control the weather, you have no choice but to let it run its natural course.

I sigh unhappily. Locket and I have a complicated past. A few months after he killed Ivana, I was navigating the back streets of Q Sector. Actually, Q Sector is all back streets with open spaces piled high with litter and waste. That's why they call it the Dump. Everything in the City that's thrown into a Collection bin eventually ends up on one of the piles. Afterwards, it's sorted and sold to different sectors depending on need. When I met Locket for the second time, I was out on my very first lone job. Some woman from the Court had lost her expensive ring down a bin chute and contracted a Criminal boss to get it back. Not wanting to send any of her real employees, Alison Diego hired me for a very small price.

She found out which Collector family handled the woman's building's contract, arranged for clearance, and sent me on my way.

I'd found the trash heap where the ring should have been. Lucky for me, this family sorted before they dumped, so an employee had already found the ring. To a Collector it's always finder's keepers. Watching from a distance, I saw the young girl show it off to the older man sitting next to her. He was smarter than her and made her put it back in her pocket before anyone else noticed.

At their lunch break I *borrowed* a sorting outfit, bumped into the girl just as she was finishing up her nutrient bar, and deftly slipped my hand into her pocket. It really was a little too easy. The ring was mine and I was pretty sure that I was home free.

Walking—all right, I was swaggering—through the Dump, I wasn't paying attention to my surroundings. I was imagining the impressed look on Alison's face when I turned up with the goods. In my fantasy, she and I were more like sisters than employer and employee. Completely distracted, I turned a corner and there was Locket, covered in blood and fighting for his life. Both he and his opponent, a tough looking guy with tattoos on his face, were brandishing mean looking knives. I have a knife that I keep in my boot, but it doesn't look anything like what they had in their hands.

Both of them were exhausted. Blood was running down their faces, they had cuts all over their bodies, and they were barely able to focus. I should have known to just get out of there. But, like an idiot, I watched them with a stunned expression on my face.

It wasn't until a few moments later that the tattooed guy noticed me. "Is this one of your little slaves, Rian?"

Locket risked a glance my way. "Get the hell out of here, kid."

It was too late. The tattooed guy rushed me. I remember the disconnected way that I examined his bloody knife as he ran towards me. I was used to fighting for scraps on the street; this clash was the next step up, something far beyond anything I could understand. So I stood there like a statue, waiting for the man, and his knife, to disappear.

Locket stepped in and deflected the blow. The strength behind the attack was staggering; my unlikely champion fell to his knees. His adversary raised his knife high and drove it down, opening a horrible wound from Locket's neck down to the bottom of his rib cage.

"You always were a hero, asshole," the tattooed guy said. Sneering in triumph, he prepared for the killing blow.

Jolted back into reality, I launched myself at him. It was a stupid move, he was far stronger than me, but it gave Locket the extra second he needed. As I fell to the ground between them, Locket spotted the hilt of my knife peeking out of my boot. Quick as lightning, he pulled it out and rammed the blade straight into his opponent's stomach.

The guy didn't make any kind of a sound. He just stared into Locket's eyes as a jagged wound was carved from his navel to his chest.

"Fuck you, Paris." There was a look of pure malevolence on Locket's face as he cradled his victim. "Your brother will be happy to see you."

"I'll be sure and find your sister, too," the dying man rasped nastily. "Cumming inside of her was fucking paradise."

Locket reached his arm into the guy's abdomen, up under his rib cage, and ripped out his heart.

What do you say to the man who killed your best friend right in front of you, saved your life, just threw a human heart into the streets, and is rummaging through a butchered man's clothes?

"That guy dead?" I asked dumbly.

Locket's threatening glare made my hair stand on end. Young that I was, I met and held his intense gaze without blinking. But a small girl who doesn't know to run when there's trouble isn't going to intimidate a man like Locket.

"You didn't see or hear a damn thing," he barked. "Understood?"

Pressing my lips together, worried that I might be his next victim, I nodded carefully.

Locket's search through the tattooed man's pockets turned up nothing. Standing on shaking legs, he cleaned his blade on his victim's jacket and examined his bleeding wounds. He grabbed a pack on the ground and opened it. Right in front of me, he poured a clear substance over his torso, flinching in pain as it burned. Then he sat down, threaded a curved needle, and began sewing his neck and chest wound together. How he managed without a mirror is beyond me.

When he was done, I was beyond traumatized.

I only had one thing to offer him for saving my life. "I can get you out of Q."

He didn't have to say anything. I led him to my contact, but the pass I had was only good for one. I dropped Alison's name to the gate-keeper, the people who guard the exits and entrances between sectors, and she let us both through. Locket went his way and I gave the ring to Alison. Of course, she wouldn't hire me again when she found out that I'd used her name to smuggle a blood-covered man through a gate.

But I can't tell Lily this story. Locket doesn't want anyone knowing about that fight. If it got back to him that I was talking about it he wouldn't hesitate to cut me down. Like I said, there's no hiding from that sonofabitch. No matter where you are, he'll find you. And because I have something on him, he hates me. I've never given him a legitimate excuse to kill me but I can always sense him watching; he's waiting for a reason to slit my throat.

Besides that, I never found any information on the man he killed. It should have been easy. Most people avoid tattoos because they're symbols of enslavement. The Court and Homestead are full of slaves, and all of them bear the mark of their master. I described the tattoos to a few experts, but there aren't any families that brand their slaves on the face. It brings down their re-sale value.

Hyde motions at me from the crowd. Glaring unhappily at a rough man who bumps into him, he desperately checks his suit for rips or stains. His search reveals that his clothes are undamaged and he sighs in relief.

"I hope to keep this intact for a while," he explains.

"Luck to that," I return.

Following him through the crowd, I conquer my nerves by biting down hard on the inside of my cheek. The sharp pain helps me focus. I'm going to need all my wits about me when I come face to face with Lyons.

6

Seven years ago, a Criminal named Nick Redden hired me. I was supposed to get rid of someone who was getting in his way. I've killed in self defence, for survival, but contract killing is a different business. Some naïve, arrogant part of me thought I could do it. In the Criminal world, if you take a contract you make good on it, or your employer owns you. When I didn't deliver my end of the bargain, Redden owned me. First he raped me, and then he beat me into a bloody pulp.

For months afterwards, I walked around in a strange daze. People would be talking to me but I couldn't make out what they were saying. I'd wander the streets for hours, oblivious to my surroundings, and then realize I was circling the warehouse where I'd met Redden for the last time. My mind had erased the rape; but then it started coming back to me in small, agonizing waves. Sometimes, when I least expect it, I'll remember something he said. I'll hear his crew cheering and jeering somewhere in the darker recesses of my memory. When that happens I feel like someone has reached into my chest and ripped out my spine. My body freezes up, I lose the ability to speak and I disappear. It can take hours of concentration to put the memories back where they belong.

After the assault, I was unconscious for three days. When I woke up, I was in Lyons' infirmary. At first, I thought he was going to torture me to death, but he was only fixing me up. Apparently, someone had found me and brought me straight to him. Lyons wouldn't tell me who. I couldn't pay him for the treatment so I've owed him a favour ever since.

To make matters even more interesting, two days before Lyons gave me a clean bill of health, Nick Redden was found dead in a Collection bin. His tongue had been ripped out and his balls had been cut off. I wish I could say that I got my revenge, but what he did to me is acceptable in the Criminal world. If I'd retaliated I never would have worked again. No one ever took credit for his death, either, so whoever killed him didn't have a legitimate reason. That kind of a kill will start a war. I can't name one Criminal who wants another one of those. They cut into business and everyone starves.

Hyde leads me to the back of the bar. Madman's booth is tucked away from the rowdier areas. I'm staring down at the big guy himself. Actually, comparatively, Lyons is kind of small. He's never beefed up like other Criminals. In the last two years he's earned a few more lines of distinction around his eyes, but his face still lays claim to a touch of youth. His eyes have that deep, arcane quality—you get the feeling that nothing gets by him. And I suppose nothing really does.

He's scribbling madly on a board with charcoal and it's absorbing all of his attention. There's plenty of art all around the City. For some people it's like a virus. It gets into their system and, instead of coughing or sneezing, they paint, draw, sculpt, whatever they have to. Wulff, one of my oldest friends, is one of them. He loves colour, probably because there isn't much of it around. He loves real green especially; we all like real green.

Too nervous to speak, I hang back instead of making my presence known. I don't want to ruin his concentration. A hollow-faced, wiry man is sitting to Lyons' left. He sees me and his overly large eyes bulge out of his face.

"Hey, Copper," he calls as he puts his hand under the table. "What am I holding in my hand?"

He leers at me as his body starts to shake...it looks like he's beating off under the table. Beck is an insecure jackass. Years ago, I beat him into submission after he tried to feel me up. His ego still hasn't recovered.

Unfazed by his vulgar pantomime, I use my psychic talent to take a peek under the table.

"A salt shaker."

Flashing me a look of loathing, Beck puts the shaker back on the table. Now Madman knows that I haven't lost my psychic talent. He's still working away with the coal and isn't looking up. Running my hand anxiously through my hair, I study Madman's tough looking bodyguards; they're standing behind the booth and looking at me with equal parts interest and distrust. Along with their scarred knuckles, muscular bodies and mean expressions, I can see fierce loyalty burning in their eyes. One false move from anyone and they won't hesitate in cutting them down.

"I can never quite get the eyes right," Lyons finally says. He rubs his fingers over the board he's holding. The coal has gotten all over his hands and shirt. When he wipes his face a streak of black appears on his forehead and cheek. He holds the board away from him to examine his work. "You should sit down, Daryl. Beck was just leaving."

Throwing me a malicious glare, Beck slides out of the booth, buttons his withered jacket, and disappears into the crowd.

"I need your opinion," Lyons says.

Too tense to say anything, I sit down and watch him draw. Every time I shift I cringe at the noise that I make. The split vinyl covering the bench squeaks uncomfortably, making the hairs on the back of my neck stand on end. I can't get out of here soon enough.

"How does it look?" Madman asks. He turns the board so that I can see his work.

My own face, captured exquisitely on the yellowish-brown wood, peers out from its rectangular jail; there's an ethereal yet wholly lifelike quality to my features. I look young, mischievous, elated—a far cry from what I've become. Sorrow erupts in my chest. Shaken and irritated, I allow myself a catty response.

"You missed the sarcastic smirk and the smart-ass attitude. Did you mistake me for someone else?"

"When I thought of you this was the image that came to mind," he replies, unfazed by my bitterness. Amusement glitters in his mysterious eyes as he studies the portrait. "But now it's all wrong, isn't it?"

Madman extends his hand behind him. Producing another rectangular board from his jacket, one of his bodyguards places it into his boss' palm. Focusing intently, Lyons begins another masterpiece and does not look up at me again. His coal rubs madly against the solid wood, his artist's face twitches and contracts as his vision slowly takes form. A few more moments of this and I'm liable to jump out of my skin. Finally, after what seems like hours, he tells me what he wants.

"I need you to get in to A Sector."

Funny, he doesn't look like he's joking.

"Cop Sector...?" He doesn't react to my incredulous tone. I have to assume that he's serious. "Nobody gets into Cop Sector."

Studying the board with a squinted eye, Madman grunts disapprovingly at his work. "*You* did."

"I got *out* of Cop Sector. There's a big difference."

"You grew up there, Daryl. Long before you decided to become a Criminal you were a little baby Copling, learning how to get paid by catching us *evil-doers*." He never lifts his gaze to catch my eye; his work is absorbing his attention. "You know the way they eat and sleep, the way they work and play; you know what *Cop* Sector looks like and how Cops act when they're not working. That's a step above every other Criminal, wouldn't you say? And, if there's a way out, there must be a way in."

I must admit, it's hard to argue with his logic.

I had hoped that people would forget about my origins over time. I never advertised that I was from Cop Sector, but it didn't take long for others to find out. *Coplings*, as Madman so accurately put it, are trained from birth to hunt and catch people with non-lethal force: more pay if the Criminal is in good working order when you get them to the Prison. The Cop fighting technique is distinctive and easy to spot if you've fought one before. In my first few public fights (I managed to avoid them for years), somebody recognized it and that was that. Being the only Cop turned Criminal has never been easy. For a few years, I was everybody's scapegoat.

Madman finally puts down his coal and board to look at me. "You owe me. I want a line into A. You have three days."

He wants what Heathcliff Jackson has to F—a path into a heavily guarded sector that can provide him with a monopoly. Madman could make an astounding amount of credit and maybe, just maybe, entice more Criminals into his *protection*.

There's just one catch. I wasn't joking when I said no one gets into Cop Sector. Madman has just given me a bullshit job.

My mind buzzes miserably as I put the pieces together. He already knows I can't deliver; he either wants me under his thumb or out of his way. If I don't give him what he wants I belong to him…just like I belonged to Redden all those years ago. That sadistic bastard's sweaty face flashes through my brain. Gasping anxiously under my breath, I put a hand on the table to steady my trembling nerves.

Fuck that. I'm not going to belong to anyone ever again. My only choice is to go into hiding. That's the only way I survive Madman's trap. It's risky, but I've got no problems with disappearing.

My tenuous control over my roaring anxiety is slipping. I get up without waiting to be excused. Lyons doesn't react. Jamming my hands into my pockets so that no one will see how they're shaking, I retreat into the crowd.

Lily and Hyde are waiting for me in a small booth.

Hyde gestures at all the people in the bar. "You're already a Legend, Daryl."

Looking around, I realize that gazes are pointed in my direction. They all think I'm back in action. That's big news. I'm supposed to be half-dead. Amongst the crowd I recognize a malevolent stare and tip my head to Beck. He's glowering at me with pure hatred.

"Be careful of that one," Lily warns. "He's out for blood. Hyde overheard him talking to Cullen."

"Tonight…?" I ask.

"I don't know." She shrugs helplessly. "Don't fight him. Let's get out of here instead."

A thrill of excitement shoots up my spine. My hands stop shaking when I think about crushing Beck's face. I see my arms wrapped around his neck, his face turning blue before I drop him with a quick jerk. His body falls to the floor in a heap as I watch him take his last breath. Sweet, intoxicating power flows through my muscles...*I'm alive again.*

"Daryl...?" Lily puts her hand on my shoulder. "Are you all right?"

Pulling myself out of my fantasy, I nod. "You're right. I just have to hit the bathrooms first."

"We'll meet you at the bar," Hyde calls after me.

The crowd swallows me whole and I have to push my way through the mass of bodies. I'm starting to get used to the crush. Actually, the noise and violence is becoming a comfort. I used to thrive on it. Braggs Bar is an unofficial let's-even-the-score zone. People meet, others lay down bets, and then they have a no rules fight. There have already been a few tonight, but I've been so preoccupied I didn't really notice them. To my left, two women are slugging it out and Braggs' other patrons are yelling and shouting at the top of their lungs.

"Three hundred credits on the blonde!" an overly excited man calls from right behind me.

Elbowing my way over to the bar, I spot Theo chatting with Locket. She's gracing him with her world-class sexy pout and coy, come-violate-my-innocence gaze. *Wow.* I'm not usually attracted to women, but that look would get me out of my clothes pretty quick.

I have to walk by them to get to the bathrooms. Theo sees my approach and pretends she doesn't know me. Locket stares as I walk past. I shoot him an unpleasant look before continuing on my way.

The bathroom is crowded and noisy, just like the rest of the bar. Urinals line the wall to my right and stalls line the wall to my left. Most people aren't here for the toilets so I find an empty stall. Just as I open the door someone grabs me from behind. Shrieking in protest, I struggle helplessly before I'm pushed towards the toilet. The stall door bolts shut with gruesome finality.

I finally snap. This day has been too much for me. It's been one thing after another, with no rest and no peace. Releasing a horrific, ravenous battle cry I dig my nails into my attackers flesh.

Swearing under his breath, he lets me go. I swing at him without thought, reaching for his face and kicking at his legs. But my opponent is a clever bastard. Grabbing my wrist and shoulder, he spins me into a painful shoulder lock, neutralizing my fists. It's the kind of move I was taught back in Cop Sector. There's no getting out of this without severely crippling myself. It's that thought, and that thought only, that forces me to calm down. I swallow my panic. Gasping pathetically, my head bent towards the toilet bowl, I silently ask Luck for a quick death.

I want something quiet, serene...maybe even ironic.

"Madman wants you dead," Locket whispers.

When I recognize his voice I feel curiously relieved, as though he isn't the cold killer that I know him to be. When I relax he slowly lets me go, allowing me enough room to turn around.

His cold blue eyes drive into mine.

Straightening his six-foot-five frame, he glares down at me. "You go into hiding and he'll send me after you."

"*Bull shit*," I rasp. I can't stop shaking...I feel like I'm about to cave in. "I'm nothing now. If you're a General he won't waste you on me."

"You're more of a threat than you realize, Sewer Rat." He uses my old nickname because he knows it pisses me off. Leaning towards me, he presses his body against mine and continues to stare hard into my eyes. "You can't hide from me."

The warmth of his skin calms my shaking, but I'm still terrified. If he were lying I would feel a warning in the back of my head. My instincts would tell me not to listen. I desperately wait for it to come, to release me from this trap, but it is cruelly silent.

Locket is right—I can't hide from him. No matter what I do, I'm dead.

We silently stare at each other, neither of us willing to move first. That's when I notice how close he is. This stall is a tight fit. I can't move without touching him, can't shift without getting closer. His warm breath brushes over my forehead, making my blood pump faster through my veins. There's something intoxicating about his effortless strength. Caught in this bizarrely intimate moment, I'm intensely aware that I've hardly been touched in the past two years.

Great, this is great. I'm attracted to my would-be executioner. I am seriously *fucked up*.

Locket shifts, bringing his strong, warm body closer to mine. Hating my traitorous hormones, I breathe in the musky scent of his skin and clothes. It's bringing new life to my ruined world, convincing me that this man isn't a threat.

I have to get him out of this stall.

"What's it like being Madman's new pet?" I ask.

My vicious words would cut to the quick of any independent's ego. Locket winces and moves away, but he's only damaged for a moment. A superior, yet captivating, smile spreads over his face.

"I think we should make it look like we were having a good time in here," he decides.

To my astonishment, he unbuckles and unzips his pants. Unlocking the door, he steps out into the noisy bathroom. Deliberately making eye contact with a tough-looking woman, he slowly walks past her, brazenly closing up his pants and fixing his hair. He shoots her a charming wink before walking out of the bathroom. Admiring his muscular body, the woman watches him leave before turning to me.

"You're Daryl, aren't you?" she asks. She eyes me curiously. "And that was...Jace Locket...wasn't it?"

I'm not in the mood to make a friend. Still reeling from my lust, I close and bolt the stall door.

7

Like they promised, Hyde and Lily are waiting for me at the bar. Thankfully, Theo's nowhere to be seen, so I can avoid that little drama. Just when I think I can get out of this place unscathed, Beck steps out in front of me.

He stares down at me with arrogant zeal. *"Place your bets!"*

The crowd around us roars in anticipation. I glance around, too stunned to move, as they clear a space for us to fight. Lily jumps to her feet, ready to grab me and run. She starts pushing her way through the crowd, but Hyde takes her arm to stop her from getting in the way. He shakes his head gently. The crowd will tear me to pieces if I back out. It's fight or die.

This is the day that will not end…I'm moving past the point of exhaustion. I watch Beck dance around on the balls of his feet, his muscles jumping with anticipation, eagerly awaiting his chance to destroy me in front of the crowd. Compared to him, I'm a wreck, a starving kitten thrown into a pit with a rabid dog. I don't stand a chance and there's no way out.

All of this suddenly strikes me as incredibly funny. Even if Beck doesn't kill me, I'm still caught in Madman's web. There's no way to get into Cop Sector and I can't hide from Locket. No matter what, I'm dead. Eyes filling with desperate tears, I start cackling and snorting with laughter. Catching

Beck's confused expression, I try to wipe the smile off my face, but it's impossible. I'm about to go into hysterics.

"You *really* want this, Beck?"

Suddenly unsure of himself, my opponent takes an uneasy step back. It's not just my laughter that's unnerving. An absurd grin is spreading across my face. I move towards him and he steps back again.

"Come on, let's go!" I bring my fists up, inviting him forward with a wave of my hand. Still smiling, eyes glittering with amusement, I relax into the Cop fighting stance. "I'm ready when you are. Make the first move."

Beck tentatively hops into hitting radius. His left jab flashes through the air. For a moment, it all seems like slow motion as I duck underneath and ram my knuckles into his throat. Shocked, Beck bends over and starts coughing. Taking my opportunity, I grab his head and smash my knee into his nose twice. Blood gushes to the floor as Beck stumbles backward.

"Fucking bitch!"

The sight of the blood forces me back to reality. My knuckles throb from the punch to his throat. Circling each other in the small space, the crowd screaming and jeering at us to kill each other, we recognize that we *are* fighting to the death. I don't want to live if I lose, and I'm not letting him walk away if I win. There's no rule that says we have to kill each other, it's just what's going to happen...whether or not that was Beck's original intention. He probably only wanted to humiliate me. He should have learned a long time ago to leave me the fuck alone.

Beck is having difficulty breathing because of the strike to his throat. The blood from his broken nose is making matters worse. He may have taken my hits, but he's suffering. He continues to jab but I dodge easily. The object of my fighting style is to never get hit or grabbed. I can't take the battering that Beck has already survived. I have to be quick enough to get away from him and sneak in my attacks while he's still recovering. Optimally, I should keep him off balance to create more opportunities for myself, but he's improved and now he's fighting for his life. He won't be making many more mistakes.

One hit pops me a little on the nose, but I manage to back out of the strike before it can do any real damage. Sinking down to strengthen my stance, I wait for him to attack. I want him to come at me with everything he has.

"You must have a lot of fun having a woman kick your ass," I mock. A look of intense humiliation invades his focused gaze. "I already have your balls. What do I get when I beat you down this time?"

Growling, Beck takes an uncontrolled swipe at me. I evade it easily. I dance around the floor while dodging his blows. Risking a glance over my shoulder, I take note of what's behind me.

"Come on, shouldn't you at least have hit me once by now? People are waiting for you to do something."

His intense roar of fury makes my hair stand on end, but I welcome his crazed battle charge. Reaching out with his hands, he tries to take me down. I step nimbly to the side. A guy with an eye patch gets clipped as Beck careens past him. They both go flying. The bystander spins around and falls to the floor; Beck's head smashes into the solidly built bar, leaving a deep impression in the scuffed wood. The impact is too much for his cranium. He goes down hard.

All muscles ready for action, smiling wickedly and wanting more, I wait for my opponent to stand up. His body is still moving; his hands are grasping for something to help him. Groaning, he shakes his head, grabs onto a bar stool and somehow pulls himself to his feet. He can't quite focus and he's reeling from the impact, but he's standing. The fight's not over until one of us doesn't get up.

The bar has suddenly gone quiet. Everyone is watching Beck stagger towards me. Ablaze with excitement, I settle back into my fighting stance and wait for him to get close enough for the last hit. One shaky step into my strike zone and my boot crashes into his face. Blood spatters across the crowd as he falls to the floor.

Straddling his prostrate form, I put my hands around his head. He's lying unconscious on his stomach, unaware that he's taking his last breath. All it takes is one quick jerk; the small pops in his neck satisfy a base and desperate craving.

It's like taking a breath after being underwater for too long.

I cradle his head for a moment, savouring the juice that comes from taking somebody's life. I was never this vampiric before the Prison. It's something new...something wholly unsettling.

Beck is dead. The crowd roars.

I can barely hear their shouts of excitement. People I don't know are clapping me on the shoulders, yelling their congratulations as I study my victim's motionless body. One of the bartenders grabs Beck by the feet. His worthless corpse is dragged into the back of the bar. By tomorrow afternoon, he'll be drying out somewhere in the Desert.

I'm still laughing. I don't know how I won but I'm happy that I did. Even with Madman's powerful grip slowly squeezing me, I'm happy to be alive. That's good to know. Yesterday, I wouldn't have been so sure.

Hyde and Lily don't say a word when I walk up to them. Taking Hyde's drink from his hands, I toss back the sugary liquid, and brush the back of my hand over my mouth. The adrenaline rushing through my veins is staggering. Bubbling with glee, I place the cup on the bar and stare at my hands. For now, all my fear is gone. The sweet ecstasy of gaining victory over impossible odds has me enthralled.

"You just made me an extra two thousand credits," Hyde says. He leisurely brushes a spot of dust from his suit.

Lily's eyes are as wide as saucers. Awestruck, she studies my exhilaration. She's never seen me fight before and I can tell I've frightened her.

"A Legend," she breathes. "The Whisperers will be telling stories about you."

"Whisperers," I echo. I slam my hand down on the bar with excitement. "That's where we're going tonight. We're going to see a Whisperer. Do you guys know where any are performing?"

Hyde nods distractedly: he's picking a hair off one of his lapels. "Marietta is in her haunt. If we hurry we might catch the show."

"Perfect."

I smile at Lily and she nods her agreement. The three of us make our way through the crowd. Opening the front door, I usher my companions into the night before taking one last look at the noisy bar. Another fight has broken out somewhere at the back. My victory is a distant memory.

Somewhere in the mass of people, I see icy blue eyes staring out at me. *Locket.*

I don't hold his gaze this time. He's reminded me that I only have three days to enjoy this feeling of resurrection.

8

Every Cop dreams of arresting a Whisperer: they're worth a fortune in the Prison. They aren't aggressive or violent; they don't incite riots or abuse the system. In fact, they live in every sector and have no Criminal background. Why is it so lucrative to haul one in? Despite their passive ways they violate the first universal law of the City—only appointed lecturers are free to tell stories about the past.

Sectors create their own laws. They have to obtain the Court's approval, but more often than not they're left to find their own balance for their citizens. The universal laws are the ones that no sector can overrule. The law criminalizing Whisperers is considered the most important.

What's so scary about history that only certain people can teach it? I don't know. History is boring: *the City born from the ashes of a ruined world, humankind working together for survival*, blah blah blah. From what I've seen, Whisperers are harmless; mainly, they embellish stories about dead people who were somewhat interesting in their day.

Marietta is probably the most harmless of all. She's a fiery old woman with wavy grey hair and twinkling, mischievous eyes. But tonight, gaining access to what Hyde calls her haunt is a painstaking affair. She performs in B Sector, so we don't have far to go, but it doesn't have any community light. We have to pick our way through the dark streets using our mediocre flashlights. Once we get there, a stocky fellow informs us that the Whisperer hasn't invited us. Like all good doormen he is completely deaf to Lily's pleas.

"She knows us, Klem. *You* know us! We're not people walking off the street, we're almost family." Klem, an impressively muscled man, can't help but smile at Lily's desperation. Her hands are flying dramatically in all directions as she makes her case. "I've been coming here ever since I was a little girl, and this is Daryl! You know that Marietta would want to see her."

"She didn't give me your names, sweetheart." Klem acknowledges my presence with a quick look in my direction. "Good to see you again, Daryl."

I nod back respectfully. The adrenaline from my victory is beginning to wear off. I'm not so sure of myself anymore, and Klem is an intimidating guy.

When I went into the Prison he didn't quite have the testosterone to grow a full beard. Now he's a full-blown giant. Despite his intimidating shoulder width, however, I can still see the characteristic gentleness in his eyes. This doorman is still the orphan boy living on the streets who gives his hard earned food to the people who can't fend for themselves.

Shrugging apologetically at the three of us, he continues to bar our way. Our destination, a horribly scarred and dented steel door, is beckoning at us from the alleyway. Klem decides the conversation is over and stops acknowledging our presence.

Lily stomps her foot and groans in exasperation. Tossing her hands in the air, she paces aimlessly for a few minutes. Then her eyes suddenly brighten with a plan. She returns to Klem's side and fixes him with a haughty stare.

"Do you *like* Lenny's food, Klem?" Her words hit home and the doorman throws her a suspicious look. "You know, there are lots of people he won't serve these days. It's too bad, too, since you can smell his food half way across this sector. Not to mention, he knows all the other cooks. Credits don't mean much to him where family is concerned. You're one of our best customers, but when he finds out that you got in my way you won't be able to step foot in any restaurant, least of all ours."

I can see tears in Klem's eyes.

"Just imagine all those pancakes and pies, the rich cheesecake, grilled steaks and fresh vegetables. You'll never taste them again. You'll walk by hoping for just a glimpse, a whiff of his freshly brewed coffee, but Lenny has cut you from his clientele. He'll never let you back in."

With every mention of the succulent dishes Klem's eyes cloud over. His lips smack absent-mindedly as though he can taste every dish, every mouth-watering morsel. Remembering Lenny's food isn't strengthening his resolve. Losing his job might very well be worth a serving of mashed potatoes and gravy.

Watching Klem wrestle inwardly with her threat, I sympathize with his predicament. After his family died he hardly ever had enough to eat. Being an orphan is illegal in the City; it's a harsh universal law. I can tell you for a fact that Cops don't take them to the Prison. I don't know where they go. There are specialized Cops in A Sector who pay well to have orphans delivered to them. And then...who knows? My point is that Klem couldn't register his name for his ration of nutrient bars.

Lily isn't willing to wait for Klem's answer. She gives him five seconds and turns on her heels.

"Fine then," she calls blithely over her shoulder. "It's not like Lenny's freshly baked bread is all that delicious."

Klem's will snaps like a dry twig. "You can't let her see you."

Did I mention that Lenny and Lily are unofficially the most influential people in B Sector? Never underestimate the power of a delicious meal. This is the first time I've seen Lily use access to her restaurant as a bartering tool, and I'm impressed.

"Pulled out the big threat," Hyde remarks to Lily, holding the door open for us to pass through.

"He pissed me off," Lily growls. Stalking into a dark hallway she heads for Marietta's haunt.

"Any bite to that bark?" I ask, thoroughly amused.

"Only if she doesn't get her way."

Marietta's haunt is a windowless, dimly lit room decorated with mismatched chairs. The people have already taken their seats and they all have their backs to us. Normally there's only standing room for one of Marietta's performances. The chairs confirm that this night was invite only.

Our entrance goes unnoticed as the people talk politely to one another from their seats. Motioning to a corner, furthest from any curious eyes, Hyde leads Lily and me into the darkest shadows. From a somber perch on a small wooden shelf in a corner, the Whisperer's favourite seat presides over the haunt's cramped interior. A tall, ancient lamp, sitting forlornly next to the chair, is the only source of light.

"I hope she tells the Legend of Kyle and Rosa," Lily whispers. Leave it to her to want a love story. She grips my sleeve as she nearly bursts with anticipation. "I always want to faint when Rosa gives up her life in K Sector to join Kyle in Q. But then her father finds them and threatens to have the Cops throw Kyle into the Prison, forcing Rosa to go back home.

"Kyle can't stand not having her in his life, so he pays a crew of Criminals every credit that he has to find her, but she won't go because she's afraid of what her father will do." A dreamy expression spreads across her face as she puts her head on Hyde's shoulder. "But the crew convinces her to go back and all the citizens of Q Sector help hide them from the Cops!"

"You might let Marietta tell the Legend," Hyde teases, but Lily is lost in her own world.

"Did you and Locket have a tragic love affair?" She sighs romantically. Hyde sniggers at my horrified expression. "Is he suffering for you the way Kyle suffered for Rosa? I saw the way he ignored Theo and followed you into the bathroom, the way he watched you fight. You should have seen the smile on his face when Beck went down. I bet he would have pulverized that bastard if he'd actually hurt you. Oh! It must have killed him when you went into the Prison!"

Hyde's shoulders are shaking with amusement and my annoyed expression is only fuelling his mirth.

I roll my eyes. "Laugh it up, jack-ass."

"Women are way more fun than men." Clapping a hand over his mouth, Hyde smothers the sound of his laughter. His face reddens with the effort to stay quiet. "I can't imagine you with Locket. Remember the time he threw you into a Collector's bin and locked the lid?"

"You were there for that?"

"Yeah, but I didn't know you and only an idiot takes on Locket without a crew to back him up. Word has it the Collectors who found you tried to sell you at a slave auction."

"Q Sector bastards will try to turn a profit on anything they find."

"But you got away. When you bumped into Locket the next day he stole your identity card and left it at the scene of a crime. The Cops came looking for you instead of him."

"It took me months of hiding and scraping to organize a new alias."

This particular memory still leaves me loathing the very mention of Locket's name. Every citizen has two cards, a credit balance and an identity card. The credit balance keeps track of a person's funds; only the identity card contains personal information. Some Criminals base their entire careers on stealing rich citizens' credit balances. When Locket stole my identity card he did more than just lead the Cops to my doorstep. That was the first time the Cops caught me and the first time I managed to escape custody. In the long run, I gained new respect from Criminals, but that doesn't mean I didn't want to damage Locket afterward.

Hyde is gleefully remembering all the crappy things Locket has ever done to me. Apparently, most of the stories are common knowledge. Who knew that Locket and I have an audience? Everyone's waiting for me to retaliate and wondering why I haven't yet. They don't know that he saved my life.

Hyde's white, toothy grin is glowing in the dim light. "You gotta hand it to the guy, he's creative when he hates somebody."

"Sure," I agree, unable to cover my sarcasm. "Creative is definitely the word I'd use to describe him."

Lily has been daydreaming for the past couple of minutes and hasn't heard a word of our conversation. Somewhere in that passionate and imaginative brain of hers she's constructing an elaborate love story. She sighs dreamily and my anger melts away. A sudden and overpowering rush of warmth settles in my chest as I watch her snuggle happily into Hyde. She makes our ugly world a place where love abounds. Even something as ridiculous as Locket and I being lovers can exist there. I don't know how to explain to her that Locket is the reason I'm going to be dead in three days. I don't know how to explain to myself that I'm going to be dead in three days.

It occurs to me that I should be frightened, maybe even hysterical. But I haven't absorbed the knowledge yet. I'm keeping it at a safe distance. It won't be long before the shock wears off, so I've decided to enjoy the time that I have. Spending it with Lily is part of that, but there are other people I want to say good-bye to, people I want to hold once more.

As I remember those that I love, my skin prickles and a deep yearning swallows me whole. Tears gather in my eyes. I forgot about love in the Prison.

Before the memories sweep me away, I dig my fingernails into the back of my hand. The pain helps me retreat back into emotional numbness. Taking a deep, steadying breath, I refuse to think about my past.

Marietta enters the room and I sigh in relief. Everyone turns around to watch her weave through the chairs and a smile of false modesty appears on her face. She's always been a sucker for adoration; the audience's respectful silence has her floating towards her chair.

From my position in the shadowy corner. she looks like the same old Marietta—grey hair, glittering eyes, and fiery soul. In her hands she's holding a small, mysterious rectangular object that sort of reminds me of a brick. My head starts to buzz; my psychic talent is telling me to pay attention. The object is cut into hundreds of thin slices that are held together at the side but, other than being peculiar, it doesn't look very impressive.

"Dar Alistair," Marietta greets. She reaches her chair and turns around to proudly survey her audience. "How lovely to see you again."

That name makes Hyde and I stand a little taller. Every sector has a Dar. They're the highest-ranking official in their sector. Dar Alistair is from the Court, making him one of the most powerful people in the City.

The man himself stands and takes her offered hand in his own. Smiling with contained admiration, a small glimmer of good esteem twinkling in his eyes, the white-haired lawmaker executes a small bow. Now that is interesting… Court citizens never bow to B sector citizens, especially a wanted Criminal. As though he's at some higher function, Dar Alistair is dressed in blue and purple clothes made from new materials. White gold jewelry adorns his fingers and wrists.

"I would not have declined this invitation for all the minerals in V Sector."

Smile broadening at his flattery Marietta bids him return to his seat so that the performance can begin. "You should enjoy this week's selection."

She lifts the rectangular object triumphantly for all to see. My head keeps buzzing and I stand up straight to get a better look. Marietta's twinkling eyes brush over the audience. Hyde, Lily and I sink deeper into the shadows. She doesn't raise the alarm, so we relax.

"You'll all remember last week that we finished Gengi's Legend and that I promised to begin a new one."

Her rich and captivating voice is already weaving its familiar spell over the audience. She hasn't even begun her performance but everyone is leaning towards her, eager for more. It won't be long before the cramped room will drop away entirely and we'll find ourselves fighting alongside Eileen Hebra in the Mole Riots, or waiting for Blaise Ali to rescue us from a Cop ambush. They've always been my favourite heroes and I'm silently hoping that Marietta will be in a battle mood instead of a romantic one. Actually, I'm a little choked that I missed the Gengi Legend. I've never heard it before.

To my surprise, Marietta sits down and gives her full attention to the strange object in her hands. This is usually the part where she puffs out her chest and dramatically throws her words out over the audience. Flipping through the thin slices of the object, making soft rustling noises, she peruses something inside.

"I would like to introduce everyone to *Don Quixote*."

She smiles in satisfaction. The people are quivering with anticipation. I, however, am utterly baffled. Where are the grand arm gestures? Where's the eye contact that can make you feel like the only person in the room? Who the heck is *Donkey Hotay*?

Frustrated, wishing she would return to the classics, I repress an angry growl. Marietta's eyes drink in the object in front of her.

"What is that?" Lily whispers in my ear.

Shaking my head, I watch Marietta turn the thin slices. Her eyes are moving quickly, her face nearly buried in the strange rectangle.

Something mysterious and mystical happens when she beings to speak. Even without the grand gestures, I am listening to every syllable. There are certain words I don't understand (buckler, greyhound, books) but it doesn't seem to matter. This madman *knight*, as Marietta calls him, has me enthralled. I can't figure out what sector he's from, but there's something about him that captures my attention.

As the Whisperer speaks, I fall into an intense trance and picture myself in a different world than this one: the air is clean, the land is green, and cool water stretches out as far as the eye can see.

It's the glorious and mythical Oasis. This is the place of legend that can't exist even though everyone secretly hopes that it does. People lost in the desert, if they're found, rave about a spectacularly green and blue mirage that kept them walking towards the east. Always just out of their grasp, they followed it until they collapsed from exhaustion.

This lunatic, this *Donkey Hotay*, has somehow caught a mirage. It's driven him mad but his tarnished conquest has me spellbound. I've been lost in the desert. I never told anyone, but I saw the Oasis shining on the horizon. It was so beautiful I thought it might be worth dying for. But then I remembered that it wasn't real, that it couldn't exist, so I turned away.

It occurs to me that Marietta's mysterious rectangle might be the source of this tale. This is the first time I've ever seen her focus her energy on anything other than her audience. The buzzing in my head increases and my curiosity gets the better of me. I want a closer look at what she's holding in her hands.

My interest doubles when she closes the sliced rectangle. "We shall continue next week."

The show is over. They all burst into rapturous applause but I am keeping my eye on the prize.

Marietta stands, accepting the attention that is being lavished upon her with artificial serenity. I vibrate with anticipation, silently grateful for her ravenous ego. People are reaching out to shake her hands. In her eagerness to accept their exaltation the Whisperer puts the rectangle down on her seat. All I need now is for her to take a few steps away.

Lily and Hyde motion towards the door. This is the perfect time for us all to sneak out so that Klem doesn't find himself short a job. Lily grabs my sleeve and pulls me with her, but I pry off her fingers.

"I'll meet you around the corner."

Lily makes a small noise of protest, but Hyde grabs her by the hand and pulls her away. Throwing me a lazy grin, he whisks her through the door. I'm eagerly watching the small crowd pull Marietta away from her seat. She's off the little wooden shelf now. This will be my only chance. I have to take it.

Throbbing with excitement, I skim the edge of the crowd. There's no reason to watch Marietta. If she catches me she catches me—I don't know how long my window is and I can't waste precious time worrying about her.

Pretending to be relaxed and dispassionate, I stroll up to her chair and brush the rectangle into my hands. It's lighter than I expected. There are little black markings throughout the slits but I don't know what they're for. My hair stands up on end when I caress its smooth surface.

There is no way I'm leaving it behind.

Everyone is still entranced with Marietta and she is soaring with merriment. Anxiously waiting for an opportunity to sneak through the cramped room, I tuck the peculiar object into my inside jacket pocket. A few people smile at me lightly. They figure I'm a member of their elite club and aren't questioning my presence yet.

"Such an amusing story," an elegant woman remarks to Marietta. "I prefer Arthur's Legend, but this is comparable to Gengi's."

"I'm glad you were entertained," Marietta returns. "Each of my Legends holds a special place in my heart."

I duck when her gaze sweeps across the room once more. Her eyebrows draw together in confusion when she notices that her chair is empty. It's time for me to get out of here. While she is weaving her way back to her chair, I weave my way toward and out the door.

Klem gives me a sour look when I brush by him. "Enjoy the show?"

"Quite a bit," I answer, hoping he doesn't take a swipe at me. "I see why it's invitation only. Don't worry. She didn't know we were there."

My words don't do anything to lift his spirits but I don't really care. The sun is already peeking over the buildings and I feel like I've been hit with a wrecking ball. The object I stole is burning a hole in my jacket, but I can't risk looking at it. I'm not in the clear yet.

Lily and Hyde are waiting for me down the street.

"What was that all about?" Lily asks.

This isn't the time to explain. Marietta already knows that her …whatever it is…is missing. Hyde notices the bulge in my jacket and does me a huge favour.

"Come on, Lily," he says, giving her a significant look. "We should get back to the restaurant."

Lily stares at us suspiciously but then relaxes. Rubbing her eyes, she grins sheepishly. "I must be tired. I thought you might get yourself into trouble."

"It's nothing you need to worry about, Lily," I assure her.

Gazing at me sadly, Lily shoots me a brave smile. "That's what Radcliff always used to say."

Lily isn't worrying about nothing; angering a Whisperer can bring down a world of trouble. Not that it matters much. I'm dead in three days anyway.

9

After a delicious breakfast of freshly brewed coffee and omelettes, I decide not to tell Lily about my little side venture. She needs the Whisperers. If they find out that she was involved with the theft they won't let her in to their performances. That would just about ruin her. Insanity and depression are also universally illegal; Lily wouldn't last one minute in the Prison.

"I've never heard that Legend before," Lily says into her third cup of coffee.

"I don't think any of us have," I reply. Leaning back in the booth, I rub my sore neck. If I'm not careful I'm going to pass out in what's left of my omelet. "I get the feeling that it didn't even happen here."

"You too?" Lily yawns as she slumps a little lower in our booth. Large, black circles have settled underneath her eyes and she is struggling to keep herself awake. "You mean it might have happened before the City? Whatever that was…"

Her eyes drift closed, her head slumps onto Hyde's chest and her breathing deepens. She's out.

Hyde, on the other hand, seems to be doing just fine. He's flung his suit jacket over a coat rack and rolled the sleeves of his beautiful shirt up to his elbows. Brushing Lily's hair out of her face, he tenderly kisses the top of her head.

Rosamund, one of the waitresses, comes over to fill my coffee cup.

"You need anything else?" she asks. I shake my head. Leaning in, she pretends to wipe a coffee spill from our table. "Well, Lenny says everything is free for you guys this morning, so you might want to take advantage."

"Pie," says Hyde quickly. "Apple if you have it."

"Will do, and you Daryl?"

"Apple pie," I echo while trying to conceal a yawn. I don't think the coffee is ever going to kick in.

"Two apples, great; I'll tell him to put on whip cream and ice cream too." She walks away with our orders.

Hyde and I sit in silence. We don't have anything to talk about…or so I think.

"Lily's been ordered to procreate," he states.

I offer Hyde hollow congratulations. The word *procreate* makes me nauseous. Curling my lips in distaste, I shift uncomfortably in my seat. Orders of this kind are standard practice for women who are over twenty-two years old. I manage to avoid it because I always pay extra to make my alias barren. Pregnancy wouldn't help me any. Besides, someone coming by one day and ordering me to have a baby doesn't sit well with me. It doesn't even matter to them whether or not you have a man in your life. They'll provide one for you.

After another extended silence, Hyde continues. "I don't exist."

I shrug at his predicament. It has nothing to do with me. A man has to apply to impregnate a woman. Once he's been accepted there aren't any problems. But Hyde is what Criminals call a ghost: he doesn't have an identity on the system. Ghosts live in hideouts, like Jack and his crew. I'm what's known as an alias: I rent a box above ground. It exposes me to Cop radar but I don't run the risk of being executed. The Prison incinerates anyone caught without an identity.

Hyde is staring at me and I realize that he wants to keep talking about this. Unsure as to why he's suddenly so serious, I ask a standard question. "How long before they send her to a breeding house?"

"Two weeks."

Rosamund comes back with our pie. Steam rises out of the dessert and the vanilla ice cream is melting over its crust. It looks delicious but I'm suddenly not hungry. We both thank our waitress and she smiles happily before leaving us to our conversation.

I can sense the tension in Hyde's body even though he looks completely calm. No Criminal relishes the idea of losing their citizen-lover to the system. Once Lily is gone, she's gone. She'll be assigned a new box to live in with whoever fathers her child. Hyde can still be in her life, but that kind of situation gets too complicated for most lovers. Considering how long they've been together, I'm guessing that Hyde isn't going to let her go without a fight.

"Are you going to make her into a ghost or make yourself into an alias?"

"It's expensive to mess with the system," Hyde says. Pushing his pie to the side, he takes out his credit balance. "A botched job will bring the Cops. I'm going to ask you for a favour."

I already know what he wants. "Keep my half of the credits from Madman's reward. I'm not going to need it."

"I also need a line to Frenzy."

That name sends a chill up my spine. *Of course*, Hyde needs a line to Frenzy; *everybody* needs a line to Frenzy. The woman walking past the restaurant's window needs a line to Frenzy; the kid being dragged to the bathroom and yelling for his mother needs a line to Frenzy; even the decrepit, old man with his nose buried in a glass of cheap wine needs a line to Frenzy.

He's is a manipulator, a Criminal who can jack his brain right into the system. It's not a rare talent, but Frenzy is a rare person. He's gifted. The system is a gigantic code—infinite, according to him. By rearranging small parts of it he changes information. He's nearly a Legend, a hero amongst manipulators, the only one you can truly count on to get the job done.

And I'm one of his precious few gatekeepers.

Even though I've been gone for over two years Hyde knows—I know—that I can still get to him. When Jack found his illegal path into the Court he needed a crew to operate it. He would only hire the best so Ash Martin, Frenzy, became part of his team. But jacking into the system is a delicate process. One wrong shift with his brain and the Cops will catch him. Certain jobs can take hours, even days, of pure concentration. Afterwards, Ash can barely talk; he hits his head against walls and tries to pull the veins out of his arms.

Hence the nickname Frenzy.

The thought of seeing him again makes my blood run cold. He's the reason I ended up in the Prison.

But this isn't about me. It's about Lily. I study her serene face, the way she clings to her lover as she sleeps. This is the woman who risked her life to save me. She didn't even know me at the time. I was an orphan running from a street gang that was going to cave my head in if they caught me. Out of breath, terrified, I ducked into the restaurants kitchen, hoping they'd run right by and I could double back. Lily had been working here for over a year, sweeping the floors and cleaning the windows. When she saw me run in she motioned me into a storage closet and locked the door.

The gang broke two of her fingers and nearly strangled her to death. Coughing and sputtering, she desperately told them that I'd run out the front door. After they left, she hid me in her small room above the restaurant. I remember how she and her brother reset her bones. They didn't have credits for even the worst doctor, so she tied her fingers to mediocre splints with dirt stained rags.

I still don't understand why she saved me. I was a worthless street kid, and I'd stolen food from the gang. They had every right to destroy me. But Lily, brave and compassionate, defied the brutal rules of the Criminal underworld. The harsh streets had toughened me. I was impenetrable and cold, always ready to fight for my next meal. But that night I cried myself to sleep.

Hyde is waiting patiently for my answer, but he already knows I'm not going to abandon Lily to the impersonal machinations of the system.

If Lily goes ghost she has to leave her life behind and be completely dependent on him for everything. She isn't suited for the Criminal life,

Hyde and I both know it. On the other hand, if he becomes an alias, Lily will still have to have a child; there's no guarantee that B Sector will accept his application.

"Ghost or alias...?" I finally ask again.

"Alias," Hyde answers. "I'm willing to take the risk. Lily doesn't know I'm asking you and I'd like to keep it that way. She thinks she's shipping off to the breeding house and she's almost come to terms with it. I don't want to get her hopes up, all right?"

I nod wearily. I would never hurt Lily; Hyde is counting on that. "How much are you offering?"

"I can pay him fifteen thousand."

"So that's how much I was worth to Madman. Seems like a lot of credit to offer for a half-dead. Give me a day."

We sit in silence for a while, finally digging in to our apple pie. Truthfully, I don't know if fifteen thousand will be enough. Frenzy has been crushing on Lily for years. There's no way to know how he'll react when I ask him.

Exhausted, I let my eyes drift shut. A pleasant sinking sensation takes over and I'm floating, gliding along without a care in the world. I jerk myself awake before my face hits the table.

"Got a place to stay?" Hyde inquires. He still looks as though he got his full eight hours.

Every smart Criminal has a stash set aside for hard times. Mine includes a small box that's paid for indefinitely, a little present from Frenzy four years ago. Unfortunately, it's with the Accountants in E Sector (otherwise known as the Bank). I have business here in B.

I toss an idea around in my head before answering Hyde's question. "Is Kentucky Jim still living in his tomb?"

"I haven't heard about him moving," Hyde answers, "but no one's heard from him for a while. He could be dead for all I know."

"That old bastard can't die. He'll have a bed for me."

"Stay clear of the north section of B," Hyde warns as I get up. "Cops have been raiding there all week."

Nodding my thanks, I go into the kitchen. Lenny's nowhere to be seen so I grab my bag from under the table. An uneasy feeling settles ruthlessly in my stomach; my breakfast is threatening to make a sudden reappearance. Reeling, I fall against the kitchen wall.

There aren't any outs. I'm fucking trapped.

All at once, my skin starts to burn. Desperately trying to keep a hold on my sanity, I slide to the ground and put my head on my knees. Without a second thought, I dig my nails into my forearm. The sharp pain helps bring me back. The room slowly comes into focus and my body temperature returns to normal. A moment passes, and then another. I'm calm now; I've got it together.

It isn't over yet, the fearless voice whispers. *There's a choice here, Madman or Locket—slavery or death. Choose. Choose before they choose for you.*

But I can't answer that question now. I need sleep before I decide which dead end to hit at full speed.

10

Kentucky Jim doesn't mess around. He changes the traps in his hideout every time someone leaves. There's a little paranoia in his work, a touch of madness that gives him the title *genius*. Anyone who's ever been caught in the foyer of his hide-out will give him a different name, which is why I was one of the only people who ever came around here.

When I slip into a back passage and open a small access tunnel, the air smells unusually stale. The old man doesn't leave his hideout unless it's absolutely necessary. He usually has enough supplies to last him a few months and he has an errand boy that I've never met.

How long has it been since someone's come through the front door? Weeks? Months?

As I stare into the dark passage, a comforting sense of security envelops me. Kentucky's hideout was my home after I managed to get off the streets. The old man took me in. He wasn't easy to live with, far from it, but his ornery nature was a luxury compared to the uncertainty of not having a box or a hideout. After a while, I realized that if he spoke to you it meant he liked you. He ignores people he hates.

I step down a metal ladder and hear the telltale clicking of a fire-trap. That noise is enough to send most people running. At the push of a button, Kentucky can burn somebody alive in this small entryway. Most people believe that he would without a second thought, but I know he's not the type to kill without reason. Amused, I stand my ground in his foyer and wait for the familiar whir of video equipment. It takes a minute for it to kick into gear. Lights turn on and a camera comes out of the wall. It bleeps at me before shoving itself into my face.

<State your business.> Kentucky's gruff voice filters through his old communications system.

"Need a bed," I say, knowing he's going to let me in. There's a long pause before he answers. I wait patiently. He isn't going to make this easy.

<Don't have a bed for you. Get out of here.>

"Give over, Kentucky, we both know you're going to open the door." I throw my bag nonchalantly over my shoulder. "I'm only coming through the front entrance out of respect."

Nobody but Kentucky's errand boy and I know about the back door to his hideout. That's how I met him; I stumbled upon it accidentally. Kentucky nearly took out my eyes but I eventually convinced him that I was more use to him alive than dead.

The camera retreats back into its home. The wall in front of me slides away and I step into Kentucky's massive hideout.

Dozens of tables, laden down with what looks like junk, spread out to my left and right, a quarter mile or so to the walls. Robots of all different sizes are sorting through scrap metal and rusted parts. They've all been constructed from this crap and look like they might collapse at any second. I know better, though. Kentucky is a man of infinite talent. These robots will be in tip-top condition long after I die.

Reassuring bleeps from the frantic robots are a soothing lullaby in this crazy place. The familiar sights and sounds add to my fatigue. Taking a deep, cleansing breath, I finally let my guard down. It's easy to forget about the outside world when I'm here. It's one of the only places I feel completely safe.

I can hear Kentucky moving from a mile away. The hydraulics of his robotic legs makes a terrible racket. He's coming up on my left and I turn to watch him clunk towards me. While inside his carefully constructed suit he stands about six feet. (I suspect that when he still had legs he was only five feet four, but I never mention that to him). The legs bend backwards instead of forwards and robotic arms stick out of a rounded core. The old man's only good arm deftly taps away at buttons inside the round compartment that he calls home. It's an intimidating contraption; Kentucky definitely didn't build it to look human.

He stops right in front of me, staring down with unmasked contempt. His grey hair sticks out of his head like wires and his white moustache droops over his lips. No matter how ugly and mean he seems, Kentucky has a gigantic heart. There's a look in his eyes that gives him away. Brimming with happiness, I meet his unimpressed gaze. He extends his only remaining limb through the steel bars of his suit. He grips my hand tight enough to hurt my bones and then drops it. The old man missed me.

"I don't like disappearing acts," he growls. "Next time you're not welcome back."

Turning away quickly, he moves down one row of tables, robots jumping out of his way as they continue to catalogue his junk. His grumpy reception doesn't bother me. If he'd greeted me any other way I'd be suspicious of his motives. In fact, his harsh ways have a strange way of making me feel welcome. He hasn't changed one bit. If he didn't look so menacing, I might give him a hug.

Glad to be back, I follow Kentucky to his living quarters. I always like to take in the smell of this place. The air is crisp, somehow smoother here than anywhere else I've been. I asked him about it once and he told me to mind my own damn business. Since then, I've minded my own damn business.

Half way across his warehouse a set of stairs descends into a carpeted room. Carpet is a luxury. Excited and relieved to be here, I fly down the stairs and throw my bag on a small table. The lights turn on automatically and I see Kentucky's half-sized cot to my right. He's added a few bars to the ceiling since I was here last. I turn to look at him when he doesn't follow me down.

He gives me a hard look before speaking. "You know where your cot is; don't say good-bye before you leave." He tromps away and doesn't look back.

"I knew you missed me!" I toss cheerily at his retreating form.

Kentucky answers with a low snarl.

When Heathcliff Jackson found Kentucky the old man was half dead and missing his legs and left arm. The wounds had been sewn and disinfected, leaving Jack more than a little mystified. Kentucky was no help because he couldn't remember his name or what had happened to him. All he did know was how to build. Hiring Jack's first crew to find the parts for him, he built his suit in a little over a month. They started calling him Kentucky because he kept muttering the word to himself, over and over. Nobody knows what it means. The old man only made sense about half the time anyway, so they just made it his name. He chose Jim for himself. When he was ready, he found this hideout and started collecting.

The walls bleep at me. As usual, their off-orange colour makes me slightly ill. The table and chairs wobble on broken legs and water damage is still soaking through one of the corners. The brown stain has doubled in size and has a mildly putrid odour. There's nothing like a small sewage leak to cramp a hideouts' style.

I press a button on the table and a cot folds out from the wall. The linens are fresh.

Like I said, the old man missed me.

11

Gasping I sit up and grab at the darkness. There's something here, watching me. In the walls, in the ceiling, in the floor, in the fucking air—I can feel it staring. My psychic talent is screaming at me.

It's here, it's fucking here.

What's next? What has it got for me this time—fire, water, blade, blunt, cold, heat, shock, seclusion, or worse. Has it brought the chair? Sweet sky! Stop staring and *go away.*

Terrified, knowing I'm caught between dreaming and waking, I ram my fist full force into the wall. Pain shoots through my knuckles and up my arm, jarring my shoulder. It hurts like a sonofabitch, but it wakes me up.

During my nightmare, I made my way to the other side of Kentucky's sleeping quarters. It isn't dark, I never turned out the lights, and it's not here. My heart won't stop pounding, but it's not here. Wiping the cold sweat from my face, I shakily return to my bed. It isn't even warm. How long was I standing on the other side of the room?

It's the same thing every night, over and over again. I don't even know I've closed my eyes until I'm back in my cell…waiting… waiting for the Prison to start another round of how-much-can-she-take-before-she-starts-trying-to-gouge-out-her-own-eyes.

Shoving the horrific memories into the darkest recesses of my mind, I search for a distraction. The object that I stole from Marietta is peeking out from under my jacket. I grab it and hold it to my chest, letting its cool outer surface soothe my terror. Rocking back and forth, pressing the object hard into my skin until my chest hurts, I force my fear to retreat. My death grip on the strange rectangle slowly eases.

This mysterious object is still making my head buzz. Carefully opening it with my shaking hands, I study the curious markings within. I don't know what they are but I do recognize numbers in the top corners. It must be some kind of code. There's only one person I know who lives, eats and breathes codes—Frenzy. If I bring this thing to him he might be able to make some kind of sense of it. Considering that I need him to put together Hyde's alias and approve the procreation application, I've got more than enough reasons to swallow my apprehension and seek him out.

Finding him won't be a problem. He'll still be with the crew: he's got nowhere else to go. Besides, Jack would never let a manipulator that good slip through his fingers. Frenzy is the only one who can get the crew in and out of the Court.

An idea hits me with such force that I'm momentarily stunned. Unable to breathe I desperately grab onto it, praying it doesn't leave as quickly as it came.

He could do it. It's a possibility; a slim chance. Small, but it's something. It's better than nothing, isn't it?

The brilliance of Cop Sector security is its simplicity. The designers assumed that, because no one can break in, there's no one inside who will try to break out. They only have a semi-permeable energy field (SPEF) in the sewers. That's how I managed to get through ten years ago: the field only keeps people out. So the trick to finding a line into Cop Sector is the SPEF. But first I have to get to the other side.

The other side…with the right information Frenzy could get you there. You could find a line into A.

I may have three reasons to see Frenzy.

Dread fills my chest like cement. I'll be surrounded by Cops. Shaking off my fear, I remind myself that Cop Sector is not the Prison. Besides, there's no guarantee I'm going to be able to get back in. If I admit defeat Madman rules me, if I go into hiding Locket kills me. Both options are dead ends.

The third, at least, gives me back a little power.

12

I wake up to metal clanking on metal. Groaning, I crack open an eye. I don't remember falling asleep.

Kentucky is using his only arm to swing out of his suit. He grabs on to a bar on the low ceiling and hops into a chair. It's amazing to watch what this guy can do with his one arm.

All through this place are hand holds and metal bars so that Kentucky can move around it if he's not in his suit. He installed them after his metal body malfunctioned a while back. I found him heaving himself around, grabbing onto table legs to move. I couldn't help him; he kept screaming at me when I came too close. In the end he taught me how to fix the suit, hollering orders from half way across the room. I try not to remember Kentucky helpless on the floor like that. He's so damn huge in that suit you forget he's missing three of his limbs.

Kentucky throws off his sweaty shirt and a little square robot, hiding in a cubby in the wall, whirs into action. A clamp attached to its head grabs the soiled garment and it pulls the worn fabric back into the wall, making bleeping and whirring noises the entire time. That's a new one! Kentucky presses a button on the table and another robot carrying a nutrient bar enters his living quarters. My one limbed friend tears off the wrapper and devours most of it in one bite.

"It true what I hear about Madman wanting you to find a line into A?" the old man asks.

I yawn and stretch as I slide my feet into my boots. Sometimes I forget how fast news travels. "Yeah."

"Never did like that Lyons guy," he comments, letting out a small belch. "Finding the line won't be easy. You'll need this."

Kentucky turns around in his chair and takes something from a front compartment in his metal suit. He doesn't even bother looking at it before he tosses it at me. The small metal gadget bounces off my palm and hits the floor. Scooping it into my hands, I examine the cloaking device. This little machine goes around someone's wrist. When it's activated it hides the wearer from Cop technology: motion detectors, heat detectors, carbon-dioxide level readers, and etcetera. These little babies don't come cheap. Mystified and touched beyond words, I watch the old man swing himself onto his cot.

How did he know I was going to try to find the line?

"You know your way out," he says.

That means I'm dismissed. Kentucky doesn't like displays of affection, so I don't throw my arms around him. Instead, I fasten the cloak around my wrist and take the steps two at a time.

The robots are still working. They don't acknowledge my existence unless it's to get out of my way. I want to head straight for Kentucky's back door but I feel a presence to my right: someone else is in the room. Looking over my shoulder, I see a striking girl sitting in Kentucky's dilapidated kitchen. She stares at me over a mug of steaming coffee, taking in my rumpled appearance with mild curiosity. She doesn't look more than ten years old...what is she doing in Kentucky's hideout?

"Who the hell are you?" I ask, unable to cover my surprise.

"Who the hell are *you*?" she returns.

Intrigued, I study her round, angelic face. Big, grey-green eyes stare right back at me. There's no suspicion in her gaze, no fear or cynicism. In fact, her eyes glow with the glory of a youth untouched by tragedy. But that can't be the case if she's sitting down here. Does she have any idea how innocent she looks?

"Someone who wants to know if there's any more coffee," I finally answer.

"You look like you need it."

Motioning towards the seat across from her, she rises and nearly floats through the run-down kitchen. I guess she knows her way around. Sitting in the offered chair I put down my bag and study the way she walks. There's something about it. Why is it bugging me?

"I thought I was the only one who ever came down here," she says, delicately dusting out a blue mug. Filling it with coffee from a decrepit pot she turns around to study me. Her grey-green eyes send a strange tremor through my body, making me suspicious of her saintly appearance. A moment later, she sits down and hands me the mug. "I've been coming here for a whole year and I've never seen anyone else."

Thanking her, I sniff the hot liquid and look around for the sugar. Kentucky usually keeps it in an old tin box about the size of my fist. Oddly enough, when I look down at the table, I find it right next to my hand. I must not have seen it when I first sat down.

The girl's eyes widen in fascination and excitement. "How did you do that?"

"Do what?"

"With the sugar tin," she explains. "It was next to me and then it slid across the table! How did you do that?"

I can't decide if she's playing a game with me. Confused, I shoot her a inquiring look. Picking up the tin she searches for a string or wire with her hands. "My brother used to love illusions. Did you learn it from a book?"

"Book...?" I know I've heard that word before.

"Yes, a b... never mind." She folds her hands on the table and demurely studies a burn mark in the decaying metal.

Shaking sugar into my coffee I search for a safe question to ask. "So... what sector are you from?"

"You wouldn't believe me if I told you." She shrugs. "You?"

"You wouldn't believe me if I told you," I echo. Despite my initial instinct not to trust her, I can feel her drawing out my softer side. "I used to be a Cop."

"You're *Daryl*, the Criminal from A Sector?" she breathes. Her grey-green eyes widen in fascination once again. She gives me another look over. "You don't look at all like I imagined you."

"And how did you imagine me?"

"I mean, the way they talk...." Her face flushes with embarrassment. "It's like you're made of precious gems or eight feet tall, or something."

I chuckle into my coffee. "The way *they* talk...?"

"The other orphans. They all tell stories about you. None of them are going to believe that I actually *met* you."

"You're a scavenger?" I ask. Each sector has a different name for its orphans. In B it's scavengers, in Q it's strays, in N it's germs. The list goes on. "The old man's adopted you?"

"I suppose," she answers, picking at a nasty scab on her arm. "I mostly live here...like you did when you first met Kentucky."

"I take it you know everything about me."

"Not everything, just a lot. It's hard not to." She studies my face and her brow wrinkles in concern. "Everyone's watching you. They want to know what you're going to do."

There's something in her tone that trips my psychic talent again. Suspicious of her motives, I take the time to study her intense gaze. The finely tuned survival instinct buried in the depths of her eyes tells me everything I need to know.

Information is power. People must be playing high stakes with my Madman drama; the whole Criminal world has probably laid down bets. If this girl could get inside info she could sell it for some real fame on the streets. She figures she's got me trusting her enough that I'll let something slip.

Irritated at her little show, I decide to teach her a lesson. Hideouts are no bullshit zones—business is reserved for topside.

"You must think I'm some shiny novice, bright eyes. I'm a veteran. I don't give away anything for free."

Her air of simple purity melts away. Fatigue and disappointment darken her clear gaze as her lips descend into a frown. Shaking her head vigorously, she rolls her eyes and lets out an annoyed sigh. "Did I come on too strong? I thought I had you."

"Are we going to trade or not?"

She pouts when she realizes that I'm not going to fall for her second trap—camaraderie. Leaning forward onto her elbows, she studies my face once more. "You're not as wrecked as you look. I'd heard you were off your game."

I won't be falling for that maneuver either. Locket and Wulff are the only ones who can manipulate me that way. "It's either a trade or nothing."

"*Fine*," she yields, exasperated. "I'll trade. What do you want?"

"I want your story."

She lets out a skeptical huff. "Yeah, right, that's all you want."

"I'm guessing you live on the streets," I continue. "You know what a good story is worth. I'm also guessing that you've never told anyone where you're really from. If you know anything about me, like you claim, you know that my curiosity gets me into a lot of trouble. I want to know your story. You can start with your name. Your *real* name, not your scavenger name."

I sit back in my chair to watch the emotions play across her face; suspicion, frustration, uncertainty, curiosity and then, finally, acceptance. Searching my idle gaze, she nods slowly.

I wonder how long she's been on the streets. It's possible the speck of optimism I can still see in her eyes is genuine, but it's also possible she's one of those people who can't stop acting. Whatever the case, I need to satisfy my curiosity. If we come up against each other again, I want to know as much as I can about her.

"What do I get in return?"

"My plans," I promise. "I have two days left but I already know what I'm going to do."

"I can live with that," she replies after mulling it over for a moment. Because I have seniority she has to deliver first. "My name is Tyler, Clarissa Tyler." She hesitates before continuing, waiting to see if I think she's lying.

"I believe you."

"I'm from the Court."

I wait for my psychic talent to tell me she's full of shit, but it doesn't kick in.

There are no F Sector would-be Criminals. Maybe my talent isn't working like it used to. Then again, I suddenly understand why her walk was bugging me. The citizens of the Court, called Lawmakers, have a way of moving. You won't find it anywhere else. It's like they're gliding across the floor, feet hardly touching the ground. The only reason I know about it is because I was Jack's second thief in his line to F—I've been to the Court. Clarissa has done a good job learning to walk tough, but there's still a bit of her old life in her muscles.

"Lawmaker," I finally acknowledge, impressed. Jack would be interested in her story. "How were you swallowed?"

"My father..." she stumbles over her words "I was seven when they arrested him."

"Arrested?"

Clarissa nods. "I never really understood what happened. Our lives were just over. My father was gone; my elder sister disappeared, I don't remember seeing her before I was taken away; my elder brother was already an adult by then, but there was nothing he could do to help us; we had no guardian so my mother and I were sold as slaves into T Sector."

Obviously unsettled by her memories, she stumbles over her words and then stops talking altogether. Her story sparks a note of compassion in my heart. I know all too well what it's like to lose your family at a young age. Still, I can't completely understand because I was never sold into slavery. The Court has a strange policy when it comes to women: no male guardian, no citizenship. I don't know much about it except that Gentry women, by law, belong to Gentry men. So, in a way, Clarissa and her mother were already slaves before they were sold.

"After a few weeks in T Sector my mother bribed a smuggler to get me out," she finally continues. "I've been a scavenger ever since."

I can only imagine what she means by *bribe*. There's something she's leaving out of her story, but I don't need the gory details. "How do you like the streets?"

"Anything is better than the grind," she replies.

That word—*grind*—abruptly ends our conversation. That's what escaped slaves call their time in T Sector. It has a double meaning. Most are worked until they can't remember their own names, but some are used for more *recreational* activities. Ex-slaves like to debate about whose worse off, the land-workers or the sex-workers.

I slowly examine Clarissa's angelic features—her bright eyes and healthy, flawless skin. Thick hair cascades in flowing waves around her shoulders. She's little more than a child but, without her carefully constructed mask of innocence, I grasp exactly what *the grind* means to her.

Sickened at the realization, I struggle not to pity her. Pity is reserved for the pathetic. As far as I've seen, Clarissa is a survivor. We wouldn't be having this conversation otherwise. Besides, sympathy will only cloud my judgment.

"If you could get back into F Sector, would you do it?"

Clarissa balks at the question. Much like me, I don't think she ever considered the possibility of going back. "What would be the point?"

"Let's say a powerful crime boss calls in a favour. It's either find a way home or die."

Her mouth falls open. "You're going to find a line into A."

I smile in confirmation. Placing my half empty mug on the table, I get up and grab my bag.

"Everyone will say I'm lying," she protests. "You only have two choices: death by Locket or work for Madman. People will rub my face into the pavement if I give them this."

"Will they?" I ask with false innocence. "Wow. I guess you shouldn't say anything, then."

"Fuck you!" She jumps to her feet. Her head barely reaches my shoulder but she's ready to hit me. My amused expression only fuels her anger. "You knew I couldn't use this info for anything."

"And you shouldn't have tried to trick me down here," I answer. "If you want to make it off the streets, bright eyes, this is your first lesson. Even Criminals have a code: we don't disturb the sanctuaries. If you're a guest in someone's hideout you don't play the game; if you're a hostess you don't play the game; if you meet another Criminal in a hideout neither of you play the game."

Clarissa visibly deflates. Hunching over, she places her hands over her stomach as though recovering from a punch to the gut. She doesn't know where to look so she fixes her gaze on her mug of coffee.

It isn't easy watching her collapse inwardly. Despite my belief that no good can come if I sympathize with her, I feel horribly guilty.

"Then again, you could take a chance," I say. "People might believe I'm crazy enough to try." My words don't do anything to improve her mood. I try another tactic. "Heath Jackson might be able to find a job for you, if you're willing. What's your scavenger name?"

She immediately perks up when I mention Jack. "Sonora."

"Well, Sonora, he'll send word by the old man."

She manages a small smile before I walk away. A warm feeling settles in my chest. Despite her manipulations, I'm fond of Clarissa Tyler.

Her story is different from mine. Nineteen years ago my mom died; seventeen years ago my dad never came home. On the morning of the seventh day of his disappearance my younger brother, Nathan, and I were officially declared orphans. A few minutes later, one of our neighbours came to claim the bounty on our heads. I was three months away from my twelfth birthday—ninety-one days stood between me and the ability to become my little brother's guardian.

Nobody knows where the orphans go; I didn't want to find out. The day I became one, I ran.

Nathan didn't want to go with me. He didn't understand the City the same way that I do; this is a place that pits neighbour against neighbour in the name of survival. My harmless ten-year-old brother trusted the other Cop to help us. While I was throwing clothes and tools into a bag he called me paranoid and let our neighbour in.

I think the tranquilizer dart must have killed him. When I say *I think*, I mean that I don't *know*—I can't be sure. Nathan went down so quickly. Mier, the desperately poor guy who lived in the box above us, was a giant fuck-up. There's no guarantee he adjusted the dosage to fit a kid's metabolism. As he stood over Nathan's motionless body he prepared the dart that was meant for me. I didn't wait around long enough for him to catch me.

When mom died my dad moved us into a poorer area of Cop Sector. I spent most of my time exploring the air ducts and basement passages of our run-down, piece of crap building. I scrambled into an air duct, took the quickest route to the basement, squeezed through the bent bars of the basement door, and ran. Somewhere in the middle of my panicked escape I found myself in Cop Sector sewers. A few hours later I came up for air and I was in B Sector.

I never saw my little brother or my dad again.

From then on, I learned the hard way. I had no credit balance so, like Klem, I worked for food. It isn't hard for a scavenger to figure out that the best way to make a living is by helping others break the law. But nobody trusts orphans. They don't see the big picture because they're starving. Most of them die before they get a chance to prove themselves.

Despite the differences in our stories, however, I feel a certain kinship with Clarissa. Her family is gone, just like mine; she's using her talents to eke out a living, just like I had to. And she's making it work. The streets are a brutal place. If she hasn't died yet, there may be a future for her in the Criminal underworld. Depending on what happens in the next few days, I'll see what I can do to ease that transition.

At the back wall I step behind an industrial storage unit. Bending metal away from the wall, I slip through a hole that serves as Kentucky's back door. There are handholds all through it to help the old man move through in case of emergency. It's a maze of tunnels but I know which lefts and rights to take. Before long I emerge into the streets. It's a bright afternoon by the looks of it.

Jumping over Kentucky's getaway vehicle—a seemingly rusted out piece of metal that can actually get about ten feet in hover and ninety in speed—I head for the messier streets of B.

It's time to visit my old crew.

13

Getting to Heath Jackson's hideout is more uncomfortable than it is hard. It's in the rough area of B. Gentler sorts don't come here. Someone might decide to smash your head in if they decide they don't like you. When last I was here a man named Gullet owned these streets. He gave Jack's crew freedom to roam as they liked. I don't recognize any faces and it's likely that Gullet is dead. Street bosses, like orphans, never last too long.

Rough looking men scan my body as I walk past. Nervously stepping over a stoned user, I make sure to keep my head down. If a woman is walking down one of these streets she's probably selling sex. I get more than a few offers for a quickie before I manage to get down the first block.

"Once you see the size of my dick, sweetheart, you'll thank Luck for sending me your way," one heavily muscled man taunts as he leers at me. "I could split that fine body in two and still have you begging for more."

I stare uneasily at the street and pretend I don't hear him. Sexual harassment always put me on edge. It brings back memories. The big talker guffaws before getting out of my way. He's impressed his buddies enough, he doesn't need to make good on his claim. Relieved, I scurry away from him and his sniggering gang.

There's a group of four scarred and ragged men up ahead. My psychic talent buzzes—some idiots you can walk right by, others refuse to be ignored. Unluckily for me, they're loitering in front of the alley that leads to Jack's hideout.

"Now you I could ride for hours," one guy loudly remarks when he sees me coming their way.

"I get her first. All I need is a minute," a tall, hollow-faced man promises. "I'll just slide in and slide out. She won't miss a step."

Disgusted, I shake my head. "Just let me through."

His hand slides over my shoulders, down my waist and over my hips. Bringing his fingers back up to rub my neck, he runs his tongue over cracked lips. My skin crawls at the unwanted contact, my stomach churns with revulsion. These guys need to learn to keep their hands to themselves. While the men continue to taunt me, circling me like their next meal, my mind retreats into menacing stillness. I can't hear them anymore. All I know is that one of them is still touching me.

He'll be the first to go down.

I'm carrying my bag in my right hand so I casually grab his wrist with my left. It takes very little effort to put someone into an arm lock if you know what you're doing. He grunts in pain as I kick out his knees. When he falls to the ground, I put my foot on his back and pull back on his arm. His shoulder pops out nicely from his body before his scream echoes through the afternoon heat. My instincts sharpen as his pain filled cry fills the uncaring streets; power surges through me as his arm flops uselessly at his side.

But I should have made this first encounter bloodier. Blood tends to make others hesitate.

Turning to my next attacker, I easily duck under his ill-aimed punch. A moment later my fist rams into his nose. The cartilage breaks with an exquisite crunch and blood pours down his face.

The third guy grabs me from behind while his buddy stumbles backwards. I drop my stance and ram my fist into his balls. His grip slackens and he slides to the ground, squeaking. When I turn around I coldly watch his eyes rolling back into his head.

I ready myself for the next attack but it doesn't come. Whipping my head around, I see the fourth man, pasty faced and unhealthily skinny, standing there with an astonished look on his face.

He shakes his head dumbly. The first attacker can barely stand, the second is still clutching his nose, and the third isn't moving at all. Nobody has come to see what happened because nobody cares; that's why Jack chose this part of B.

Emerging from my detached state, I take terrible delight in this man's fear. I savour his friends' intense agony. The three wounded men, moaning and whimpering, are slowly crawling away from the alley.

"You want to follow your friends the fuck out of here?"

I don't bother to watch them leave. They're nothing but a waste of skin and space.

Striding down the narrow alley, I take a left, right, and another left before I reach a dead end. I remove a brick from the wall to my right and press the flashing button behind it. The lift activates as soon as I put the brick back in its slot. Holding onto a rail that looks like it belongs to a fire escape, I'm lowered into the foyer of Jack's hideout.

14

When my head clears street level another lift takes it place. That's a new feature; the crew has been busy.

"Fancy shmancy," I mutter as I'm enveloped by darkness.

The lift moves fast for a piece of crap. It only takes a few moments to get me two stories below ground. I could take out my flashlight and have a look around, but the black is so comfortable. Besides, by activating the lift I've automatically triggered the hideout's traps. Someone must be inside because the lift wasn't disconnected. They'll be waiting for me to use a light source so they can have the tactical advantage.

Stepping off the lift, I walk forward eight steps, turn to the left and walk five more. I could use my psychic talent to see in the dark, but that talent tends to give me a headache if I abuse it. At any rate, it wouldn't help me. I already know every nook and cranny of this place. Even with the lights out, I know that directly ahead of me there's a steel door. Beyond it is Jack's hideout.

I wasn't sure how I would feel once I got here. Nostalgic, I guess, maybe even a little sad. There are parts of me that are made of steel; I figure their sufficient protection from any part me that's still connected to this place.

Standing in the dark, I hesitate on the threshold of my past.

Wulff pleaded with me for months to accept Jack's offer of becoming part of the F Sector crew. Back then I wouldn't even consider it. I'd decided never to work with others, to make my way as a loner even they usually end up crazy or worse. Then the Criminal world discovered my Cop origins. Overnight, I lost nearly every connection I'd made in five years of clawing my way off the streets. A few people stood by me—Lily, Kentucky Jim, Wulff—but they couldn't give me work. They were struggling, just like me. I was going to starve if I didn't do something.

I know now that the only reason Nick Redden contracted me was because he guessed that I wouldn't be able to kill in cold blood. He wanted me to fail so that he could avenge everyone he'd lost to the Prison.

I suspect that Wulff was the one who convinced Jack to renew his offer. I was in rough shape, but Jack decided my A Sector background would be an asset to his team. He didn't see me as an ex-Cop who needed to be beaten into oblivion. I was a source of previously inaccessible information. I could teach him about Cop fighting techniques; I could help him anticipate Cop strategy; I could design new ways to infiltrate Cop security. But the truth is, I didn't take his offer because of his clever speech. I took it because he fascinated me.

Jack isn't an easy man to describe. When we first met I admired his quiet strength. He has a calming effect on people—on me. I felt safe around him. There was something about the way he treated me; no psychological fight for dominance or deliberately sexual scan of my body. He just held out his hand and warmly asked me if I needed work. When I hesitated he launched into his speech, but it was his gentle confidence that prompted me to accept. I was completely disarmed.

Years of working and living with him turned my admiration into a deep and aching respect. He would sit across the table from me, cleaning his equipment, while I pretended not to be totally aware of everything that he did. Those were interesting hours.

We also I played games like siblings. There are some people I can't sense with my psychic talent. I don't know why, it's a conundrum. They're invisible to my inner radar. Jack is one of them. He used to milk his gift for all it was worth. Scaring me out of my wits was one of his favourite past-times. I used to check every corner no matter where I went but he still managed to get me. Punching him afterward only made him laugh harder. He loved that I was such an easy target.

One morning I didn't hear him coming up behind me. I was concentrating on my tea, listening to Wulff tinkering in the garage, laughing at Frenzy's nervous good-bye as he left to get his oatmeal snacks. It suddenly occurred to me that I was happy. That kind of realization is Luck's greatest temptation. I froze in terror.

A few minutes later and it wouldn't have happened. I would have filed it away for a moment alone. But Jack came up behind me and gave me his brotherly shove. His touch threw me into a state of shock. All I knew was a terrible and hollow sense of loss. I had reached that inner void where my brother lay dying on the floor; where Ivana's neck snapped like a twig; where Nick Redden grunted on top of me. I was the nine-year-old who watched her mother die and the eleven-year-old waiting for her father to come home.

Jack carried me to my room, wrapped me in a warm blanket, and stayed at my side until I came out of the shock. I only knew one thing when I did: everything was going to slip away. My happiness guaranteed it.

This memory shakes me to the core. For a moment, I consider stepping back onto the lift and disappearing. Locket will find me in two days, but I could spend those days in a blissful, drug-induced euphoria. Forget Lily, forget the City, and forget the slim chance of sidestepping Madman's trap.

Torn between my loyalty and my fear, I stand wretched and alone in Jack's foyer.

<Copper...?> Frenzy's rough but hopeful voice filters through the com-system. <Are you out there?>

I don't know if I should answer. Before I can make up my mind, whirs and clicks echo through the large cement room—the traps have been disabled. I can hear the wheel on the steel door turning. When it opens, Frenzy pops through, the light from the hideout creating a bright halo behind him; his familiar, deep brown eyes welcome me home.

A strange mixture and relief and pain settles around my heart as I study my blurry-eyed, messy-haired, lean-bodied friend. I want to pick him up and spin him around, like in the old days, but I can't move. There's too much to feel and I'm too exhausted to do it. I quickly retreat behind a stony façade, leaving his warm-hearted expression hanging in the cool foyer air.

Cocking his head to one side Frenzy gawks at my haggard face. "We didn't think we'd see you again."

"I'm here on business," I state, hating my brusque tone. "I'm sure you guys heard about Madman's little *errand*."

"We heard," Frenzy answers. "We figured you'd choose Locket."

"Well, I've got two days," I snap. "I haven't really made up my mind yet."

Frenzy stands uncertainly on the threshold of Jack's hideout. He doesn't know me anymore. That doesn't concern me much, though, because I can still read him. His cautious behaviour screams that he's alone and that I'm making him nervous. I torture him by letting the heavy silence stretch on. Being here on business, it isn't my job to make him feel better.

"I've still got your tea," he finally offers. Stepping to one side, he hesitantly ushers me in. "I'll make you a cup."

A long, white hallway leads straight into the common room. I'm instantly enfolded in the masculine smells of Jack, Wulff and Frenzy. Wulff likes to shave with a strong, mint soap; the invigorating smell helps soothe the tension behind my eyes. Surrounding it is the rich aroma of Frenzy's favourite oatmeal snacks, hand made by Lenny. Frenzy uses them as an excuse to flirt with Lily in the mornings. Lingering beyond the mint and oatmeal is the earthy smell of Jack's leather cleaner.

To my left and right are the cubbies where the crew sleeps. Cubbies are big enough for bunk beds and a dresser. I lived in the second cubby on the left, right next to the bathroom, the worst cubby in the place. Someone would flush and the ghastly noise would wake me up every time. I remember, about a month after I moved in permanently, Wulff came back from Bragg's Bar staggeringly drunk. He didn't want to wake me so he went into the kitchen. The sink was too far away so he ended up puking all over the floor. We found him the next day, passed out on his stomach. His face was covered in vomit and he was muttering about how everyone got a good night's sleep. The funny part was that I wasn't in my cubby that night. I'd stayed out late with Lily and crashed on her floor.

My old cubby is tidier than I left it, but my stuff is still here. Picking out one of my favourite old shirts from the dresser, I press the soft cotton against my cheek. Wulff dyed it purple when I complained about the faded brown I always had to wear. Sick with nostalgia, I cram the shirt into my bag. Jumping onto the top bunk, I move a piece of the ceiling up and to the side then peer into the darkness. Every cubby has an escape hatch. They lead to the hideouts back door. I was using this space to store my black boots.

After I escaped from Cop Sector I couldn't wear them anymore: only Cops can wear black boots. It's illegal to even own a pair. I don't know why I kept them all this time, but I'm glad I did. My feet stopped growing when I was eleven, so they still fit nicely. If Frenzy agrees to help me I'll be ready to find the line into A tomorrow. In fact, it's lucky that Frenzy is here alone. I don't want the others hearing what I need from him. If they can't talk me out of it they'll insist on helping me, and that's the last thing that I want.

Stuffing the boots into my bag, I walk into the bright blue common room. Wulff changes the wall colour when he gets the urge. The year I was arrested they were bright yellow, the year before that bright green, the year before that bright orange. The big table sits where it always did, six chairs tucked neatly under its scarred, wooden top. Behind that is Frenzy's workstation, a wall of bleeping lights and whirring computers. The helmet where he jacks his brain into the system sits on his giant, wing-backed chair. His straightjacket is carefully draped over one of the chair's arms.

"Still no cream and sugar?" Frenzy calls from the kitchen in the corner.

"I've learned to appreciate those things."

I'm standing near the table, facing him. Directly behind me is the door leading to Wulff's garage, where he keeps all his vehicles in top condition. Two years ago he had six different models: his favourite junker for casual rides; the hover vehicle for desert jobs; the classy, low-riding two-seater with the perfect paint job and leather interior for the upper end jobs; what he always calls the packer, his big truck for heavier loads; and two crap cars for jobs that require a switch. If I wasn't struggling so much with memories of him, I'd open the door and take a peek. I'm curious to know if he ever got around to painting the packer.

I take a seat when Frenzy offers me a mug full of steaming tea. My old companion has cooled it down with a little cold water, making it the perfect temperature to drink. He gags when I take a tentative sip. The familiar, pungent flavour assaults my taste buds and I sigh happily. This stuff is almost better than the chocolate Jules shared with me in the desert. It's an acquired taste, I admit that, but it's wonderful.

"I still don't understand how you can like that stuff."

"It's what my mom always drank," I explain for the umpteenth time. "It kept her from ever getting sick, and it does the same for me."

"Bullshit." Frenzy grunts disapprovingly as he sits down and leans back in his chair. Running his hand roughly through his short hair he crosses his arms over his chest. "You drink it because you know it makes the rest of us gag."

"*Anything* to get a reaction out of you."

Despite my initial coldness, I slip back into our old pattern. Taking a large portion of the tea into my mouth I stare cheekily at Frenzy as I swish it around. He grimaces, so I tip my head back and start gurgling. After a few moments his face squishes into an expression of revulsion and he has to turn away.

Amused, I swallow the tea noisily and smack my lips. "Best I've ever had!"

"Disgusting."

"I'd bathe in this stuff if I could afford it," I claim, relishing his gasp of horror.

"It smells like *sewage*!"

"Sewage with cream and sugar," I correct. I hold my mug under my nose and take a deep breath. "There's a reason they used to call me Sewer Rat."

"You're insane!" Frenzy starts laughing. "Just can't help yourself, can you?"

"Never can, never will."

"Fine," he concedes. "You can have your stupid tea."

I smile triumphantly and we descend into comfortable silence. How many times have we had this conversation? I remember having it whenever I was recovering from a night out. Frenzy always had the tea ready before I woke up. His shy smile let me know he wanted to hear about where I went and what I did. The poor kid doesn't like to leave the hideout. His past makes him fear the outdoors.

Frenzy and I sit together like old times—no words, no movement. We used to do this when no one else was around. When you live in an underground space with three other people there's never a quiet moment. If Jack and Wulff went out, Frenzy and I would haul ourselves out of our cubbies, get a few drinks and just enjoy the silence.

But this silence is heavy—awkward. Frenzy's gaze fills with regret and the merriment drains from the room. I wish I had the fortitude to comfort him, but I'm struggling against my own pathetic remorse. There are too many things that need to be said, too many apologies that we have to make. Neither of us is brave enough to step up and be the first. As soon as someone does we have to acknowledge the past, and we're not ready.

The day the bounty hunters caught me, Frenzy made a mistake. He doesn't make them often. The crew was heading out for a job in K Sector. It was a standard grab and go, nothing fancy. We figured we could be in and out in a few hours, but Frenzy wasn't having a good day so Jack was thinking of saving the job for later. I, however, was in a rush. I hate K Sector: the Scientists freak me out with all their little rules.

In K there are areas where you walk south and areas where you walk north; lanes where you walk slowly and lanes where you walk quickly; places where you don't talk and places where you can have a low conversation. Try going against the rules and the entire populace will freak out. And their *laws*! Days are colour-coded. If you can't afford the colours of that day you're not allowed to leave your box. Hairstyles must be short, no facial hair, nails must be trimmed, no stains or wrinkles on your clothes, any visible scars must be covered (some people have to wear masks), no jewelry. There's an absence of life there that leaves me feeling grotesque. Even the streets are pristine. B, Q, and C are messy and falling apart. The people in the streets are loud, always in your way and never moving directly from one place to another. There's something comforting about that kind of chaos.

K Sector not being my favourite place I just wanted to get the job over with. I told Frenzy to suck it up. He was hurt, but he did what I said.

The identity card he made for me was faulty. To get from one sector to another you need permission. It was Frenzy's job to convince the system that I was somebody with clearance. The gatekeeper swiped my card and knew right away. He still let me through, but the bastard tagged me. If a gatekeeper suspects anything illegal he, or she, can stick a locator on the identity card. It immediately sends a signal to whichever bounty hunter pays the gatekeeper for the information.

Bounty hunters are smart. They knew to follow me before pouncing. Having a forged identity card means that I'm connected and might lead them to other Criminals. But my psychic talent let me know they were behind me. I never made it to the rendezvous with Jack and Wulff. I led the Cops in the other direction, hoping to shake them and use the sewers to get back to B.

With three bounty hunters on my tail I never had a chance. They took me down when they realized I was aimlessly wandering the streets.

Frenzy has always been hard on himself. The smallest mistakes send him into dark emotional pits of self-loathing. It's written all over his face: he blames himself for my arrest. For a while, I did too. It seemed horribly convenient that, out of everyone, I was the one who was handed the faulty identity card. But two years gives a person the chance to go over every detail of how they were caught. Frenzy knew he wasn't up for the job and I shouldn't have pushed him.. Guilt is the most uncomfortable emotion. It's hanging over him like a lead weight, making his chest cave and his shoulders sag. I'm not doing much better.

I don't know how to talk to him. My mind is drawing a blank, the words I need are eluding me. I open my mouth a few times but nothing comes out. Frenzy is sinking further into himself. If we're not careful, we'll sit like this, waiting for forgiveness, for hours.

"My friend Hyde needs an identity card," I finally say.

Grateful for the distraction, Frenzy launches himself into the task at hand. "Is he a Fix-it?"

"He's a ghost."

"Not a switch but an insertion. That'll be a little tricky."

"He also needs approval for Lily's procreation."

"Lily's been ordered to have a kid?" Frenzy gasps. His eyes look like they might pop out of his head. "Does she know about what this guy wants to do?"

"Hyde is her lover," I answer carefully. "You know I would never hurt Lily."

Frenzy nods unhappily. It's obvious by his pained expression that he's having trouble thinking of Lily with anyone other than himself. "She could have come to me. I would have helped her if she'd asked."

Without even mentioning payment, he gets to his feet and heads for his workstation. He takes a metal disk from a stash that he keeps under his seat and sits down. Strapping on the helmet, which covers his eyes and ears, he inserts the disk into a slot on his workstation.

I don't know how Frenzy gets his job done. It's something to do with how the helmet interacts with his brainwaves. What I do know is that he always hums while he works. There are some great bars in B Sector where musicians get together and play all night. It's his favourite past time to go and listen. With the exception of Lily, he'll ignore anyone who tries to talk to him.

Eventually there's a small whirring sound. The flat, unmarked metal pops out from its slot. Frenzy pulls of his helmet, grabs the disk and tosses it at me.

"His new name is Sohrab Adam," he grumbles, "I hope he likes it."

"And the approval...?"

"...on the card."

I can't help but be concerned about Frenzy's state of mind. Little disappointments can send him into fits of depression, there's no telling what this news will do to him when he's had a chance to think about it. "Hyde's offering fifteen thousand for this."

"No charge. It's for Lily."

His despondent expression is making me feel horrible for bringing this job to him. Falling back on teasing, I try to cheer him up. "Would you even know what to do with a woman if you had one?"

"Still think you're fucking funny, don't you?"

I don't honour his anger with a response. Instead, I choose to distract him. Pulling out Marietta's rectangle, I present it to Frenzy for examination. "This is entirely between you and me."

Frenzy inspects the objects hard outer surface. Sliding it out of my hands, he opens it and grunts with curiosity.

"I've never seen anything like this before. What are all these markings?"

"I figured you might be able to find a pattern. Could it be some kind of code?"

"Maybe," he mutters as he flips through. I can practically see his neurons firing as he tries to understand the mystery he's holding in his hands. "The markings aren't random, that's for certain... Wait a minute."

He sits there thinking, lost in the dizzying passages of his mind.

"Wait a minute...?" I repeat.

Ignoring my impatience, Frenzy leans back in his chair. His eyes dart back and forth and then he springs to his feet.

"Brilliant," he whispers as he paces around the room. "I never realized that the lines of code could be broken down into individual markings before. I always assumed they were incomplete if they weren't together." He's talking to himself now. If I say something, he won't hear me. "I thought I was manipulating huge symbols that couldn't be broken apart, I thought they were what made up the system, but now I see that they can be broken down even further. There are individual characters, small but vital. Imagine! It's like when Wulff starts painting the room. Each stroke creates the bigger picture, but without the strokes there could be no bigger picture."

He's growing more excited and more agitated by the moment. He bumps hard into the table and doesn't notice. Turning to me, he throws his arms out dramatically.

"Frenzy, what the heck…?"

"Copper, this is huge! If I'm right then this will cut down the time I need to manipulate codes! Instead of cutting out huge sections I'll only need to substitute the smaller markings." His eyes continue to dart back and forth. "Yes! Yes, yes, yes, yes, yes, yes, yes! I see it now, I *see* it now."

I couldn't understand his babbling if I tried. It looks like he's ready to explode.

"Do you know what this means, Copper? Can you believe what this means!"

"I can say with absolute certainty that I don't."

"I have to practice," he announces as he disappears into his cubby. "I have to test the theory. I might be getting ahead of myself! I might be jumping to conclusions. But I can't be! I can't be! What should I do first? Something simple, that's right, something simple."

He flies out of his cubby and straps his helmet back on. Annoyed, I sit back in my chair and grumble angrily under my breath. I can't disturb him while he's working, that could screw with his brain. Instead, I have to watch him giggle happily to himself for the next few minutes.

I guess his theory is working.

"You have no idea." He looks like a crazed maniac when he finally brings himself back out. "This is so amazing. It will take me a few days to reassess everything on the system, but once I have…the possibilities are endless. This might put an end to my crazy days. I might be able to cut the straps off my bed; I might not have to use this bastard anymore!"

He grabs his straight jacket and bundles it up in his fists. His excitement is infectious. My irritation drains away. Thrilled that he's found so much in something so small, I lean forward eagerly.

"So, what is it?" I ask.

"What?"

"The…thingy."

"Oh!" He cocks his head to the side. "I have no idea."

"No idea."

"None whatsoever; I've never seen anything like it."

"Do you know what it means?"

"Nope. Where'd you get it? That might give me an idea."

"One of Marietta's performances," I answer. Then I notice he isn't carrying it anymore. "*Where* is it?"

"Oh, you want it back!" He nervously peers over his shoulder and into his room. "Can I keep it for a few days?"

"You put it in your cubby, didn't you?" I cry. "You thought it was yours! That is so typical."

"You didn't know what to do with it," he mutters sheepishly.

"I'm still the one who had to steal it from Marietta."

"You *stole* it." His eyes widen in surprise and fear. "From one of the *Whisperers*? Are you kidding?"

"What?"

"Don't act like it's no big deal!" For a moment, I think he's going to leap at me and grab me by the shirt. He stays in his seat, but he leans forward so that I will understand how upset he really is. "Whisperers have powerful friends. If Marietta finds out you stole her…whatever the heck it is—she might be angry enough to do something about it."

"She didn't even know I was there."

"Well, well, well," says Frenzy, eyes shining impishly. "Still crazy, I see. No wonder Madman wants you."

"He's not going to get me!" Staring intently into Frenzy's warm gaze, I fold my arms over my chest. "I'm going to need your help to get into Cop Sector."

"Nobody gets into A." He sighs and fixes me with a curious look. "What do you think you need?"

"It won't be easy."

"That's obvious. What do you need?"

Taking a deep breath, I think over what he should know and what he shouldn't. He needs enough information to get the job done properly, but I can't give him anything that will tip him off about the line. In other words, he can't know anything about the SPEF.

"Do you know why Cop Sector security is so hard to infiltrate?" I finally ask.

"Simple," Frenzy answers, "biorhythms."

"Exactly. A good manipulator can convince a security system that my thumbprint or my retina scan belongs to someone with clearance. They can't do that with biorhythms. They're too complex to mess with and too complex to fake."

"I remember," he says. "I got cocky and nearly didn't come back from it. I thought I could manipulate a part of the code and convince the system that the biorhythm belonged to someone else. But I missed something...well, a lot of somethings. There were too many things to change at once. I lost my grip." A chill runs up his spine and he shakes it off. He looks at me suspiciously. "What does this have to do with how I can help you?"

"You learned first hand not to mess with Cop security, no matter how good you think you are. But with your help I could get back into A." My words hang between us for a few moments. "Your brain's been inside Cop security before."

"Only for a few minutes," he objects.

"That's all you'll need."

"I'm not following you."

Mentally going over everything I have to gain from pushing Frenzy, I let him sit in suspense. I can tell he doesn't want to know what my plan is: he's avoiding my gaze and squirming uncomfortably in his seat. But I'm starting to feel giddy. My plan is exciting, even if it is doomed to failure. It provides me with that coveted third option, something outside Madman and Locket.

"Cops are allowed access to Cop Sector because their biorhythms are on the system," I finally reveal. "They're scanned when they're born.

Every time they go into A, the security system checks to make sure there's a match."

"You told us all as much when Jackson first hired you. A biorhythm is more accurate than a thumbprint but Cops are the only ones with the technology. No one outside of A knows how to replicate it."

"You won't need to *replicate* it."

"What do you mean?"

"I was a Cop for eleven years, Frenzy. My biorhythm is already on the system. All I need you to do is convince it that I'm still alive."

"I can't do it," he protests. Nervously running his hand over his sweaty temples, he shakes his head. "There's no guarantee I'd be able to find what you need. And even if I did, I wouldn't know how to do it."

"Don't give me that," I shoot back. He's starting to piss me off. "You know exactly where the Cops keep the biorhythms; you found them in half a second last time you took a peek. With the right information, you could find mine."

"They probably erased it when you disappeared!"

I'm doing my best to keep my voice calm. Frenzy knows more about the system than I do. He will win this argument if he senses any doubt on my end. "You told me once that nothing can really be erased from the system; it can only be put somewhere else."

Frenzy looks like he's ready to scratch out his own eyes.

"All you have to do is look," I persist.

"I swore I'd never go back in there," he cries through shallow breaths. He balls his shaking hands into fists. After a few moments of silent, inward struggle, he's breathing normally again. "I can't self-destruct again, Copper. When I came back out I wanted to die, just like I did before I met Jackson."

I shrink away from his argument. Death wishes aren't uncommon in the Criminal world. Before Frenzy took Jack's offer he was throwing himself into suicidal jobs. He never found anything that could destroy him, that's the irony of how good he really is.

Frenzy won't look at me. He knows I'm dead if he doesn't help.

"I'll need to know your second name," he rasps. "That's the only way I'll be able to find what you're looking for."

I'm suddenly hesitant; I've never told anyone my second name before. When a new citizen is born the system names them. That name, their first name, is only used for official business. Most everyone goes by their second name—the name their parents gave them. If they don't it's because they despise their parents.

My father told me that he named me Rhys because it reminded him of how he grew up, whatever that means. Apparently, he was so insistent that my mother didn't know how to object. She wanted to name me after her grandmother. It never occurred to me until now how deeply personal my second name truly is.

"I'm not going to leave you dry," Frenzy insists. "Give me the *name*."

I search his determined gaze. "Rhys."

"Daryl Rhys," Frenzy repeats. Going over to his seat he straps on his helmet one more time. "Let's see if I can find you."

Frenzy hums nervously; the computers make bleeping and whirring noises; the time ticks away.

"You're still in here," Frenzy says. "They haven't erased you, but this will still be tricky. I can't make whatever I change stick for long. You'll have…twenty minutes. Any longer and they'll know I'm in there and start hunting."

"I have to be in by tomorrow anyway," I say, even though he can't hear me.

Removing his helmet, Frenzy tosses it irritably to the side. "0600. I'll start then. Do you really think you can do this?"

"I don't have a choice," I reply.

This mission is voluntary suicide. I already know that there's no way I'm going to make it back. But, oddly enough, I'm at peace with that.

15

Unlike the rest of the crew, Frenzy didn't choose to enter the Criminal world. He was barely eight years old when his dad first jacked him into the system. Everybody knows that kind of stimulation can severely damage a growing brain. Frenzy's dad didn't much care. He was a poor Mole who was told he was having a kid. When the mother died in childbirth, he was forced to care for his unwanted child. When he first realized that his son was a near genius his first instinct was to figure out how he could make credits.

That's when Cremin enters the picture.

Like rape, hitting your kid isn't universally illegal. Discipline is discipline, but some parents take it too far. Frenzy doesn't have full movement in four of his fingers and can't turn his head fully to the left; just a few parting gifts from his dad. In some ways, Cremin was a step up for little boy Ash, but in others, not so much. Unlike Frenzy's dad, Cremin didn't kick or slap when the boy got in the way. He didn't want to damage the merchandise.

When Cremin first met Frenzy, he had Frenzy's dad strap the boy down and jack him in. According to Frenzy, it was Cremin's way of probing for paternal love. I'm convinced that Frenzy's dad didn't flinch when Frenzy shrieked and passed out from the pain.

Cremin was a Hack, but he wasn't a fool. He couldn't jack into the system anymore, a year in the Prison had seen to that, but he still knew how to make a fraudulent living. Teaching kids like Frenzy the barest of manipulator skills, he rented them out as decoys for Criminals. Every sector has manipulators that legally jack into the system; Cops have manipulators who are there to protect it. Cremin's decoys were instructed to do whatever the Criminal manipulator was doing. The theory was Cops would find the decoy first and try to flush it out, giving the real manipulator the time needed to get the job done. When the kids' brainwaves were found in the system they were jammed (unable to send signals to the rest of the body) and then a patroller would be sent over to collect the prize. Unfortunately for the kids, their brains would be mush by then.

But eight-year old Ash Martin was never caught. His brain never turned to mush. Cremin taught him the basics and the little genius figured the rest out on his own.

After a disappointing night of trying to get Lily to notice him, Frenzy told me that he tried to teach the other kids what he knew. They weren't supposed to talk to each other. If they were caught breaking the rules they would be bumped to the front of the decoy line, but Frenzy didn't much care. He figured that if he was going to join the brain-dead it might as well be sooner than later. But there wouldn't be a job that he couldn't handle. Cremin eventually stopped buying other kids; Frenzy was all that he needed.

In the end, Cremin underestimated what his slave's capabilities. Over the next few years, he worked Frenzy until he could hardly remember his own name; there were days when his eyes and ears would bleed. At twelve, Frenzy was working codes manipulators three times as experienced were still trying to master; at thirteen, he was pulling jobs Criminals swore could never be done; at fourteen, he bared his teeth and killed Cremin.

Well, tortured and killed is more accurate.

I was nineteen when I first saw Frenzy. He was walking a few steps behind his master, eyes darting around uncontrollably and limbs quaking with fear. It was Cremin's belief that his slave needed at least an hour of sunshine a day, so he had a perimeter-node implanted in Frenzy's cheek. If his slave wasn't within ten feet of the node's control it would fire electricity into the surrounding muscles, causing them to cramp and lock his jaw. It isn't the most pleasant piece of technology. Frenzy still gets agitated when he's outside.

At that point in my career I was making a good name for myself. I'd managed to get out of running encrypted voice messages about two years earlier. But then my parentage caught up with me. Nick Redden wanted to destroy me, so he contracted me to kill Ash Martin. He made up some bullshit story about how a fourteen year old was cutting into his business. I didn't believe him, but I needed the credits. I took the job.

At night, Cremin kept Frenzy locked in a cage that was barely big enough for him to lie down in. I don't know what I thought was doing. The night I snuck into Cremin's hideout I picked the cage lock, opened the door and stepped out of the way. It just had to be done. Frenzy looked just as confused as I felt, but once he saw I wasn't going to get in his way, he didn't waste any time.

I left before he took his revenge. Apparently, a manipulator has to operate on a specific, personalized frequency or risk eventual brain disintegration. Nobody understood this fact better than Frenzy. How many nights did he spend, fantasizing about how he would destroy Cremin? As sensitive and compassionate as Frenzy can be, as big as his heart is when it comes to his loved ones, I've never seen anyone take more joy in crushing his enemies.

If I'd stuck around that night, I would have witnessed the slow and painful annihilation of Cremin's already warped brain. Frenzy took his time—two days and one night. Then he left him, a quivering and unresponsive mass, on the floor of the hideout.

I never told anyone that I was the one who let him out. Redden got a story about how the kid had already disappeared by the time I got there.

Jack found Frenzy after a few months and hired him. I became part of the crew half-a-year after Lyons Emmett gave me a clean bill of health. I wasn't sure if Frenzy would remember me, but when I walked into the hideout he couldn't place me.

He never place me, either. Eventually, he just gave up, muttering that his brain was fried. It felt too weird for me to tell him outright.

This particular memory has always been a favourite of mine. I've done a lot of things that I'm not proud of; becoming a Criminal means crossing the line that shelters you from all the things you thought you weren't capable of. Remembering that I didn't kill Frenzy is a comforting thought for someone like me.

Frenzy has zoned out, which usually happens to him a few times a day. It's probably from early damage, having been jacked in at such a young age. You just have to let him leave for a while. I watch the tears spill from his unblinking eyes and feel my own water with compassion. It never occurred to me until now how strong Frenzy really is. Eight years of torture at his father's hands, followed by six years of torture at Cremin's hands, but he hasn't let it destroy him. He struggles and sometimes he falters, but he's survived. Inspired, I suddenly feel honoured that he considers me his friend.

A low rumble makes the hideout shake. Frenzy snaps out of his trance.

"That's the lift," he says as he scans the room. It takes him a moment to fully recover from his space-out. Wiping his sleeve on his moist cheeks, he shoots me a confused look. "I must have dozed off?"

I don't tell him he was crying. No one ever does. Forcing my own tears back, I shoot him an encouraging smile.

A sharp buzzing noise invades the hideout: the traps have been deactivated. Frenzy pushes a button on his wall. A black panel slides to the side to reveal the monitors linked to the cameras. The metal front door swings open.

"Get out of bed, Ash!" Wulff's heavy boots echo down the hallway and stop at Frenzy's cubby door. There's a pause when Wulff realizes that his friend isn't in there. "Damn it, Ash, are you in Copper's cubby again?"

I shoot Frenzy a questioning look. He avoids it but his face turns bright red.

"Not in here, either. You're going to *love* this one. I mean it. Our little Copper is back in business. She's going to find a line into Cop Sector!"

Wulff strides into the common room—my heart jumps into my throat.

He doesn't look any different, as though I've only been gone for a day instead of two years. My arms and legs go numb with anticipation as he throws a bag onto the table. Casually acknowledging me with a small wave, he unzips his jacket and pulls a bottle of his mint shaving cream from an inside pocket. He must have been running errands today.

Grinning wickedly at Frenzy, he nods towards me. "Does Heath know you brought a woman down here, Ash?"

"Wulff…" Frenzy shoots him a significant look.

I shakily get to my feet, not knowing what kind of reaction I want from my closest friend. The tall, muscular man takes a moment to look me over. It isn't until he searches my eyes that his mouth drops open in both amazement and horror.

Quaking with emotion, I find the courage to greet him. "Hey, loudmouth."

The shock doesn't keep him quiet for long. Nothing ever does. That enthralling, nothing-held-back, exploding-with-joy, you'd-forgive-him-anything grin bursts over his face. Before I can react, he whoops excitedly, crosses the room and catches me in a bone-crunching hug. I groan in discomfort but Wulff has no intention of letting me go. Lifting me off the floor, he dances around the hideout.

I can hear myself laughing—Wulff's natural enthusiasm is as infectious as ever.

Dizzy from the exhilaration of being held by him again, I cling to his arms so that I don't fall over. Steadying me with a hand on the small of my back, Wulff studies my uncertainty.

The excitement in his eyes lends me a little strength. Bolstered, I open my mouth to say hello. Wulff puts his hands on either side of my face and presses his lips against mine. I sputter at first, but the fierce kiss is sending waves of buzzing energy through my limbs. My exhaustion melts away and my greeting is completely swallowed. Next thing I know, he puts me in a friendly headlock and drags me back to the table. Grabbing me by the legs he throws me over his shoulder. I struggle playfully without any real intention of getting out of his grip. I love it when he throws me around like this.

"Ash, we're going out!"

He slides me down his chest and puts my feet back down on the floor. Looking me over, he playfully flicks me on the forehead.

"Still in one piece," he decides. Pulling me into his arms he holds me in a warm embrace. It feels so good to be in his arms; I nuzzle right in and close my eyes. Wulff rests his cheek on my head. "Do me a favour, Copper," he whispers into my hair. "Never disappear like that again."

16

I've had a total of two lovers in my life. Wulff was my first.

I met him in a small pub in E when I was seventeen. He and I would go there for drinks. Theodora was a bartender who'd hired me to sit with her on her breaks so that the men wouldn't automatically assume she wanted *company*. That neighbourhood's entire male population would go down there every night to watch her pour alcohol. She wouldn't choose to become a prostitute for another year or so, but the men were always looking for a few minutes of her time. I liked it there because it wasn't a Criminal hangout. There was no repressed violence in the atmosphere, just Accountants unwinding from long days. Theo didn't pay well, but it was an easy job that didn't require too much effort.

Wulff is an Accountant turned Criminal who used to visit old friends. If you're born in the Bank you become an Accountant. Just like if you're born in N Sector, the Hospital, you become a Doctor. It's just the way the City works. Wulff hated the Bank; his passions were vehicles and art. He had to become a Criminal to do what he loved.

One night, the first night of many, his friends didn't make it to the pub, so he introduced himself and offered to keep me company. It's very hard to say no to Wulff when he turns on the charm. I was captivated from the beginning.

I was crushing on him for a few months before I worked up the nerve to pounce. Wulff is ten years older than me. Generally, it's considered taboo for a man to proposition a woman that much younger. If anything were going to happen I would have to seduce him. And I wanted to. *Sweet Sky*, how I wanted to! It got to the point where just knowing he was somewhere near made me weak in the knees. So, one night I followed him to his box.

The two years I spent as his lover feel like a separate life. They're sacred and incorruptible. In the end, I fucked it up. But I suppose that was inevitable. You don't become a killer without carrying a certain amount of baggage around.

What confused Wulff was my total lack of remorse. I never went looking for fights, but I didn't prevent them either. If someone died at my hands, I didn't go over the details wondering how I might have prevented it. It didn't take long for Wulff to realize that I had a bit of a death wish. I must have driven him crazy. When he ended it, I was wrecked, but I couldn't lose him. I swallowed my disillusionment and concentrated on being his friend. My broken heart healed eventually. Despite the pain and confusion, there isn't anyone in the City I trust more than Wulff.

Walking into the pub with him, I don't feel raw and exposed anymore. His presence allows me to sink back into who I used to be. It's so natural. I feel so confident that I barely realize it's happened.

Wulff grabs a petite waitress around the waist and pulls her towards us. "We need beer, Astrid!"

"First you have to promise me a dance later." The pretty blonde pouts flirtatiously. "Otherwise, I'm ignoring you all night."

"You could never ignore me," Wulff returns. He picks her up with one arm and carries her to an empty booth.

Shrieking with laughter, she playfully hits him with her tray. "Careful or I'll tell Jules to shave off your hair! You want a blistered head?"

"She'd never do it. She loves me too much." Wulff sets the waitress back on her feet as I slip into the booth.

"Where is she anyway?" Astrid asks, fixing her hair. "I've got news for her."

"Haven't seen her," Frenzy answers.

"She was out testing her new ride yesterday," Wulff offers, "but I haven't seen her since she took off."

"If you do see her, let her know that Liam has a huge crush on her. With a little flirtation, he might give her free drinks."

"I'll flirt with him if it means free drinks," Wulff avows.

"Take a seat, you lush!" Astrid pushes him into the booth and leaves to fill our order. "*I'll* buy your first round."

"You're beautiful, sweetheart."

"Anyone who buys you beer is beautiful," she tosses playfully over her shoulder.

"She knows you too well," I say.

"Astrid's a good sort," he replies. "Sit down, Ash!"

"What's Locket doing here?" Frenzy asks. "I thought he rooted in the Hospital."

My heart immediately starts banging against my chest. Madman's General is casually sitting at the bar and we all know this isn't a chance encounter. He's reminding us that he's watching, patiently waiting for the clock to run down.

Unnerved, but also annoyed, I refuse to give him the satisfaction of staring at him. Frenzy adopts a protective stance but Wulff is unconcerned. At first, I don't question his composure. One of the reasons Jack hired Wulff is because he always knows everything. It's a natural talent—one of the side benefits of being charming. If he isn't worried then he must know something that I don't.

After a moment of quiet contemplation, he gives Frenzy an answer. "He moved here a few months ago."

"And you didn't tell Jackson?" Frenzy's mouth drops open in shock.

"Why would he have cared?" Wulff shoots me a teasing glance. "*Heath* and Locket never had a problem with each other."

I reply by sticking out my tongue at him.

"I think Jackson would have wanted to know that one of Madman's Generals is rooting in B," Frenzy insists.

Wulff concedes the point with a shrug. "You're right. Locket is one bad motherfucker. Heath would have wanted to know."

"I need to pee," Frenzy says. He shoots me a worried glance. "You okay with *him* here?"

"I'm not going somewhere else just because he's sitting at the bar," I reply. Sure, every nerve is screaming at me to get out of here, but he'll just follow me wherever we go. "I still have a couple of days before he's allowed to touch me."

Frenzy sees through my bravado but he can't force me to leave. One eye on Locket, he retreats to the washrooms.

Wulff continues to watch Locket, making it impossible for me to ignore my stalker. Getting to his feet, Locket walks over to our booth. Without warning, he pushes me out of the way and slides in beside me. Outraged, I push back. He retaliates by squashing me into the wall. I look to Wulff for help but he's grinning mischievously. Hurt and confused, I watch him greet my long time nemesis with a handshake.

I growl at Locket, wondering what the heck he thinks he's doing. "Do you *mind?*"

"Not really," Madman's General replies.

"What's the news?" Wulff asks Locket.

"McNally wants me to tell you that she was more than satisfied with your work on the last job," Locket says.

"It was a pleasure doing business with her," Wulff returns.

"First round!" Astrid arrives with our beers. Scanning the muscular man squashing me into the wall, she graces him with a flirtatious smile. Looking to Wulff, she waits for an introduction.

Wulff obliges with a wide grin. "Astrid, this is Jace Locket."

"Jace Locket?" The awe in her voice is enough to make me gag. She leans closer. "I'll let Liam know you're here. Obviously, you drink for free." Locket barely acknowledges her presence. Undaunted, the cute little waitress tosses her hair suggestively. Wulff chuckles openly at the show. "Just call if you need anything."

"McNally is a nice woman," Wulff continues once she's gone. "Anyone would want to work in her shop."

"She'll be glad to hear that," Locket answers.

"I won't be able to work for her anymore," Wulff admits, searching Locket's stony expression. "She's with Madman now. My loyalty is to my crew."

"McNally works for Madman…?" I nearly tip over my beer in surprise. Locket finally gives me more room so I shove my elbow into his ribs. Next thing I know, his fingers have found a pressure point in my wrist. Sharp pain shoots through my arm. *"Ow! I give!"* Shooting him a menacing look, I twist my hand under the table until he releases me. I rub at the sore spot he created. "I thought McNally was a legitimate Fix-it. She cornered the collector truck business *years* ago. Why would she work for a Criminal?"

Neither of them gives me an answer. Locket nods thoughtfully at Wulff before sliding out of the booth. Before he leaves, his cold gaze settles on me. We don't speak; we don't have to. He's already heard I'm going to try and get into Cop Sector.

Fronting a confidence I don't own, I silently challenge his smug expression. Something I can't identify flashes through his eyes. It retreats as quickly as it surfaced, however, and he walks away.

"Lovers quarrel?" Wulff asks.

Confounded, I shoot my friend an angry glare. "What?"

"News travels fast, Copper. Everyone knows you guys are an item. I can't believe you didn't tell me about it. When did you two hook up, anyway?"

"Lily opened her big mouth!" I growl angrily. "I could kill her. You know Locket's going to kill me if I don't find a line into Cop Sector."

"As if he would. He'll steal you away to a place where no one can find you.

You'll build a beautiful home together and raise violent children."

At a loss for words, I stare dumbly at Wulff. His eyes sparkle in roguish amusement. Frenzy returns from the bathroom and slides into the booth next to me. Taking in my shocked expression, he casually looks to Wulff for an explanation.

"Ash, do you remember that time Daryl took that crazy Hospital job? Remember what happened when Locket found out about it?"

"Yeah, how could I forget?" Frenzy laughs at the memory. "He had a manipulator change her clearance after she got in. She couldn't get back out."

"She still made it, though," Wulff says with pride. "Then there was Alison Diego's enforcer, that big guy...what's-his-name?"

"You mean Hector?"

"No, the *big* guy, the one who used to drink his victim's blood..."

"...oh... Sherman." Frenzy shudders with revulsion.

"Right, Quentin Sherman."

"Locket stole Sherman's favourite knife and told him that he saw Daryl with it," Frenzy recalls. "He challenged her to a fight."

"And she took him apart," Wulff narrates, growing more excited. "That was an awesome battle. She did us all a favour when she broke his neck. There weren't too many people who wanted him back in action. They say he used to eat his victims while they were still alive."

Suddenly moody, I grimace at the thought. "That asshole deserved to die."

"All those years of hating Locket must have been pretty good foreplay," Wulff says.

"Foreplay...?" Frenzy blinks in confusion. "Why are you talking about foreplay?"

Wulff ignores Frenzy's question. "For all his hatred, though, Locket did save Copper's ass in the desert."

"What?" Fuming, I turn on Wulff. "What are you talking about? I saved myself out there."

"Nuh-uh." Wulff disagrees with an annoyingly condescending grunt. "You took that crazy Scientist job even after I told you it was a mistake. You went to find those cacti with the special needles and got lost. How long did you wander around before Locket found you?"

"First of all, I found those needles; second of all, I was never lost. I knew where I was the entire time. My problem was that *somebody's* precious hover called it quits when I was on my way back!"

"There was nothing wrong with my hover vehicle. You just don't know how to drive. The engine overheated when you pushed it too hard. I never got it back, by the way."

"I can't believe you're still whining about something that happened that long ago."

"That's beside the point." A superior look spreads across Wulff's face. "Locket is the one who found you and brought you back in. He *saved* you. Is that when you two became lovers?"

Horror-struck, Frenzy chokes on his beer. "Lovers...? You and Locket are lovers? That's seriously fucked up."

"Locket was the one the Scientists contracted to bring the needles to K Sector! That's why he went looking for me." I'm ready to tear Wulff's head off. "And just so you know, Locket had no idea I was the one the Scientists had hired. It's not like he saved me out of the goodness of his heart."

"So you admit he saved you."

"Hold it!" Frenzy is ready to break bottles over our heads to get our attention. "Copper and Locket became lovers after he saved her?"

"He didn't save me!" I cry.

"But you *are* lovers?"

"No! I hate him. I wouldn't sleep with him if somebody paid me."

"That's not what Jen tells me," Wulff interjects.

"Who...?"

"Jen saw you with Locket at Braggs Bar." Wulff leans conspiratorially towards Frenzy. "She says they were having a little fun in a bathroom stall."

Frenzy shakes his head. "This isn't making any sense."

"You mean that woman who saw me with Locket in the bathroom?" I ask.

"So you *were* there!" Wulff lets out a whoop of triumph. "I wasn't sure if I should believe her. Copper, you should have told me."

"There's nothing to tell! Just get it out of your head, Wulff. I am not, never was, and never will be, Locket's lover."

"Whatever you say, Copper, whatever you say. For whatever reason, you don't want others to know. I won't spread it around."

But, knowing Lily's mouth, it's already everywhere. Frustrated and angry, I put my head on the table and groan. Unfortunately, there's a big part of me that wants to laugh, but if I do it will only encourage Wulff. This is the first time I've seen him in over two years and we're back to our old routine. That realization alone makes me chuckle.

Lifting my head up, I raise an eyebrow at Wulff's impish smile. "You know I've never slept with Locket."

Saluting me with his bottle, Wulff leans towards me over the table. "There's no way you could have hidden something like that from me."

"Lily hasn't been spreading this around?"

"No one would believe her if she was."

"You're a jerk," I say without malice.

"You love me," he returns.

"I missed you."

"Just don't let Madman get hold of you," he charges. Shifting uneasily he disguises his sorrow with conviction. "If anyone can find a line to A, Copper, it's you."

"Maybe you two can tell me why Madman wants to get hold of me." I fix them both with a serious stare. "Locket said something about my being some kind of threat. Who in their right mind is afraid of a Hack?"

Wulff's face falls. "I assumed you already knew."

Intrigued, I lean forward. "Assumed I knew what?"

"About six months after you went in Lyons Emmett made his move on Madman. Heath had been expecting it, of course, but it took everyone else by surprise. The smartest thing he did when he took over was recruiting Locket."

"Recruit...." I repeat, trying not to sound too incredulous. "Locket was a respected independent when I went in. What could Madman possibly offer him?"

"Absolute power," Wulff answers. "Lyons has been a Criminal for what...twenty-five years? He hardly took a credit of payment that entire time. He helped people who had futures instead of funds."

"There aren't many Criminals in the City that don't owe him," Frenzy puts in, "just like you do."

"So he starts calling in his favours, one by one," Wulff continues. "Using the Cop Sector bullshit job, he starts absorbing the independents into his organization. The ones who go into hiding…"

"…Locket is sent to find and kill," I conclude.

Wulff salutes me with him bottle once more. "You still catch on quick."

"Not one person has even tried to go into hiding," Frenzy says.

"No one, so far, has gotten out." Wulff brings his bottle to his lips and drains it. "Locket is Madman's trump card. As long as he's a General there's no stopping Lyons. He aims to take over the Criminal world. He'll do it, too. When his organization is big enough, other Criminals won't be able to work around him."

"That's quite the ambition." I shudder at the thought. "I still don't see what it has to do with me."

"You may be a Hack, Copper, but you had a reputation before you left." Wulff signals for another round. "People heard about you stealing that hover-board and they started talking…hoping. They started calling you a returning champion. There was no way Lyons was going to take the chance."

"A returning champion," I echo. My guts churn with nausea. "The hero who arrives in the nick of time. Hyde called me that yesterday but I didn't catch on. I thought he was making fun of me."

"Even the citizens are watching you, Copper," Wulff says. "They need you to slip through Madman's fingers."

"They want a hero?"

"They *need* a hero," Wulff corrects. "There aren't many citizens who don't use Criminals to work around the system. Legitimate business people are already being absorbed into Madman."

"McNally…?" I venture.

"Croft, Wu, John, Busch…just to name a few others."

"But I'm not a returning champion," I protest. "This…display isn't real. I just didn't want to choose between slavery and death, so I *invented* a third option. The smart people are betting on Lyons. *You* should bet on Lyons. This is the end of the line for me. One way or another, the Cops will catch me trying to get into their sector, and there's no way I'm going back to the Prison. I'll die first."

"Whatever you say, Copper." Wulff can't meet my gaze.

Ominous silence dominates our conversation. Wulff stares aimlessly at people in the pub while Frenzy toys with a loose thread on his jacket. I'm too distressed to talk.

How could anyone place their hopes on a Hack? Furious at being given this responsibility, I curse their desperation. But the magnitude and brilliance of Lyons' plan is staggering. By controlling the Criminal underworld, Madman will control a greater portion of the City. Even the Hacks will belong to him. And what if, by some miracle, I do create the line into A? With a path into the heart of Cop Sector, Lyons won't fear the law. How long after that until he absorbs Heathcliff Jackson's crew? Jack is the smartest person I know. I have to believe that he already has a plan to keep his crew safe from Madman.

I finally break the silence. "I need to talk to Jack."

"He's been gone for about a week," Wulff answers.

"Gone?"

"You know him," Frenzy shrugs. "He'll be back."

"He still takes off for weeks?" I ask, exasperated.

Wulff nods, a humorous twinkle in his eyes. "He picked a hell of an exciting time to disappear, didn't he?"

17

Hyde rolls me from B Sector to the Bank for free. His play is simple but effective. For years he's been collecting crates of all shapes and sizes. These are top of the line parcels, designed for safety and durability. They don't come cheap. Every few months, he hires manipulators to give each crate round-trip clearance from B Sector to whichever sectors a client requests. Luck blessed Hyde with powerful foresight. He's been investing in his business for over ten years and he's the only one with anything like it. According to Carlos, one of his delivery boys, the scope of his operation is starting to catch people's attention. The Criminal bosses have started giving him major contracts.

I'm in a deluxe package, with soft foam interior to keep me cozy. Hyde was really happy that Frenzy made the identity card for free. It hasn't been a short ride, so I'm grateful for the comfort. There are lots of ways to travel from one sector to another, but without my credit balance, and with my doom extremely fucking imminent, I took what Luck gave me. Cramped spaces don't bug me, but two hours in this crate is a little much.

I sigh in relief when Carlos finally pops open the lid. A wide grin is splitting his face.

"Welcome back to the Bank, Daryl!" he says.

"Are you paid to be this happy, Carlos?"

"Nah, I just love it here. Amanda is going to flip when I tell her I got to roll you through. We're betting that you make it into A. Her sister thinks we're wasting our credits, but I think it's a sound investment. Safe journey, Daryl!"

"Safe journey," I call back.

Rolling my head from side to side, I stretch out my neck. Despite the foam, my body is stiff from the ride. Luckily, my box is a hop, skip and a jump from where I've been delivered. I toss my bag over one shoulder and exit the building.

As I walk towards my box, I start to understand why Carlos is a fan of the Bank. E Sector is cleaner and brighter than B Sector because Accountants pay more taxes to their administration. With the added funds, the Bank Government hires Collectors to keep the streets free of garbage, Fix-its to keep communal devices working, and the Gentry to keep streetlights on all night. B Sector citizens hire Collectors independently to remove unwanted garbage. There are no communal devices, like swings in parks, and they don't care about communal light. As a result, B taxes are more manageable, but the public areas tend to fall apart.

But even though it's cleaner, I miss the messy B streets. There's a sense of community there that you don't get here in the Bank. Accountants have an unofficial hierarchy based on the success of its citizens. Wulff and his childhood friends were swept into it soon after they matriculated. When Wulff decided to become a Criminal so that he could stay in B Sector, his friends slowly stopped meeting him for drinks. They were all higher-ups so they couldn't associate with him anymore. Wulff never talks about it, which is how I know it still bugs him.

The only reason I sometimes root here is because Accountants mind their own business. No matter what I look like, they keep their eyes forward and ignore me. That means I don't have to sneak through back alleys to get home. The Bank workday has just ended, I'm not alone on the streets, but even though I am obviously not one of them, they don't question my presence. Successful Accountants are heading off to bars and restaurants to socialize and unwind from the days work. The less successful ones are running home to enjoy a tasteless nutrient bar and a tepid glass of water; exactly what I'll be doing after I take a shower.

The lift in my low-end building takes me up eight stories. I am tired: the last day and a half has been more fun than I can handle. With a flick of my key card, the door to my box slides open. I don't bother turning on the lights, my box isn't hard to navigate. Straight ahead, directly under the only window, is my single bed; to my right is the closet where I hastily stow my jacket, boots, and bag; to my left is an open door that leads to my toilet and shower. Everything else is irrelevant right now.

I'm about to slide off my shirt and pants when the sight of the City outside my window catches my eye. The sun has set and night has enveloped the buildings. Bright lights are filtering into my room, making it easy to make out my few pieces of furniture.

Hushed and peaceful, the world turns without me.

For weeks after I was released I stared hard out the window, willing myself to move beyond my fear. There were days I didn't believe I was out. I thought it was some psychological game the Prison was playing with me. It was going to pull me back in as soon as I allowed myself to believe it was over. Eventually, I stopped waiting, but that place is still stalking me. It's nipping at my heels, breathing down my neck. It's crawling around in my brain. When I close my eyes, it finds me again.

An unexpected knock on my door saves me from my memories. Portia, her stunning black hair flowing down to her shoulders, smiles from the hallway.

Accountants are what hold the Criminal world together. Without them our financial trails would lead the Cops right to us. They hide the credits for us, creating reasons for the transfers so that they go unnoticed. Portia was the Accountant I left my stash with. Technically, she isn't a Criminal. She handles my account numbers. There's no law against that.

Usually, she has her hair pulled out of her face. She must be meeting her lover later. When women can't afford new clothes they use their hair to catch a lover's eye. Portia is wearing a faded blue shirt tucked into a worn skirt, but her long, glossy hair will be enough to let him know she wants to be noticed. Greeting her with a small nod, I step to the side to let her in. She declines my invitation by putting up her hand.

"I heard about the line to A. What's going on?" She obviously isn't happy. When I don't reply right away, she keeps going. "There must be some way out of this. Everyone's laying bets. They keep talking about the returning champion. Sweet sky, Daryl! What happened?"

"I went out," I explain lamely.

"You went out...? That's it? I didn't think you would ever..." She puts a hand over her eyes and takes a deep breath. "They didn't see you when you got out. They don't know the shape that you're in. But, it'll be OK. I'm going to bet on you."

I'm about to protest but she throws her arms around my neck, squeezing me tightly. Performing an old blessing, she places her hand on her heart and then touches my chest.

"Luck," she mutters before turning away.

She races down the cramped hallway. Bewildered, I watch her as she impatiently waits for the elevator. When it arrives, she steps into it with an anxious backward glance.

Dazed from her whirlwind visit, I retreat into my box. Wulff wasn't wrong—the citizens are watching me. Lyons has turned the Madman organization into a monster, and the people think I'm going to save them from his terrible hunger.

18

I'm back on *my board, flirting with the cliffs. The freedom is addictive. I can go over if I want. I can crash into the wall if I want. It's all about me—me and my board, me and the curving road ahead.*

There's no danger here. If I go over I can fly; if I crash I won't break. I'm free. Blissfully free. I can do anything.

Enraptured, I tilt my head to the sunless sky. I'm following the road that curves forever. My curiosity keeps me moving, keeps me on the path. Eventually, the road narrows. It narrows until it's barely the width of a spider's web. Still, I keep on the gas, moving faster and faster, hoping to catch a glimpse of what's beyond the bend.

The board disappears and I'm coasting through the desert. My feet are attached to rails that move into a blistering sun. Afraid of burning my retinas, I hastily cover my eyes. Directly ahead, sparkling water laps against dark sand. There's a tall, masculine figure up ahead, looking directly into the blinding light. He's waiting for me. I can't tell who it is, I just know it's someone I trust.

I reach out to touch him; my fingers are a hair's breadth away. But then someone is touching my shoulder. Confused, I look to the mysterious figure and find that he's gone. He's standing behind me now. I don't look back. Whoever he is, his touch is giving renewing my strength. I look directly into the sun and watch the Oasis spring up from the dusty earth.

"They believe," he whispers into my ear.

"They're crazy," I answer.

"The essence of faith…."

I turn to look at him. Even though his hand is still on my shoulder I see him, standing with his back facing me.

My heart beats heavily in my ears. Gasping, I sit up on the bed and grab my shoulder. I can still feel the pressure of his hand.

You were dreaming. Remember it!

I was on a hover-board. I see the cliffs—*what was the rest?* Straining my memory, I try to grab the tendrils of the fading dream. The harder I concentrate the more it slips away. I've lost it. But I still feel the comforting hand on my shoulder.

The morning sun streams into my room. Staring at the small clock on my wall I watch the seconds tick away.

0435. Time to get ready.

This is my last job. It makes no sense, but I'm nervous. There's nothing to fear when you already know what's going to happen. Pulling on my clothes, I retrieve my credit balance and identity card from the bathroom. I left these bastards on the counter by the sink the other day.

Everything I need is in my bag, but I can't shake the feeling that I'm forgetting something. Before leaving, I turn to examine my box. The stillness saddens me. This miserable little space was my refuge. Leaving like this feels anti-climatic.

Forget it. It's time to go.

19

In theory, the plan is simple—get to a Cop Sector gate and go through it before time runs out. But no job is easy. There are no exposed main gates. A two-story building called the Perimeter surrounds Cop Sector. The gates are inside of it and they look like normal doors. Only trained people can tell the difference between a gate and a door; I'm not one of them.

Citizens go to the Perimeter to register complaints. For instance, maybe your vehicle was stolen or your neighbour is harassing you. Just register a complaint with one of the clerks and a Cop will look into it. The best part is that you don't have to pay for the service: Cops never charge for volunteered information.

The only time the victim pays a fee is if they press a panic button. Companies inside of A hire and train patrollers. These Cops make big pay if they're first on a panic scene. There are panic buttons in every Sector and citizens knows where they are. They always keep a certain amount of credits on their balance so they can use one. If you're in trouble, you run straight to the button. Within minutes, seconds depending on how far the nearest patroller is, a Cop shows up.

It's actually illegal for a Cop to stand by and watch someone being attacked. It's also illegal for them to join in. Once they show up they have to restrain the perpetrator or risk paying a hefty fine. Fellow Cops have no trouble asking for it. However, if the victim doesn't have the credits then he or she is hauled off with their attacker. The attacker goes straight to the Prison but Cops will usually keep the victim until a loved one pays the panic fee. Sometimes they end up hauling the victim to the Prison too. A Cop has to be a real asshole to do that. I've noticed that the City is full of assholes—too many of them are Cops.

Getting to the Perimeter is incredibly easy. Cops want citizens to be able to register complaints so there are tunnels running from every sector straight into the building. All I have to do is take E Tunnel and I'll be right where I need to be. It's a long walk, but it gives me time to finalize my plans.

Before my mom died, she worked guard duty. She was one of the Cops responsible for protecting the Perimeter. When I turned five, she started bringing me to work to begin my training. Cop-lings, as Madman appropriately called them, are trained in a variety of ways. The most common is parent's bringing them to their work place. I had an exclusive view of how the Perimeter operates. I know the building. Its depth is divided into three distinct layers: the foyer, the workspace and the garage. In the foyer, citizens register complaints with clerks; the workspace is a common area, designed for both business and pleasure; the garage is attached to the Cop sector wall. Outside of the buildings design, however, I also know that the first two layers don't have video surveillance.

Why not? Because this is the building that Cops pass through in order to get to work. There are never less than a few thousand of them swarming around inside of it. Other than me, who would be stupid enough to infiltrate it?

There being no cameras, I should be able to get into the workspace through the air ducts. As a kid, when my mom couldn't watch me, I decided to face my fear of the dark. The best place for that was in the Perimeter's walls and ceilings. I'd get lost every once in a while and pop up in the strangest places. Those years of exploration are going to come in handy.

I've already neatly glued brown fabric over the black boots that I'm wearing to prepare myself for the job. No sense changing footwear and wasting precious time. I don't have the standard black Cop uniform; I'll be blending in with the clerks.

My mom always warned that the clerks were the unluckiest Cops in the City. They've pissed off some Cop politician and are now doomed to sit in little booths for the rest of their lives. They're also the only ones you'll see out of uniform in the Perimeter. They're not even allowed to own one because it's illegal for them to leave A. Dressed in citizen clothing and wearing black boots, I'm hoping that no one will question that I'm a clerk.

Up ahead I see lights flashing against E tunnels cement walls—I'm almost at the Perimeter.

When I spot the guards my heart leaps into my throat. I suddenly lose all my confidence, so I drop to one knee and pretend to tie my shoe. Fidgeting desperately with the fabric glued to my boot, I struggle with the fear. I want to run. More importantly, I want to slap myself for stealing the hover-board. If I'd just stayed in my box I wouldn't have to walk straight into the jaws of the beast. Cursing Luck, I slowly gather the last vestige of my courage.

I casually glance up at the guards. They're leisurely waiting for me to get up, unconcerned with whether I come or go. Getting to my feet, I consider retreating—*but where to?* By the end of tomorrow I'll either join Madman or finally die at Locket's hands. No, I can't accept either of those options. Forward is the only way to move.

Tightening my grip around the straps of my bag, I stride towards the guards. According to my identity card I'm Yulie Thorp from E Sector. I'm a normal Accountant who has a complaint to register with the Cops. They have no reason to believe otherwise.

Nervously reaching into my pocket I take out my card. A guard holds out a black-gloved hand for my bag so I carefully pass it over. While she rummages through my stuff the other one waits for the go ahead. All I have in there a change of clothes, a nutrient bar, my canteen, and a flash-light. After carefully searching the contents, the Cop nods to her partner. He swipes my card through a silver machine.

The system's calm, feminine voice identifies me. <0589. Yulie Thorp. E Sector. Access Granted.>

Waving me through, the Cops give me back my stuff. The door behind them slides open and I step through the X-ray frame. No warning bells go off and no lights start flashing. According to the machine I'm completely clean. The easy part is over.

The system thinks Yulie Thorp is in the Perimeter. It's waiting for her to leave. I have one hour to make my complaint. If I don't swipe out before time runs out the guards are notified that I haven't left the building. That's when they lock it all down until I'm found. If they don't find me they send a team over to my E Sector box. By then I won't need a place to live anymore.

As I examine the Perimeter's E Sector foyer, my fear melts away. The job has begun. Shutting out distractions, I focus on the task at hand. To my left and right thick cement walls prevent citizens from gaining access to other sectors of the Perimeter. Directly ahead of me clerks sit inside their small booths, busily helping people register their complaints. There are maybe thirty citizens waiting in the lines. None of them look my way as I pass by on my way to the washroom. Two guards flank the door so I groan and clutch at my stomach as I race in. They won't be expecting me to come out any time soon.

Once inside I immediately check for other people. Closing my eyes, I reach out with my psychic talent. There's only one person here. In the second stall a middle-aged Accountant is silently crying. This situation isn't optimal, but I don't know how long I have before someone else comes in. One person isn't bad and he doesn't look like he's coming out any time soon. Drawing strength from my rising excitement, I search the ceiling for access. The metal panel isn't hard to spot.

I don't give myself a chance to think. Quickly moving into the stall below the panel, I carefully step onto the toilet and reach towards it. I remember these panels from when I was a kid. They aren't screwed in or nailed down. It's easy to slip in and out. But it seems so much smaller now; my hands look gigantic next to it. Sliding it to the side, I push my bag through first. I place one foot on one side of the stall, my opposite hand on the other and push myself up. A moment later I put my other foot on the stall. My head and shoulders disappear into the ceiling. I'm just about to pull myself in but chills of disaster race up my spine—someone is staring at me.

My fear is quickly replaced with acceptance. There's no way to explain my actions. This job was over way before it began. Looking down into the bathroom, I prepare myself for the inevitable. But the guards aren't there. I'm staring straight into the Accountant's confused, blood-shot eyes.

The worst part about this situation is that I might have to kill him. If I'd been quicker, quieter or luckier I wouldn't have to consider it. But he isn't running out and sounding the alarm. He's studying my compromising position, intrigued with the inelegant way I'm balancing on the sides of the stall.

"I've...never met a Criminal before."

Relieved that I won't have to hurt him, I quickly reply. "Sure you have. You just didn't know they were a Criminal."

"Daryl...?"

I don't have time to chat. Shooting him a cocky grin, I throw him my identity card and get back to work. Effortlessly pulling my whole body into the ceiling, I silently replace the panel.

The narrow space is disorienting. My knees are practically at my ears. I used to have enough room to move unencumbered up here. The Accountant titters excitedly, washes his hands, and leaves. I listen nervously as the door opens and then closes. If I was wrong, the Cops will rush in and pull me out. There won't be any opportunity to escape.

I hold my breath and count to five, deliberately placing giant gaps of time in between the numbers. Somebody walks in and goes directly into a stall. For the first time in years, Luck has favoured me.

Stealthily moving through the ceiling, I focus on the rays of light shooting through other panels up ahead. I *remember* this area. I'm crawling through a relatively empty space between the main storey's ceiling and the second storey's floor. If memory serves, my destination is straight ahead.

The workspace is the biggest and most confusing area in the Perimeter. It's where guards go on break and wait for shift change; it's where patroller crews gather before heading off into their sectors; it's where bounty hunters gain legal access into a sector. It's where protectors, Cops who work independent security, swipe in and out of A; it's where the Criminals are processed before they're sent to the Prison; it's where you'll find the clerk locker rooms.

Pulling my bag along behind me, I carefully stop over a panel and peer through. Directly below I see a metal bench—I've found a locker room. Clerks don't leave anything valuable in this place. The locker rooms are where they store what they don't want in their booths.

Closing my eyes, I reach into the room with my psychic talent. A red-haired woman closes her locker and walks away. A bored looking man puts on his jacket and shuffles in the opposite direction. A moment later he's turned a corner and I take my chance.

Tense but focused, I rip off the fabric I have glued to my black boots. Stuffing it into my bag, I take one last look with my mind before making my move. I grab the panel, lift it up and carefully slide it to the side. Before I can doubt my decision, I slip my bag over my shoulders. Holding onto one edge of the hole, I soundlessly lower myself onto the bench. Nobody comes around a corner and nobody calls for help.

I put the panel back in place and step off the bench. Noting how quiet it is, I take a quick look around.

Everything seems so small. Running a hand over the dented metal of a locker, I remember my eyes being level with the cheap, dial locks. I finger one absent-mindedly, feeling clumsy and over-sized. I never expected to be disoriented in a clerk locker room. It doesn't feel like I'm in danger, but I'm standing in the one place where I should never feel secure.

Shaking my head to clear it, I force myself to concentrate on the task at hand. My skin prickles with anticipation. When I walk out of this locker room I am looking for a gate. If Frenzy has done his job I'll walk through without a scratch.

Whatever I do, I can't look like I don't know where I'm going. At this point I'm hoping to recognize something that will lead me in the right direction. Maps are universally illegal, no matter where you are. There won't be anything on the walls to give me a clue.

An middle-aged female clerk walks into the locker room. Opening her locker, she stiffly pulls on her jacket and grabs a small bag. She sighs dejectedly before retreating back into the workspace. I make a quick decision. Following her is my best option.

Silently asking Luck for one more favour, I move deeper into the belly of the Perimeter.

At first, I don't let my surroundings overwhelm me. The bustling, spacious centre of Cop life hardly penetrates my focus. But what I didn't count on was my memories. It's the *smells* that hit me first. The familiar aromas wafting through the air ensnare me—a strangely gratifying mixture of coffee, multi-purpose cleaners, warm food and recycled air. Somewhere amidst it all, I recognize the spicy sausages I begged my mother to buy me every morning. They were delicious with warm, buttered bread and freshly cooked eggs. She would pull me along, grumbling that she would be late for work, but always got them for me in the end. We weren't wealthy, but we could afford certain luxuries. Those sausages were my favourite indulgence.

Flashes of messily eating breakfast while my mom enjoyed a cup of her favourite tea sweep my original plans away. Overcome by the dangerous familiarity, I follow the mouth-watering smell. The middle-aged clerk disappears into the crowd as I walk in the opposite direction. The restaurant was just around this bend, I think. It had orange paneling and yellow furniture. Some of the tables were outside, which is where we used to sit. Mom made her own tea, so she wasn't allowed stay inside the restaurant.

My excitement mounts as I search the open design of the workspace. There are tables and chairs everywhere, but I can't find the restaurant. The Cops, walking around with their helmets hooked to their belts, almost looking like normal people, lull me into a false sense of security. I grew up here. Everything seems so tiny now, but I know this area of the workspace. There are only a few restaurants in this section. It's dominated by rental space. Privates, Cops who work alone, rent the space and put up makeshift walls. Packs, groups of Cops who work together, rent space as well. They always set up shop in this area because it's so open. It's also where there's the highest concentration of guards: professional rivalries can cause problems.

I step around a group of people and spot the orange paneling up ahead. It's just the same! The smell of the sausage grows stronger and I race towards it recklessly. The yellow tables and chairs are still here. It's been over fifteen years, but they're still here! Sitting down, I tenderly stroke a familiar table, remembering how my mother, agitated, traced the rough top.

This was where we spent our last morning together.

One of her superiors had sponsored me into a bounty hunter academy. Mom was proud but sad, and gently explained that I'd be living with the other trainees. I'd be too busy to see my family. It was a great honour, she kept saying, it was for the best.

I was seven years old. Two years later, when my mom died, my dad couldn't make enough credit to pay the academy's fees, so I went home. Mom was gone, but I never forgot our morning ritual. The memory made— makes—me happy.

Something fierce awakens inside of me. Careful not to draw attention to myself, I watch the Cops meander towards restaurants and rental spaces. Some wander up to the second floor while others chat with friends and colleagues. Surrounded by the enemy I am completely invisible. With my abilities as a Criminal I could live comfortably in the Perimeter, free from both Madman and Locket. All I need to do is steal a few credit balances.

I carefully consider the idea. The Perimeter wraps around Cop Sector, it's gigantic. I could keep travelling around it, sleeping in air ducts, using their facilities and stealing my food. With a little diligence, I could make it work. Getting to my feet, I eagerly study the workspace.

This is my way out.

My first task is to know my environment. Emboldened by my new plan, I move into the steady flow of Cops walking through the workspace. I quickly investigate the layout of this area, noting restaurants, locker rooms, air duct passages, and rental spaces. Grinning wolfishly, I make a small but vital mistake… I make eye contact with someone.

The Cop runs his eyes appreciatively over my body before flashing me a ravenous smile. Shocked, I stumble over my own feet—he's a bounty hunter. Trying to pass myself off as shy, I bow my head and walk away. The last thing I want is to be noticed.

"It's okay to run away from Rodney," an alluring voice remarks. "I react that way to him all the time."

Startled, I quickly look around to find the owner of the voice. A tall, striking man is walking next to me. Obviously amused by my quick retreat, he chuckles at my confusion. Meeting his captivating gaze, I reply without thinking.

"Run away...?" My voice warbles anxiously. I clear my throat. "What are you talking about?"

"Rodney gave you the *look*. It sends nine out of ten women screaming for their lives."

"And the last one...?"

"...is looking for trouble."

I laugh quietly; his sense of humour is disarming. A gentle yet enticing smile spreads across his face. His soft manner, however, can't conceal the arrogantly charming glint in his eyes. Unfortunately, it's that glint that I'm finding so beguiling. Cursing myself for being too friendly, I carefully study his armour. The superior shock plates are a dead give away. This guy is a bounty hunter too. And like any good bounty hunter he's thriving on the chase.

"You must be a new clerk," he says. "I'm sure I would have noticed you otherwise. If your shift is over we could..."

"...I'm sorry." I put up a hand to show my resistance. "I have to go home."

My immediate refusal intrigues him. His smile broadens. "All right, I'll walk you."

"Hey, Selim!" a voice calls. My admirer turns around. A brash looking man runs up and punches him in the arm. "Are you coming or what?"

"Not today, Ellis." Selim's captivating gaze brushes over me. "I'll be there tomorrow."

"Right, right, tomorrow," Ellis echoes. Unabashedly looking me up and down, he gives a low whistle. "You know, gorgeous, you don't have to be impressed just because he's a bounty hunter. Has he gotten to his *it's a dangerous life* speech yet? Don't fall for it. He gets himself a new woman every week. A humble patroller like me has way more to offer than this clown."

Selim chuckles good-naturedly. "You can get out of here now."

"I'll tell the others you're indisposed." Ellis offers me a conspiratorial wink. "Remember, a new woman every week. Look me up when he breaks your heart."

Despite myself, I smile at Ellis' retreating form before looking to Selim. "What are you missing for the pleasure of my company?"

"Friends and alcohol," he answers. "Shall we?"

I motion for him to lead the way. Luck might give me a chance to lose him. This area of the workspace is bustling with activity. Every few moments someone hails Selim, preventing him from focusing entirely on me. But when I think I see an out he looks over, making sure I'm still with him. Admittedly, I'm not exactly suffering; it's entertaining to watch him socialize. His greetings are understated but he obviously thrives on his popularity. Despite myself, despite this fucked-up situation, I'm enjoying his company. I'm slowly being lulled into a false sense of security. As if I never left A—as if I'm still a Cop.

"Where do you live?" Selim finally manages to ask.

I wasn't prepared for any questions so I say the first thing that comes to mind. "3rd block."

"That's a close-knit community."

I burst out laughing. "Are you trying to put a positive spin on one of our crummiest neighbourhoods?"

He answers with a shrug and a lazy grin. "I've been to worse places in this City."

"Is this the beginning of the speech your friend warned me about?"

"Not even close. I would never rush into genius. You've got to let me warm up first."

My admirer holds a door open for me. I step into the small restaurant beyond and a strange vibration assaults my bones. My teeth rattle in my mouth. Looking back at the door, I flash Selim a curious look.

"It makes my flesh crawl, too," he says, before walking through himself. "They should be replacing this one soon."

I stand there with a dumb expression on my face. That was an older gate, they replace them when you start to feel the scanners. My eyes widen when I realize that I've just made it into Cop Sector.

Horrified, I try to retreat from the nearly empty restaurant. "What time is it?"

He looks at a small screen stitched into the base of his glove. "0619... No, wait! 0620. Forget something?"

"No," I answer. Swallowing my disappointment, I force myself to stay calm. "Everything's fine."

"That sounded convincing." He studies me as I stare longingly at the other side of the gate. "Let's go back."

"No, seriously, there's nothing I need back there." I flinch at my abruptness. "It can wait."

"All right," Selim replies. "How are you getting home?"

I shoot him a suspicious look. "Walking."

"I'll give you a ride."

"I don't need one." But for some reason I'm not turning away. "I'm sure you have more important things to do."

"Well, that isn't fair. You're not giving me any ins."

Frustrated at my thwarted plans, I offer him a predatory smile. "Is that what you want? An *in*...?"

He chuckles at the sexual connotation. That charmingly arrogant glint returns to his eyes. Taking a step forward, he boldly studies my face. "You have no idea what I want."

My breath catches in my throat. Am I actually considering letting this Bounty Hunter into my pants? "I don't have time for this."

"So let me give you a ride."

"There must be other women you can flatter."

"Of course there are," he says, "but you're the one who sparks my curiosity."

Is it really *so bad* that I'm enjoying his attention? I don't want to say no. Sensing that my defences are crumbling, Selim continues.

"What's the worst that happens?" He flashes me a rakish smile. "You make it home in a fraction of the time? Once we get there, if you decide you still don't want anything to do with me, I drop you off. We say good-bye."

I'm still shaking my head but I already know he's got me. "It isn't a good idea."

"Are you going to make me follow you home?" he asks.

"You wouldn't!"

He leans in, his eyes gleaming with mischief. "No, I wouldn't. But I really do want you to change your mind."

I believe him and sigh in relief. But now I'm thinking that a Bounty Hunter escort to my destination is a great idea. No one, is going to question someone he's with. Finally, with a small nod, I agree to his plan.

Selim smiles in excitement. He motions to a set of double doors at the back of the restaurant before taking the lead. Pushing them open, we walk into the garage.

I am not exaggerating when I say that this place would be Wulff's dream home. The windowless steel and cement walls are begging to be painted. Thousands of models of vehicles are parked, row upon row, as far as the eye can see. Some Cops walk to the Perimeter, but most choose to ride. Their vehicle is usually their pride and joy.

As I follow Selim, I keep my eye on the Cop Sector wall. Sunlight is streaming through an open garage door and my location is starting to make me nervous. Hiding in the Perimeter was one thing, but I wouldn't last if I tried to stay in this sector. There are undercover Cops, known as detectives, who do random sweeps in here. They keep the peace in A. Like everyone else, my mother and father were terrified of them, and I'm not above what they taught me.

"Here she is!" Selim announces as he swings his leg over a motorbike.

I carefully study the rubber tires. "What, no hover?"

"I like the feeling of the road," he explains.

Unhooking his helmet from his belt he straps it on. A huge dent mars its otherwise flawless workmanship. I shrug on my bag, swing my leg over the bike, put my arms around his waist and ask him what happened.

<I was tagging along on a desert sweep with a friend>, he replies through his helmet mike. < They stopped a tour bus for a toll and a couple of hover-boarders were there. I was bored out of my mind but then one of the boarders actually *jumped* over the side of the cliff. I wasn't expecting it, so when I jumped to attention I slipped on loose stones. Next thing I know, I'm crashing head first into a rock. I'm lucky my helmet is top of the line.>

He turns on the bikes, pulls out of his stall, and motors out of the garage. I hold on tight, thankful he can't see my astonishment.

My situation managed to get a whole lot more interesting.

20

I love having the wind in my face. It's a rare pleasure.

Watching the buildings flash by, my nerves take a vacation, and I forget that I'm an intruder in this sector. Small pleasures tend to keep me calm. Being a street-raised Criminal, however, I haven't forgotten about the job. The way I figure it, Selim taking me to 3rd block is the best possible set-up. I actually did live there with my father and brother. Familiar territory can't hurt me at this point. Besides, I have unfinished business there.

Selim brings the bike to a gentle stop and takes off his helmet. Awestruck, he stares off into the distance. "Take a look at that."

All I see is Cop Sector. It looks a lot like the Bank. There are large buildings and small buildings, the streets are clean, and citizens are always out no matter what the time. The difference is in the details. Cop Sector streets are made of black pavement; the Bank's streets are made from yellow stones. Cop streetlights are painted green; Accountant street lights are painted grey. I could go on, but Selim is motioning to a section of the desert sky.

In between the tall buildings, I glimpse a rare storm brewing. The intense, dark blue swirls of dense cloud are breathtaking.

So far, the storm hasn't reached the City. It'll probably pass us by. The last time we had rain it filled the streets and created lakes outside the walls.

People who usually hide from the desert were racing into it in droves, gigantic mobs flocking to the pools of water. Moles from C Sector were showing off; they splashed around and gave people swimming lessons. I dove in just to know what it felt like to be immersed. I almost drowned, but it was worth it.

That was years ago, but every once in a while you can hear the storms off in the distance. I wish it would rain here again.

"Hold on!" Selim puts his helmet back on. <We're going to the Observatory.>

He doesn't give me time to protest, not that I would have. The gathering storm has me spellbound. There's nothing I would rather do than get a better look.

The Observatory is located on the tallest building in Cop Sector. It's about thirty stories. Originally, the Observatory was just for the owners; it was a place of privilege. Then they realized they could make major credits by charging the general public access fees.

Selim swipes his credit balance to pay for us both and we ride up to the top floor.

The dark storm has drawn more than a few Cops to the Observatory. The sky is usually clear, not a cloud to be seen in any direction. This inspiring show is the most entertainment some people will get for months. Flashes of lightning illuminate the clouds from within, making the viewers gasp in fear and excitement. The tall windows offer a full view of the awesome spectacle, but Selim heads directly for the door that leads onto the balcony.

This is where I hesitate. There are guardrails around the edge but I'll lose control of my legs anyway. Thirty stories is a *long* way down.

Selim opens the door for me. Thunder echoes into the room. "What's the point if you can't feel it?"

I admit, I want to go outside. There's no way of knowing if I'll ever have another chance like this. Aching to feel the wind, I slowly follow Selim. Once I'm through the door, however, my limbs feel heavy and weak. My escort, oblivious to my difficulty, walks directly to the guardrail.

Determined not to show him weakness, I take one step forward and then another. It's a slow process. Every time I gain a foot my panic rises a little higher. But I rode a hover-board at break neck speeds along the edge of an eight hundred foot cliff, and I jumped off that same cliff to avoid going back into lock-up. After all the excitement, I even glided my way back to the City. By comparison, this should be easy. I take another step.

Nope, I'm going to be sick.

"You have lost all colour in your face," Selim teases when he looks back at me. "You're afraid of heights, aren't you?"

He is really pleased with my vulnerability. Reaching out with his hand, he offers me a steady body to hold on to. Annoyed at his pleasure but wanting to make it to the guardrail, I grit my teeth and put my hand in his.

"Don't look down," he instructs, smiling gently. "Just watch the sky. You'll forget all about the fear."

Pulling me forward, he tucks my hand into his arm before turning his attention back to the storm. I try to take his advice. The raw beauty in the sky has my senses transfixed, but I can't forget the drop. I'm shaking with nauseous terror, the sinking feeling in my stomach overtaking my rational mind. My fingers dig into his forearm.

"Imagine if it came through here?" Selim is lost in faraway thoughts. "My mother used to dream of rain. She'd pick my brother and me up from our training sessions and take us into the desert. For hours we'd watch the sky and listen for thunder. If we saw a rain cloud we'd chase it. And then one day, she went alone and never came back."

His story strikes a chord in my heart. Forgetting the steep drop, I study his earnest expression as he worships the dark clouds.

"My father liked caves," I suddenly blurt out. Selim gazes at me, inviting me to continue. I'm not sure why I'm sharing this with him, but I can't stop myself. "He and I would go spelunking. There are these caves to the east that he loved. We would climb the walls inside of them and once I slipped off. I fell a hundred feet into a dark pit. The ropes and knots held, but I never forgot the way it felt."

"That why you're afraid of heights?"

I nod sadly. "I never went again and one day he never came back."

Selim nods empathetically. "And your mother?"

"She died when I was nine...euthanasia."

"Wow." Selim shakes him head in wonderment. "Was she sick?"

Doing my best not to show him how vulnerable I am, I turn away. "I think she was sick at heart. She just kept saying that it was for the best, whatever that means. I don't know which one's worse... knowing what happened or not knowing."

"Not knowing drives you crazy," Selim offers. "But at least we can dream."

I carefully look at him again. He smiles knowingly and tucks a loose strand of my hair behind my ear. The intimate gesture brings me back to reality. I would move away from him, but the world isn't steady. Vertigo takes over. Terrified, I hold on to the bounty hunter for dear life.

Selim senses my fear. Gallantly, he escorts me away from the rail. The wind picks up, blowing cool, refreshing air into my face.

"Let me take you out to breakfast," Selim offers. "We'll go to the restaurant at 24th block...nothing too fancy."

He's a clever man. He's chosen a place that a clerk would definitely not be able to afford. It's supposed to inspire my curiosity. I want to go, but here's my opportunity to shake him. "Take me home and I'll meet you there."

We can't talk while Selim's driving and I'm grateful for the chance to study the familiar buildings. Not much has changed where the facades are concerned. Oddly enough, I don't feel anything when I look at them. When I returned to B Sector, I was disoriented and nostalgic. I guess I don't feel that way here because there's no one to come home to.

Every sector has numbered blocks. Only K and E have them in order. For instance, in B Sector, Heidi's restaurant is located at 31st block. Bragg's bar, which is seven streets over, is located at 2nd block. And, despite the title, most blocks aren't square. Before we got back on his bike, Selim told me he lives at 14th block. That's a nice area of A. It's also a good twenty minute ride from 3rd. 24th is somewhere in between the two.

The ride to 3rd from the Observatory takes about five minutes. Selim pulls up to it and waits for my directions.

"It's the grey one on the North West corner," I say.

Next thing I know, I'm staring at the ugly building where my life took its second major turn. The walls are still dirty, the windows are still cracked, and the steps up to the first floor are still uneven. The front doors all open into an exposed corridor. You can see them all from the street. Two stories up and three doors to the right is the entrance to my family's old box.

Pulling off his helmet, Selim studies the decrepit building with a mild look of disgust on his face. "You're sure you don't want me to pick you up?"

Assaulted by old memories, I hardly hear his question. "I'm sure."

"Hey!" he calls after I hop off the bike. "You know Ellis was just joking, right? I don't really have a new girl every week."

"Every month?"

He chuckles and shakes his head.

"Then it must be every day."

An enigmatic smile spreads over his face as he puts his helmet back on. Giving me a small wave, he drives away. A peculiar feeling of regret settles in my chest. For a while there, I was pretending that I could meet him later.

Shaking off the emotion, I scan my old neighbourhood. My body feels light as a feather, like I'm not really here. Stepping into the past will do that to a person. To my left I spot a tall, man-sized rectangle: an information box. If it's not broken it's exactly what I need.

Jogging over I tap the small screen. It slowly flickers to life.

"Patrick Meir," I say into the flat microphone.

<Patrick Meir,> the calm, female voice repeats. The only legal map in the City flashes on the screen. <3rd block, 6th building, 3rd floor, 23rd box.>

A symbol, 'X', appears where I'm standing. The computer draws a line from it to Meir's place of residence. He stills lives above my family's old box. My brother's unmoving body flashes through my mind as I stare at the run-down piece of crap building. If this whole thing didn't feel so surreal, I might ask myself what I was planning on doing. But what's the point? I'm running on instinct.

Unwilling to draw too much attention, I calmly climb the steps. There are people visiting on the streets. They're walking by on their way to work, or wherever else they have to go. Nobody is paying attention to me. That's exactly the way I want it. With mounting excitement, I casually continue on my way to Meir's box.

One, two, three doors—the number '23' hangs on the dilapidated metal like a target. Balling my left hand into a hard fist, I raise it up and knock twice. Someone shifts around inside; I concentrate on the noise.

The door swings inward and I stonily greet the skinny, balding man in front of me. The skin on his face is falling and what's left of his hair is turning grey. This old man is the same mummy-looking fuck-up who killed my little brother seventeen years ago.

His large eyebrows draw together in confusion. "You the one asking about me?"

When I asked the information box for Meir's address, the system immediately informed him that someone had looked him up. He takes a good, hard look at my face and recognition flickers in his yellowing eyes.

That's what I was waiting for.

My hands shoot out before he can react; a second later, his neck is broken and his body goes limp. In one smooth motion, I noiselessly lower him to the floor, step into his box and pull him back in by his arms. Nobody screams. There are no shouts of alarm. I don't much care if someone saw me anyway. If this is where I go out, so be it.

I stare into Meir's empty, unblinking expression. Crime is part of A Sector too; Cops get greedy, they feel anger, they have ambitions. In a week, the system will inform the detectives that Meir hasn't opened his door in seven days. That could mean he's depressed, which is illegal, or that he's disappeared. When they find his body, they'll make a half-assed attempt to discover who killed him. They won't find anything and the case will be closed.

I've met some real psychos in my life. And I'm not talking about people who torture and kill, anybody's capable of that under the right circumstances. I'm talking about those who only find pleasure in other people's pain. Most of us can deaden ourselves to someone's screams, but some feel dead unless they're making someone else hurt. That's what separates the killers from the psychos. My history is fairly brutal. In my first week on the streets of B I beat another orphan to death. We both wanted the scraps of a discarded nutrient bar—starvation is a powerful motivator. It wasn't my intention to hurt him any more than I had to, but it turned ugly. That was the night I crossed over one line and had to draw another; hence my distinction between killers and psychos.

But staring down at Meir's unmoving body, I suddenly understand how someone might take pleasure in slowly torturing a man to death. This whole situation is anti-climactic. I'm completely unsatisfied.

There's no concern here other than the dead man on the floor. Stepping out of the box, I close the door behind me. I have other business to attend to.

As much as I hated living on 3rd block I still have good memories. Nathan and I used to hangout with the kids who lived on the top floor. They're the ones who taught us how to be pickpockets. We used to practice on adults as they walked by. I nostalgically remember the beatings we caught, and how Nathan used to try and protect me. He was a good brother.

3rd block is poor, but that doesn't mean the residents don't have spirit. Every so often there were spontaneous celebrations. The Cop who lived below us owned a guitar and would start playing on the street. My dad would grab his own instrument and join in. Next thing you knew, everyone was coming out of their boxes to visit and dance. The guy who ran the 3rd block bar would wheel out the booze and drop the prices; everyone could afford to get drunk. I even used to know all my neighbours' names. There was a community living in this run-down area.

But even though I knew everyone, that doesn't mean that I trusted them. The day my dad disappeared, I understood that they had no problem turning my brother and me over to the detectives. My dad would have done the same thing to their kids. Of course, there's no proof that the orphans are taken somewhere terrible. It's the secrecy that's so terrifying.

Bringing myself out of my memories, I return to the task at hand. It isn't unusual for people who don't live in 3rd block to pass through on their way to somewhere else. My presence doesn't inspire much curiosity. A mother nods at me politely as she picks up her toddler; a middle-aged man ignores me completely as he rushes across the street; an elderly woman smacks her gums disapprovingly when I brush by her. All in all, I'd say this is a good time to find sewer access.

Making my way to the back of my old building I spot the chained basement door I squeezed through all those years ago. It feels like it all happened eons ago. I'd like to remember where I ran afterward,s but I'm drawing a blank. Any way was good back then, and it's not like I knew where I was going. At least this time I have a goal in mind.

I scan the area until I spot a drainage grate a few meters to my right. Casually wandering toward,s it I grab hold of the bars and heave it to one side. It makes a loud, aggravating noise as it scrapes along the pavement, making my hair stand on end. I slip into the sewers and pull it back into place before anyone comes to investigate the sounds.

Relieved to be off the streets, I stare into the darkness. I'm fairly certain the hard part is over.

21

There are a few people that Luck favours with a natural ability to sense which direction is which. I wish I had someone like that with me now.

Unless you're a Mole, all sewers look the same. It's easy to lose your way down here. One moment you might think north is east, and the next you're convinced that west is south. As it is, I am relying on my psychic talent to guide me through the tunnels; I can't be sure I'm getting anywhere.

In most cases, whenever I have to journey through the sewers, I hire someone who knows where they're going. Trouble with this little adventure is that nobody outside of A knows these tunnels. Moles are hand-picked early in life and disappear into places like A and F Sector. They're never heard from again. They form special sewer crews that tend specifically to that sectors water supply.

Without being able to see the sun, I have no idea how long I've been down here. Judging from my exhaustion, I'd say at least a couple of hours. Every so often, I see rays of light peeking into the gloom. Then I consider going back to the surface, but if anyone got too close they'd smell the sewer on me. I can't pass myself off as an A Sector Mole.

Using my flashlight, I look behind me and then up ahead once more. There hasn't been a bend in this particular tunnel for a while and I can't decide if that's a good thing or not. Exhausted, I lean up against the wall.

It feels great taking a little stress off of my feet. While resting, I examine the walls and wonder if Moles find any enjoyment in their work. As I imagine what it must be like to work in dark places like this, day in and day out, my flashlight begins to flicker. I glare at it, willing it to keep working. Finally, after it's dimmed to a useless glow, it dies.

Furious, I curse into the darkness. I charged this piece of crap! It should have lasted a few days. I could use my psychic talent to see in the dark, but the headache would severely hinder my progress. Angrily jamming my flashlight into my pocket, I start feeling my way down the tunnel. I can't see any rays of light in either direction. Grumbling at my helplessness, I continue the way I was originally going. I've never liked backtracking. Stumbling along, doing my best not to imagine rats gnawing on my corpse, I glimpse a faint light up ahead.

Maybe Luck hasn't abandoned me.

A few minutes later, I step up into a dimly lit section of the sewers. There's no water running along the floors and it feels warmer. Scanning the walls, I note small bulbs hanging from a wire that's been nailed into the cement. Curious—why provide light in one section of the sewer and not another?

Up ahead, I see rays of sunlight pouring into the sewers from above.

And then it hits me.

My body goes numb with fear. Stepping into the warm sun, I bite down on my lip, taste blood, and look up. My hand shields my eyes from the bright light. There isn't much to see from here, the bright blue-sky looks just like it always should. But I know what I'll find if I reach out with my psychic talent.

The Prison has a large, paved, square courtyard. In the middle of that courtyard, in plain sight and completely unguarded, is an iron grate that leads directly into the sewers. I would pass by it whenever I was allowed to go outside. The light let you see straight into the tunnels and prisoners would stare longingly towards freedom, day-dreaming of escape. And that's exactly what that place wanted. Some prisoners would suddenly snap and start clawing on the iron bars. They'd break their nails off and smear the pavement with their blood. But an energy field also protects the grate. If someone touches it for too long they lose their first few layers of skin.

I step out of the light. It wasn't long ago that I jumped off a cliff to avoid coming back here—Luck has an ugly sense of humour. I want to walk by, forget I was ever here, but I can't move. I don't even know if I'm breathing anymore. Staring into the dimly lit sewers, I wait until I can process what I've found; I wait until I understand that my psychic vibe *deliberately* brought me back here.

I stare up, once again, at the blue sky. Two years of studying that grate and now I'm on the opposite side. Sweet sky! This is a sick joke. Seething with rage, I tear my flashlight out of my pocket and hurl the pathetic piece of junk at the grate.

Burn, you fucker! I nearly cry out loud, but the broken light blazes ethereal green as it passes in between the steel bars. Stunned, I watch it fly into the air beyond the grate. It crashes to the ground somewhere out of sight. Cocking my head to one side, I study the iron bars.

That wasn't a mirage. My flashlight passed through the grate. The energy field should have blazed a maddeningly beautiful blue; the flashlight should have been destroyed and fallen back into the sewers. But it went through. Is the grate's field semi-permeable?

I can't deny what I saw. Too curious not to find out, I slowly take off my bag. Placing it on the ground, I study the hole that leads up to the grate. It's only a few meters long. There's no ladder, but it's narrow enough that I could shimmy up. I quickly calculate the difficulty and realize that I have nothing to lose.

Closing my eyes I take a moment to scan the courtyard. It's abandoned except for a few people huddled in a corner. One is doubled-over, clutching his head and muttering to himself. The others are staring at the sun, high overhead. No one is near the grate.

It's as good a time as any.

I wedge myself into the tight space. A few uncomfortable minutes later my head is inches away from the grate. I warily reach towards it. If I'm wrong the field will glow bright blue and the tips of my fingers will start to burn. But if I'm right, the field will briefly shine green, my hand will pass right through. What's a little burn compared to knowing?

Gritting my teeth, I go for it.

The field glitters green for a moment. My hand grasps the cold iron of the bars. This has to be a mistake. I just found a line into the Prison.

My heart starts beating a million miles a minute. A semi-permeable energy field—it's a semi-permeable energy field. They require less power and less maintenance, there's less chance of a breakdown. *Of course* that's what they would use.

Jumping back down to solid ground, I look up at the grate. An SPEF has one flaw, one problem in its design that can always be exploited. If there's someone on the permeable side they can reach out and pull you through. The field doesn't distinguish between two bodies if they're connected. All I have to do is grind down the cement holding the grate in place. I could reach in and pluck out a prisoner.

A feeling of terrible dread seizes me; if Madman gets his line to A it won't take him long to figure this out. Even the Prison will be under his control. That possibility horrifies me—absolute supremacy in the hands of one man. Everyone will live according to his whims. There's no one I trust with that kind of power.

Nauseated, I place my hand on the wall for support. My options are limited. I now know that I'll create a line into A. If I give it to Lyons he'll own everyone. Then again, I can pretend that I was never here. Instead of creating the line I can just walk through the SPEF.

Then it's the simple choice: Madman or Locket—slavery or death.

I should already be dead. How the fuck did I get here? Having come this far, I know I want to live. I want my freedom.

Wrestling with that weakness, I make a hard decision. I'll give Madman his line into A. I'll savour the shocked look on his face when he realizes that I've slipped through his fingers.

The future is somebody else's problem.

22

Tripping, stumbling and staggering, I slowly navigate the dank sewers. I'm moving from one patch of sunlight to another. Without my flashlight it's the only way I'm able to see. The lack of good lighting severely limits my movement. My belly starts to growl and I know I've been fumbling around for hours. Tired and angry, I growl in frustration. When is this going to end?

A tunnel to my right suddenly gets my mind buzzing. Looking down, I see rays of light some forty meters away. I'll have to be careful where I step. Trusting my instincts, I turn right and slowly make my way toward the light. I'm just about to reach it when something green flickers in front of me: the SPEF.

My excitement mounts as I carefully reach towards it with my hand. The green field flicker once more.

My search is over.

Escaped T Sector slaves always speak of holes they found in T's SPEF. I'm fairly certain those don't exist here. Holes only occur if the field isn't getting enough power. Cops wouldn't risk Criminals being able to sneak in and out of A. If I knew how to make a hole I would do it, but I'm not that talented. All I know is that a hole has to be made from the permeable side. Even if I had the training, I never would have been able to get the equipment through the Perimeter. All I have is what's in my bag and whatever else I can scrounge up from these sewers.

Still, this is the easy part. Once I place an object through the field, I can use it to get me back in. The field will think that the object and I are part of the same body. If I'm wrong, I'll only get a few burns. Despite my nonchalance, however, I know that burns are the *worst*. I've broken limbs, had my teeth knocked out, been dragged over broken glass, and been beaten to a bloody pulp. None of that pain compares to when I caught fire.

I was still sleeping in the streets back then. Even in the City the desert nights are cold. A gang of kids had started a fire in a collection bin. I remember it was just after I'd killed for a shred of nutrient bar; the others gave me a seat without a fight. I sat there watching the flames and a spark shot out of the fire, landing on my shirt. There's a reason why buildings in the City can't be made from flammable materials. My clothes went up in a matter of moments.

No one came to my rescue. I put myself out. I lost a good portion of my hair and sustained second-degree burns on my torso. When you're an orphan, there aren't many places you can go for medical treatment. Doctors can be expensive. Poorer citizens tend to make home remedies. A compassionate woman gave me some kind of oil to prevent an infection, but there was nothing for the agony Even if I could have afforded drugs I don't know if I would have taken them. Anything you get on the streets is highly addictive.

The pain from all my other injuries has faded from memory. I remember they hurt but, once they'd healed, they were easy to forget. My burns, however, have stuck with me.

Enthralled by my work, I forget all about the grim consequences of success. I reach into my bag, pull out a shirt, and hold it out in front of me. The sewers are full of debris and discarded items. It doesn't take me long to find an old pipe, about double the length of my arm, and slip the shirt over it. Carefully wrapping the cloth securely around the metal, I place the pipe underneath the water. It slides easily through the green energy. The field grabs it and tries to whisk it out of my hands, but I keep a firm grip and refuse to let go.

Securing the end of the pipe with a discarded cinderblock, I make sure it won't slip out when I'm not holding it. Satisfied, I quickly step through the SPEF. It doesn't feel like much. Mostly it just makes the inside of my ears itch. Fortifying myself against my guilt, I turn around, bend down, and grab the swaddled pipe. I take it out from the cinderblock holding it in place.

Everything has been building to this one moment.

Despite the chill in the water the shirt is warm. I may not have the training to make a hole in the SPEF, but I do know that if metal is in contact with an energy field it heats up. The shirt is a precaution against burns. The water should be enough to keep the metal from getting too hot, but you can never be too careful. Anxious to get this over with, I close my eyes and step towards the field.

My ears itch—I'm through.

I've done the impossible; I found a line into A. But I'm too conflicted for excitement. The cost is higher than I should have to pay. And yet, what's done is done. Sickened by my cowardice, I step back through the SPEF. The blue sky on the other side of the grate beckons to me from this damp tomb.

Beating back my guilt I jump, grab the bottom rung of the hanging ladder, and pull myself up. It's common knowledge that F, Y, K, W and N surround A Sector; my only question is which one I'm currently under. My first choice would be Y. The Gaffers are a friendly bunch who wouldn't think twice about my smelling like the sewers. In Y, no one ever mentions funny odours. The whole sector smells strange from the factories. It's considered rude to mention it.

Also, in Y Sector the people work but aren't paid. All credits are put into a public fund and then politicians choose where to distribute them. For instance, the door of a box won't close and a citizen wants it to be fixed. When they're not working, they go to the Y Sector Application Centre. An official checks the complaint and arranges to have it fixed. It's an efficient system that Gaffers seem to enjoy. Their neighbourhoods are absolutely beautiful: buildings with courtyards that have green community parks. They don't worry about losing their box or getting hurt. Y Sector pays their rent and their medical bills. I think it's the security that keeps them happy.

My instincts let me know that it's safe to leave. Carefully sliding the grate up and to the side, I poke my head out. Sniffing the air I wrinkle my nose: I'm definitely in Y. With a grunt of satisfaction, I jump out of the sewers and quickly slide the grate back into place.

The next thing I need to do is get a message to Locket. When I tell Madman I created a line I'm going to need proof. He'll want to hear it from someone he trusts. Locket is the only General that I know and he can get anywhere in a hurry. Once he's seen that I'm telling the truth he can escort me back to B. Running into a pub, I decide to do this quickly, before the guilt changes my mind.

Getting a message to someone in another sector is tricky. It can also carry a high cost. When I mention Locket's name to the bartender the large man nods happily.

"Sure, sure, I know someone who can get a message through. They'll want the credit up front." He leans his red face towards me over the bar. "Anything to Locket won't be cheap."

I appreciate his friendly warning. "This call is collect."

"Collect, you say?" The bartender eyes me over, a glimmer of respect in his bright gaze. "Well, I don't think I've ever heard of Locket paying for someone else's message. You must be important!"

"Not me. My information."

"Ah, I see." He wipes off a glass and sets in down in front of me. "You like dark or light beer?"

"I'll take red ale if you have it."

The bartender bursts into hefty guffaws. Alcohol is a way of life in Y. They're the ones who make it. "*If* I have it...? It's only the pride and joy of all Gaffers! What self-respecting Y bartender doesn't have red ale?"

Smiling at the jovial man's dramatics, I accept the large tankard of alcohol. I don't have to pay, food and drink is free in Y Sector. Gaffers have punch cards. They get to go out a certain number of times a week. Obviously, I don't have one of those. The bartender is serving me because he likes me. I take a large gulp of ale and the melodious flavour helps dampen my shame.

"Now, young lady, what's your message?"

"If you don't want him here, pick a different place," I say. "He just needs to know where I'll be."

Intrigued, he leans further over the bar. "And you are?"

"Sewer Rat."

"*Sewer Rat*." He groans in disappointment. "Nothing else...?"

"Nothing at all."

"You figure he'll come running when he hears that Sewer Rat is waiting for him."

"That's right."

He looks me over once again, unsure if he should believe me. "Well, that's something I have to see."

Shuffling away, I take the chance to study my surroundings. The gleaming bar, typical of a Y Sector bartender to keep everything pristine, is making me self-conscious of my appearance.

"Is there a place to grab a shower around here?" I ask.

"You can use the one here, if you want. It's just upstairs. Clarice! Clarice!" He bellows the name into the kitchen. "There's a woman who's going upstairs to use the shower!"

"Are her boots clean?" a sharp voice calls.

I look down at my soggy black boots and curse inwardly. "I'll take them off."

"She's good, Clarice! She needs a shower." He motions to the back of the bar. "Up the stairs, last door at the end of the hall."

"Thank you."

I lean over and slip off my boots. Tucking them under my arm, I charge myself to glue the brown leather around them again. It should take my message an hour or so to find Locket. First, it has to reach the right people to make its way past the walls. There are Criminals who make decent livings delivering messages. If they don't know where Locket is, they'll know how to find him.

After my shower, I sit at a table in the bar. The red ale is delicious, but the warmth spreading through my limbs isn't enough to help me forget what I'm about to do. The bartender hovers around, asking if I need anything else, but I wave him off. My mind is spinning. I keep thinking that there must be another way—a solution that doesn't give Madman the line and somehow guarantees my freedom. Lost in thought and anxiety, I lose track of time.

When a warm hand grasps my shoulder I barely take notice. "I'll come to the bar if I want something," I promise. I like the bartender but his hovering is unnerving. The hand leaves my shoulder.

"I'm not taking any orders," a grave voice replies. Turning around, I stare into Locket's unfathomable blue eyes.

"Tell that to Lyons," I say. Locket doesn't react. Looming above me, he awaits my explanation. This is it; there's no turning back. "I've got something to show you."

"Is it worth eight hundred credits?" he growls.

I don't reply. Gathering my courage, I stand and grab my bag off the floor. The bartender shoots me a nervous smile as I leave. He'll be telling stories about the woman who summoned Madman's General for months to come. I don't bother looking behind me; I know Locket is following.

The grate is around the corner. The Cop Sector wall watches us stoically as I slide the heavy iron to the side. I gesture for Locket to go first. He looks contemptuously into the darkness.

"Your curiosity brought you this far," I point out.

"Half-deads first," he returns.

I slip my bag over my shoulders and descend, once more, into the sewers. When I'm on the ground, Locket jumps in after me. Standing in the ankle deep water, his lips curl in distaste.

"I hate sewers," he grumbles under his breath.

"Stop whining," I grumble back. My guilt is making me bold.

"You're gift wrapping justifiable homicide, Sewer Rat."

"Y Sector," I identify, pointing at the ground. It's time to get this over with. Wasting no time, I grab the pipe under the water. The field glows green as I move through it, "Cop Sector."

Intrigued, Locket straightens. Stepping towards me he jumps back when the field flashes blue. "Jesus Christ!"

"Who…?"

He shoots me an angry glare. "Nobody you know."

Securing the pipe under the cinderblock, I watch Locket examine the burn on his knuckles. Hesitantly, I offer him my hand. He glares at it, not sure he can trust me. Staring hard into my eyes, he finally takes it and I pull him towards me. He resists half way through the field. Green energy glows around him; a faint buzzing sensation travels through his arm and into mine.

"A Sector," he whispers. Warily, he steps the whole way through. "How?"

The question is rhetorical. He already knows I won't reveal my secret. Letting go of my hand, he moves back through the field. With a growl of frustration he paces restlessly around the Y Sector tunnel.

"You're not actually planning to give this to Lyons, are you?" he asks.

Unsure if I heard him correctly I fix him with a quizzical gaze. "You're my proof. Why else would I bring you down here?"

"You're not stupid, Daryl." Locket pins me with his cold gaze. "You know what it means if he gets this."

I'm too confused to speak. He should be excited. Wulff explained that Locket started working with Madman to gain absolute power. This line to A is exactly what he wants…isn't it?

Holding Locket's intense gaze I step back through the field. "Why are you working for Madman?"

"None of your business," he snaps. "You just complicated everything. This was supposed to be impossible. You should have just joined Madman like everyone else."

I snarl at his threatening glare. "Or let you kill me."

"That might be preferable."

The hairs on the back of my neck stand on end. I'm in a vulnerable situation. Down here, there's nothing to stop Locket from putting me down. Where there are no crowds, there are no rules. It was my mistake bringing him here, but I thought he wanted the line. For a moment, I consider fighting. My hands ball into fists even though I know it's futile.

Then it occurs to me—this is the miraculous option I was searching for: Madman doesn't get the line to A. Uninhibited relief and happiness lightens the heavy weight on my shoulders.

"My death solves all problems," I finally agree. Locket's brow furrows in confusion. "You, of all people, must have known I would never join *Madman*. Just *do* it."

Locket step towards me; he's so close I can feel his chest rise and fall. My heart jumps into my throat. Despite my willingness to sacrifice my life, my mind is still screaming at me to run. Searching Locket's intense gaze, I wait for his hands to encircle my head. To make it easier, I close my eyes. One quick jerk and this will all be over.

"There's one chance," Locket says softly. My eyes fly open. "Lyons hasn't considered the possibility that you might find a line to A. Once I corroborate your story the surprise will throw him. His only priority is the destruction of the independents. If you slip through his fingers, you will give hope to his enemies. It's possible that he'll forget the advantage of owning the line and concentrate on capturing you."

"Get him to overplay," I murmur. Hope flares inside of me. "He might make a mistake."

Locket nods. "He's over-confident right now. You can use that."

I consider his words carefully. "I'll have to goad Lyons into coming after me in front of everyone. He's a calm man...it won't be easy. What if I fail?"

"I'll make sure I'm standing right next to him." Locket fingers the wicked knife on his hip. "Lyons cannot have this line. Even without it he's moving people around like pawns. He's driving up prices on necessities and destroying people if they can't pay."

"Destroying...?"

"Trust me, Sewer Rat," he charges, "you do not want to hear about his *little closet of wonders*. It isn't about pain with him, it's about horror. He doesn't look like much, but he's a meticulous little fuck, and I will not live under his absolute rule. If I fail we're better off dead, but if you succeed get the hell out. Afterwards, we're not friends. You give me a reason and I'll take you down. It's up to you what you do with the line. Destroy it, keep it: it doesn't concern me."

"I'll make sure to tell Lyons that I'm moving it. He won't be able to use you to get to it."

His serious expression softens. "I can take care of myself, Sewer Rat. Worry about your own neck for now."

"That's all I ever worry about," I reply.

"I'll wait here in Y to give you time to get back to B before me. The lower tunnels are best. I don't want Lyons to suspect that I withheld information. When you contact Madman ask Ishida to bring you in. He'll be quick and efficient. When I walk in late do not make eye contact, but make sure and wait until I'm there *before* you tell him."

I shoot him a teasing look. "Are you sure you thought of everything?"

Locket grabs me around the waist. Lifting me up to the hanging ladder, he offers me words of advice. "You've got strong instincts. Don't forget to use them."

It didn't even occur to me to struggle when he grabbed me to help me up. Head swimming, I climb up to the grate and look back down. Locket is staring at the shirt-swaddled pipe. He's tempted to destroy the line, but I don't wait to see if he does. Slipping back onto the streets, I head directly for the lower tunnels. Locket can do as he pleases.

23

I'm going to betray Locket.

It's an easy decision; I'm not wrestling with my conscience at all. The simple truth is that I'm better off if both Lyons and Locket are dead. When I present Lyons with the line to A, I'll put on a small show but then falter. Locket will have no choice but to kill him. Once Lyons is dead, his bodyguards will rip his assassin apart. I know it; Locket knows it. With both of them put down for good, the line to A will fall back into my hands. All those years ago, lying on a cold recovery table, I made a deal with Lyons Emmett, not Madman. It's a technicality, but the new boss won't argue. I'll be free and the secret of the line will stay with me. The only way my plan doesn't work is if Lyons survives. But I'm not worried—Locket never fails.

All that remains is to watch them die.

John Ishida finds me minutes after I contact Madman. He's a General, like Locket, so it's part of his job to escort Lyons' preferred victims to the slaughter. Quietly nursing a beer, I watch him stride into the dark pub. I don't know him very well but his immediate appearance is unsettling. The other Generals, Orion Dennis and Stephen Arik, are probably already at Lyons' side, eagerly awaiting the announcement of my failure.

Ishida scans the dimly lit bar. His empty expression falls on me and the hairs on the back of my neck stand on end. This strange, abyss-like man makes me uneasy. Years before I scraped my way off the streets, Ishida was an enforcer for Madman who silently tore out throats when commanded. He destroyed his lover's crew when she couldn't follow through on a deal. Amber was what's known as a *shadow*; she preferred stealth and avoided violence. Rumour has it Ishida didn't even flinch when he killed her.

Disquieted by the nothingness in his eyes, I hesitantly salute the impassive General. He doesn't return the weak greeting. Instead, he stands completely still by the door, waiting for me to come to him. I take one last, courage-boosting gulp of my beer. There's no time for dread anymore.

We don't have far to go. Ishida is leading me straight to Braggs Bar. For now, the booze I consumed before the General found me is enough to keep me calm,. With every step, I concentrate on my undeniable victory. I tell myself I'm going to savour their shock and disappointment before swaggering triumphantly out of their plans forever. Soon, this will all be over. I'll be free to explore a life that doesn't mess with my last shreds of sanity.

But no plan is foolproof. There's always the chance that Locket is planning on betraying *me*. In fact, that makes far more sense than him suddenly turning noble and turning down the chance for absolute power. My mind races as I try to understand what Locket's true stake is in all of this. Searching for clarity, I look up towards the bright blue sky, but a cloud is passing overhead. Dark and ominous, it heralds a troubling storm; flashes of lightning illuminate its swirling, chaotic interior. Somewhere in the back of my mind, I realize this is the storm I watched with Selim this morning. Awe-struck, I watch it bear down on the late afternoon sun.

News is spreading fast. B Sector has been waiting for my return. People on the streets point our way. They run into buildings and, when they come out again, scores of others exit with them. Whispering amongst themselves, they wait until I pass before joining the growing mass of people who are following me. A little girl runs ahead, shouting at the top of her lungs.

"It's Daryl! She's back! Everybody, it's *time*!"

Citizens poke their heads out of their windows. Gasping in excitement, a woman yells at her friends to save her a space. Others take one look at the crowd and rush out of their homes.

Scowling unhappily, Ishida raises an eyebrow. That's interesting: there aren't many things that unnerve him. Wary of his presence, the people keep their distance. When Ishida glowers at them they instinctively move back a few paces. But he can't make them scatter. There are too many of them now.

Daunted by the commotion, I instinctively stay close to my escort. Clarissa Tyler told me I was being watched, Wulff warned me the people needed a hero, but I didn't understand their desperation until now. But I should have known. They hung their hopes on the belief that a Hack can slip through Madman's fingers. By some miracle, I pulled it out, but their anticipation is still crushing me. I never asked for this responsibility and I hate them for placing their future in my hands.

When we reach Bragg's Bar, Ishida ushers me in. Unable to trust the crowd behind me, I instinctively hesitate on the threshold. The air is too still. The people aren't talking, they aren't moving. I can feel their eyes on my back, pushing me into the bar's darkness, urging me to rescue them from their fate. But I'm not sure what my success truly gives them. Hope? How long before they realize that Madman still has just as much power as it did before I walked into this bar? The citizens are as shortsighted as the orphans right now. They're living too close to ruin to understand that all they get from my success is the illusion of freedom.

A cool and terrible gust of wind races through the streets. Howling around us like a crazed animal, it laughs mockingly at my cynicism.

"Let me through," a familiar voice demands. People yelp in protest as somebody elbows them aside. "Get your arm out of the way or I'll break it. Sir, you'd better hope your first punch puts me down. Matilda! Save me a dance later."

Wulff bursts out of the crowd. Flashing me a confident look, he takes his place at my side before giving my hand an encouraging squeeze. Now that he's here, my pessimism is slowly draining away.

"Sorry I'm late! Let's get this over with, I need to fix the trucks transmission."

Ishida places his hand on Wulff's chest. "You're not invited."

"You don't really think I'm going to let her go in there alone, do you?" Wulff doesn't bother removing Ishida's hand. "How many Generals are in there? All of them, I'm guessing. Lyons gets his side-kicks, she gets hers."

Wulff tries to move past him but Ishida stands firm. "Only Daryl...."

"Oh, come on, Ishida! If I were Heathcliff Jackson I'd understand the caution. But I'm not. I'm Heath's *mechanic*. Besides, Lyons and I made a side-bet over Copper's adventure. I'm here to collect."

Ishida wavers. After a moment of silent deliberation, he removes his hand from Wulff's chest.

I shoot my friend a suspicious look. What does he mean *side-bet*? As I anxiously search his face for a clue, the dark clouds reach out and enfold the sun. People gasp as the day is suddenly cast in shadows. Glancing at the sky, I realize a major storm is going to hit the City.

Aggravated by both the weather and Wulff's claim, I finally step into the bar.

It's nearly empty save a waitress and a bartender. Lyons is sitting at the same booth, flanked by the same bodyguards.

His last two Generals stare at me arrogantly, confident that I've come to admit defeat. Orion Dennis, her long blonde hair falling down her back in a loose braid, is sitting on the back of Lyons' booth. The ex-Mole rests her hands on the hilts of her infamous blades. She is legendary with a knife. Slowly carving away at flesh, confident in her throwing accuracy, she makes it impossible to run. It's either fight to the last or die with a knife in your back. Stephen Arik, adorned with his expensive jewelry, leans on a table to Lyons' left. He rose from the pits and dust of V Sector. Like all Miners, he believes in the bone crunching power of knuckle-dusters. His weapon of choice, however, is encrusted with uncut diamonds; his fists both shatter and shred his opponents.

Locket is nowhere to be seen; I made it here before him.

Seeing Lyons in the nearly empty bar makes him appear vulnerable. He's so small compared to everyone else. As I study his boyish features, I try to imagine him as a man with a *closet full of wonders*; someone with sadistic needs and a terrible appetite for pain. Locket told me that Lyons is about horror, but I can't see it in his face. I understand that he's maddeningly patient. I understand that he doesn't make many mistakes and that he has a hard-on for power, but I can't find his brutality. And it occurs to me that his ordinary mask is his greatest asset. Nobody sees him coming.

When my host beckons me forward. I keep my distance. Ishida remains a few inches behind me, hands folded in front of him.

"I was told you have some news for me," Lyons says. "It's a bit early, but I can assure you that you must honour your debt. It's either the line or you die."

I bristle at his admission. It was never Madman's intention to recruit me—Lyons wants me dead. Orion and Arik shift where they're sitting. They're aggressive stance sends a warning chill up my spine. Wulff tenses. Looking over my shoulder at Ishida, I study his soft hands. He could take me down in a heartbeat if Lyons gave him the nod.

That's when I hear metal sliding through leather.

"Before you break out your knives, Orion," I say, still looking at Ishida, "Madman should hear what I have to say."

"I'm not interested." Lyons waves me off. "If you don't have the line than we have nothing to discuss. Your life is forfeit."

"Life is forfeit…?" Wulff echoes.

"Armin Wulff," Lyons identifies. "I assume you've come for Jules?"

My companion shifts uncertainly. "That's right."

"Someone go and get her," the Criminal boss orders, a smug glint in his eyes.

Orion stands and disappears into another room. When she returns, she's half-dragging Jules. The dark-haired beauty is bound with rope and her mouth is taped shut. Looking first at Wulff and then at me, Jules cries out in pain when she's thrown to the floor. Wulff immediately steps forward to help, but Orion puts a knife to Jules' right eye, daring him to come closer. Growling under his breath, Wulff puts up his hands and steps back.

Bewildered by this turn of events I lick my lips nervously. *Where the fuck is Locket?*

"What's going on?" I ask.

"A little wager," Lyons replies, smiling serenely. "If you found the line Jules goes free. If not, Wulff joins Madman. Then Jules..." He makes a cutting motion across his neck.

"That wasn't the deal," Wulff protests.

"She belongs to me," Lyons says. "I can do with her as I please."

"Belongs?" I turn to Jules but she can't look me in the eyes. Infuriated, I turn on Wulff. "When did this happen?"

"The day you came back," Wulff answers, face twisted with concern.

"I called in my favour," Lyons explains. "She was sent to bring you in and she came back empty-handed. I don't tolerate failure."

Lyons gives me the time I need to process everything that's happening. This is why Jules was desperate enough to come to those roads alone. When I jumped off the cliff, I ruined her chances of discharging her debt and, knowing that she was trapped, she went to Wulff for help. He never abandons a friend in need.

So here we are.

This is why I don't like softies. They always pull others into their mess.

A door in the back opens and Locket saunters in. Relieved that he's finally arrived, I struggle not to show my happiness. Unconcerned with the tense scene, he nods to his boss. Lyons motions for him to take his place. The tall General stands behind Madman's booth, hand resting innocently on the hilt of his knife.

I have an important decision to make but no time to consider consequences. All the times Locket could have killed me—*should* have killed me—but let me go; the day he stepped in and took a near killing blow to save me; the day he pulled me out of the desert when he could have left me for dead. I'm now certain that he meant everything he said in the sewers.

He's willing to sacrifice his life to prevent Lyons from getting the line. It's a humbling realization. I was going to hand it over and let the City burn. But my newfound shame isn't the issue here. The real question is: am I going to let Locket die?

This is no time to hesitate. I make my decision and deny myself the chance to change my mind.

"You're fucking *crazy*!" I round on Wulff. Shaking with fury, I ball my hands into fists. My friend's hope filled gaze falters. From the corner of my eye, I see Lyons smile triumphantly. "I told you not to bet on me. Bastard! I told you not to.

"That fucking crowd out there, they don't know me. They don't know a damn thing. *You* don't know a damn thing. Who the hell told them that I could do this? *Who*? I know it wasn't Jack. He's not around. Frenzy barely comes up for fresh air. Who rallied them behind me? Don't turn away from me, Wulff! You shouldn't have put all this on me. You shouldn't have placed all your hopes, all their hopes, on a Hack who barely remembered her name a few months ago. That's right. I didn't remember who I was. I crawled, naked, out of an alleyway when the Prison turned me loose.

"I'm a fucking half-dead, you idiot."

Wulff puts his hands on my face. Wiping away my angry tears, he puts his forehead against mine. "It doesn't matter what you say. I'll always bet on you."

"Fuck that." I place my hands on the back of his head. "Next time, I may not be able to deliver."

Wulff stiffens. Pulling away he looks into my eyes. "Next time...?"

"Right. Next time. I created the fucking thing."

There's a heavy silence before Lyons speaks. "You'll have to repeat your claim."

"I *did* it," I affirm. "I created a line into A, you fucking asshole. You don't get any part of me."

Lyons face falls. "It's impossible."

"Just ask your General," I say, motioning to Locket.

"That's why I wasn't here," Locket confirms. "She showed it to me earlier this afternoon but wouldn't allow me to escort her back here. Something about not trusting me..."

Sneering at Lyons, I savour his humiliation. "I'm going to go out there and tell the crowd that I won. A fucking *Hack* has destroyed decades of planning. I guess you have every reason in the world to fear me."

"Fear you...?" Lyons eyes narrow in fury.

"Fear," I confirm wickedly. "Everybody knows it. And it doesn't matter what spin you put on it, you are *terrified* of a Hack."

Lyons doesn't lunge at me. He's too controlled for that, too cold. When beaten, he retreats into his mind to search for a way to win. "You think your job is over?"

"My job *is* over," I assert, leaning forward in anticipation. "You said you wanted me to find you a line into A, I found you a line. *I've* delivered."

"Your job includes procuring the items that I desire," Lyons charges. "The line was only the first part."

"What *items* would those be?" I'm trying not to jump for joy.

"I want to know where the orphans go," he says. "Bring me evidence of where they're taken. Then it will be over."

I answer with a laugh and then a whispered: "fuck you."

Ishida grabs me from behind, Orion places her blade on Jules' throat, and Arik clenches his hands into fists. But I remain perfectly calm. Lyons has risen to the bait.

His calm expression finally slips. "May I assume that's your final response?"

"The deal was I find you a line into A," I insist. Ishida's hold threatens to dislocate my elbows and wrists; I grunt in pain. "I *found* a line. Kill me if you have to. But remember, *you* were the one who made this public. You should have been clearer about what you wanted. No one is talking about me finding orphans—no one will see this as a clean kill."

My subtle threat has the desired effect. Everything is business. If he kills me people will go out of their way to take jobs away from Madman. His employees will lose confidence and their disloyalty will destroy the organization from within. Slowly but surely, Madman will lose its grip on the Criminal underworld.

Lyons puts a hand up. Ishida immediately releases my arms; Orion takes her knife from Jules' throat.

"Your dogs are well trained," I taunt. "These unprovoked, aggressive actions are the *end* of our association. The line belongs to me."

I don't wait for Madman to agree. Stepping triumphantly towards Jules, I help her to her feet. Wulff cuts the ropes with his knife and pulls the tape from her mouth.

"Are you all right?" he asks her.

"Time to go," I order.

Wulff nods and escorts Jules to the door. Refusing to turn from the Generals, I slowly back away. Before I make it to the door my eyes flick over to Locket. The cold, hard stare hasn't disappeared but the left side of his mouth turns up—he's smiling at me.

A flash of lightning followed by a loud clap of thunder makes us all jump. It sounds like the dark clouds are right above us, and no one is used to being this close to a storm. I shut out my own fear and continue towards the exit.

"That was dramatic," Wulff says.

"Fucking thunder," Orion Dennis rasps.

Outside, the cool air makes me shiver. Looking up at the sky, I examine the swirling clouds. It doesn't feel like it's going to rain. This is just a lightning storm.

The crowd is waiting. Wulff motions for me to talk, but I'm dumbstruck. I've walked out so they already know that I've succeeded. What are they waiting for?

Still reeling, I turn to Wulff for help. "I'm fucking exhausted."

Clearing his throat, my friend gives the crowd a simple nod. It's the only encouragement they need.

They burst into raucous cheers. Pulling me into their celebrations, they grab my limbs and lift me into the air. Before I can protest, I am gaily paraded through the streets. The citizens sing and dance; they're shouting at the top of their voices. I can't understand, I'm too disoriented. The world is spinning uncontrollably. Taking a deep breath of cool air, I feel the strength ebbing away from my limbs. My eyes roll up; the earth is dropping away and I'm falling a million miles into nothing.

I don't fight. Lightning flashes, thunder rolls, and I lose consciousness.

24

Groaning, I shift around in the bed. I don't want to open my eyes. I'm so cozy and warm and the sheets smell of Wulff. Nothing can go wrong if I stay here. Comfortable with sleeping forever, I snuggle deeper into my sanctuary.

It must be a day off. I can sleep as long as I want to. Later on I might visit Lily, or maybe I'll hang out with Wulff in his garage. Frenzy will insist on training with me again. Amused by my skinny friend, I remember the last time he tried to do a chin-up and giggle into my pillow. His face turned bright red as his legs kicked furiously. I was doing my best not to laugh, but Wulff walked in. He took one look at Frenzy's flailing body and burst into hysterics. That was it for my self-control. The both of us rolled around on the floor for what seemed like hours and Frenzy angrily let go of the bar. We tried to apologize but kept breaking into uncontrollable guffaws. That was when Frenzy vowed he'd learn how to do a chin up. He won't leave me alone until he does.

It's also possible that Jack might need help today. He never stops working. The Court line is time sensitive, so we can only go in every three months. As a result, we take other jobs to keep us sharp. Jack plans them all but I try to help when I can. There's always something to learn from him.

Or maybe he's gone this week, out on one of his secret tasks. If he is then I'll take the break to visit friends in other sectors. I could use a vacation. Jack has us lined up for another K Sector job next month. Fuck, I hate that place. I always feel like I'm not going to make it out of there. Wulff says I'm just being paranoid. He might be right, but I still want to get it over with.

"Twenty-four hours," I hear Wulff say. I groggily open my eyes. He's sitting in his comfortable chair, weaving strands of dark brown leather together.

"Hmmm...?" I yawn and stretch contentedly in his bottom bunk.

"You passed out twenty-four hours ago."

"Was I drinking last night?" I mumble, confused. Wulff shakes his head. "What happened?"

"You were exhausted," he replies.

"Exhausted?"

"Did Kentucky Jim give you this?" He holds up a thin metal strap: a cloaking device. My brow furrows as I study its shiny surface.

"I...." I've never owned a cloaking device, have I? No, I don't think so. So why does it look familiar? Why do I remember Kentucky Jim tossing it at me? He doesn't give gifts. Why did he give it to me?

It all comes rushing back—an avalanche of misery. One by one the memories crash into me, pinning me under their crushing weight. The Prison, the presence in the wall, the chair, all those people.

None of this is real. The hideout, the sheets, Wulff—it's all in my head! I'm still in my cell. Fuck, it got me. This fucking place got me again.

You can smell the fires. But there aren't any fires. It's just something in your head. Listen! You can hear them talking—that's real. The fires aren't. They put them there to screw with you. Listen to the voices. Follow them home.

"Daryl! Daryl, you're all right. Snap out of it. Shit, you're pulling your hair out."

I follow his voice. Wulff is holding me, crushing me to his chest. Looking at my fingernails, I smile at the hair and blood.

That's right. It's the blood that brings you back.

"What are you talking about?" My Wulff hallucination is scared, but the Prison has fooled me for the last time. I need to bleed.

"I wasn't talking."

"You were mumbling about fire," he insists.

"No, I wasn't!"

I understand with blinding clarity what I need to do. Tearing myself out of his arms, I rush at the nearest wall. With a determined leap, I ram my whole body into the hard surface. Wulff's room, my cell, shakes from the impact. I don't know why the Prison does this, why it torments me with hallucinations. There's no greater agony than thinking I'm free when I'm still locked in this place.

My Wulff hallucination grabs me from behind, preventing me from throwing myself against the wall again. I struggle half-heartedly, already sluggish from the impact to my head. Wulff is breathing hard, holding me so tight I almost think that he might be real. But I'm not falling for it; I'm never falling for it ever again.

The cell door opens and Jules rushes in. Frenzy is seconds behind her.

"You're not here!" Tears blur my vision. "Sweet sky, you're not real! Fucking illusions ... in my head... it's all slipping away."

"Daryl," Jules coos. She steps towards me with her hands out. "Everything is going to be okay. Put down the knife."

"I don't have any knife! You're a fucking crazy hallucination! What are you doing here, anyway? I don't even *like* you."

"Daryl," Frenzy begs, "look at your arm."

I glance down. Blood is running down my forearms and dripping to the floor. "I need blood. Get out of my head, get out of my head, *get out of my head*. I don't want you here."

"We're not in your head," Wulff whispers in my ear. "Just give Jules the knife, Copper."

I stare at his rough, oil-stained hands clasped around my middle. I know these hands so well, but they're gone forever. I'm never getting out of here. My agony and loneliness knock me to the ground. Why can't I just *die?* "I don't have a knife. You're all in my head. Just like always. I want you all so badly that I dream you up. Go away!"

"Please, just give it to me," Wulff pleads.

I can't banish him. Why won't he leave? He's so warm I could drift away. Without warning, I surrender, and the knife in my hands falls to the floor.

"Where did I get the blade?" I ask. "From Kentucky?"

Wulff shakes his head, "my boot."

"Oh…" I chuckle softly to myself.

This isn't the Prison. You can come back now. You can let them take care of you…

Wulff's room is exactly how I remember it. Every square inch of wall is covered with colourful works of art. He uses whatever he can to create what he sees in his head. In H Sector, where the Weavers live, he learned how to dye fabric. Then he went back to learn how to make clothes and rugs. He never was any good at sewing, but the one rug that he made is spectacular; a myriad of breathtaking colours woven together in an abstract, captivating vision of the Oasis.

"Because it doesn't really exist," he explained. I was draped over the fabrics, fascinated with the way the individual colours bled together. While looking at it I felt energized and calm at the same time. "And because I want it to."

Grinning at the memory, I lie down on the rug. I always found it so funny that Wulff made something so beautiful for people to walk on. We used to tell him to hang it on the wall, but he refused.

Jules grabs the knife and Wulff grabs me. Neither of them feels like an illusion. Yelling at Frenzy to get the medical kit, my strong friend carries me out to the common room. He places me on the table and Frenzy rushes over with the kit.

"Apply pressure," Wulff orders. Jules places clean gauze on the wounds.

"I didn't cut deep," I mutter. I'm lazily drifting in and out of reality. "I never cut deep."

"What the fuck was that?" Wulff asks under his breath. Grunting unhappily, he examines the tidy scars on my arms.

"Psychotic break," Frenzy answers, "her mind couldn't take it."

"Couldn't take what?"

Frenzy shrugs. "I don't know. She just crashed."

"Sweet sky," Wulff murmurs.

"The bleeding is slowing," Jules offers. "Luck is on her side. I don't think she needs stitches."

Relieved, Wulff sits down in the nearest chair. Placing his head in his hands he sighs deeply. He doesn't know, he can't know; what just happened was a gift. I'm not in the Prison, I'm free and they're really here. It's like waking up from a nightmare. That's all that matters.

"Hey," I call. Wulff warily meets my gaze. "I missed you."

My words only fuel his concern. I wanted to comfort him but he can't understand.

None of them can.

25

They're talking. I can hear them through the hideout's thin walls. Sitting on Wulff's top bunk, I fidget with the cloaking device fastened around my bandaged wrist. The dressings go all the way to my elbows but I'm hardly aware of them. Wulff, Frenzy and Jules are discussing whether or not I need a straight jacket. That's far more interesting than my self-inflicted wounds.

I mean, *obviously*, I need one. But that doesn't mean I'll calmly slip into it.

Cheerlessly examining Wulff's escape hatch, I prepare for the chase. Jules is quick. She'll be right behind me. Also, Wulff knows the lock down code. Once the hideout is sealed there's no getting in or out. Even the emergency escape route will be useless. I'll only have a few minutes. It would be easier to go before they come, but I'm waiting. I want to know what decision they make. Anxiously holding my breath, I watch them with my psychic vibe.

"Maybe she won't do it again," Jules says. Who knew she was an optimist? "It might have been a one time deal."

"You saw the scars," Wulff counters. "Next time, she might kill herself."

"Or somebody else," Frenzy mutters, wretchedly looking back at Wulff's cubby door.

"Or somebody else." Wulff agrees.

They sit in silence, nobody wanting to say what needs to be said—Daryl is crazy. And there's no telling when I'll lose it. With Frenzy, at least, they know when to break out the straightjacket. I am an *unpredictable* menace.

"We'll watch her," Jules finally proposes. "There's no reason to bind her all the time. You saw how quickly she calmed down. If we think she's going to lose it we ask her to get into the jacket. She knows what she's capable of. If either of you guys asks, she'll do it."

"I don't think the jacket will work with her," Wulff argues. Sweat is beading on his forehead. He doesn't like what he's determined to do. "I was thinking... she should be medicated. Heath has a box with a few doses. I'll get whatever else we need from Locket."

Frenzy gasps. "Medicated? Give over, Wulff. She wouldn't even take painkillers for her cuts. Jules is right. We should ask her to wear the straightjacket. Daryl could never get out of it before. Why would she be able to now?"

"I wasn't suggesting that we *ask* her to take the drugs," Wulff says.

"Well, we're not going to force her," Frenzy asserts.

"It isn't that simple, Ash."

"Why not?" Frenzy demands. "Daryl can't get out of the straightjacket. Let's just ask her to use it."

"It was too quick," Wulff replies, trying to stay calm. "I didn't know anything was wrong until it was too late. And it wasn't like what happens to you, Frenzy. We can see your episodes coming a mile away. Don't you get it? There aren't many people in the City that can take her down. Not only is Daryl freakishly strong for someone her size, she's also better trained than any of us. Don't take it personally Jules, but you're nowhere near her. You're strong—Daryl is scary. We'll medicate her until Heath gets back."

"Why don't we just ask her to wear the jacket?" Frenzy questions stubbornly.

Wulff hesitates with his answer. I'm listening so hard that I'm afraid to breathe. There's a chance I'll say no to the jacket, but it's better than trying to medicate me, isn't it? What is my oldest friend thinking?

"What I'm going to say will be hard to believe. I need you both to listen."

Frenzy leans in. "What's going on, Wulff?"

"Daryl was on the other side of the room when she took my knife."

"You mean she went back for it?" Jules asks.

"No. The damn thing flew across the room. One moment it was in my boot, the next it was sailing through the air. It went *straight* into her hand."

Shocked, I nearly fall off the top bunk. I don't remember!

"Telekinesis?" Frenzy doesn't look convinced. "You saw her move an object with her mi...?

"...but that's impossible," Jules interjects. "That kind of talent is an illusion, it doesn't exist."

"I know," Wulff says. "I thought it was some kind of trick, too. But I've gone over it again and again in my mind. I know what I saw. If she can call the knife out of my boot, she can undo the jacket's straps."

"Shit," Frenzy mutters.

Jules shakes her head. "You must have seen it wrong."

"I didn't see it wrong." Meeting her incredulous gaze, Wulff silently asks her not to question him. "And I don't have any answers."

"If this is real..." Frenzy begins.

"...then we have no choice," Wulff finishes.

The silence that descends is thicker than cement. Wulff has become the unofficial leader, but he's loathe to do what must be done; Frenzy is tearing at a hole in his sleeve, desperately searching for another solution. Jules is studying the scarred table, dreading the idea of facing Crazy Daryl once more.

"I can't do it," she says. "You heard her. She doesn't even like me. That means she won't have any trouble kicking in my face if I try anything. But you two...she might be gentle."

That's right softy, I think, laughing at her cowardice, *just back out of the hard parts. This doesn't concern you anyway. Fuck! You have a lot to learn.*

"Frenzy and I will find a way," Wulff replies. But still, he doesn't move.

Their inactivity amuses me. Jack would have dosed me before the others could argue. He knows I can't sense him and he's clever. I would have been under before I knew what had happened. As much as I love my friends, however, they don't have a chance and they know it.

Jumping off the bunk, I grab my bag. I'm going to get out of here before they get hurt.

A sudden and intense pain slices through my chest. Grabbing at my heart, I fall to my knees. I *know* this pain. It is a serious and heavy warning—something horrible is coming.

The power goes out. Emergency lights flicker for a moment before failing. The hideout is now blacker than pitch. Wulff grunts in confusion as the others cry out in alarm, but only I can see the bounty hunters sneaking into the hideout. On instinct, I tap my cloaking device to life. Huddling in terror, I cower in Wulff's room.

They're quiet bastards, smoothly opening and closing the steel door without alarming their prey. One, two, three of them enter. The infrared sensors in their visors tell them exactly where the Criminals are. They bypass Wulff's room completely: my cloaking device is working.

I'm too scared to intervene. Helpless to stop them, I watch with my psychic talent. The bounty hunters are moving down the corridor; Frenzy is stumbling around the common room; Wulff reaches out and grabs Jules' outstretched arms.

"My tools are in the garage," he says, unaware that they're not alone. "Everybody stay calm, just stay in your seats. I'll have the lights back up soon."

The bounty hunters pounce.

Their technique and execution are perfect—things of rare beauty. All three of their victims go down at the same time. Cops don't like to knock people out: bruises bring down the price. Knowing they are in complete control, they each grab a Criminal. They lock elbows and shoulders, force their prey to their knees, and tell them not to struggle. Not that they could if they wanted to. As their captives grunt in surprise, the Cops lock their hands into cuffs.

<OK, Leonato, you can turn on the lights.>

The power kicks back in. My limbs unlock. I can escape if I go now.

Taking a deep breath, willing my heart to slow down, I quietly climb onto Wulff's top bunk. The escape hatch lifts open without a sound.

My brother's limp body suddenly flashes through my brain. I squeeze my eyes shut. Sweet sky, I'm half way into the ceiling. Get out of my brain!

One by one I see their faces, contorted with fear and surprise. Wulff is straining against the cuffs. He doesn't understand that it's useless. Cursing himself, he grunts in pain when the metal bands tighten around his wrists. Soon, they'll cut off circulation and his hands will turn purple. Jules cries out in alarm as the hunter holding her pushes her face into the floor. Running his hands over her body, he searches for concealed weapons. A growl of frustration erupts in the back of Jules' throat. Frenzy is the only one who isn't bothering to resist. He's staring at the wall in front of him, glassy-eyed and shattered.

Taking control of my psychic talent, I force it to power down. There's no way I can go back for them. The hunters will get us all and *then what?* This way, I can get them out of the Prison later.

That's what I'll do. I promise. That's what I'll do.

But I know that's a colossal lie. I'm incapable of willingly stepping back into that place. If I abandon them now, I abandon them forever. Torn with indecision, screaming inwardly at my cowardice, I pull at my hair. What the fuck! What the fuck am I supposed to do?

Kill them… Kill them all.

An eerie calm spreads through my mind and body. I can do that.

Careful not to make any noise, I lower myself back onto the bunk. The bounty hunters don't know I'm here. They won't see me coming.

Like all doors in the hideout, Wulff's door opens noiselessly. Taking in the scene, I stare at the bounty hunters' backs. The hunter closest to me has a knife strapped to his calf. That's all I'm going to need.

<Weren't there supposed to be four?> the woman holding Wulff asks.

<We'd have sensed someone if there were,> her colleague, still running his hand over Jules, answers.

<Maybe the girl had it wrong,> the second man suggests. Forcing Frenzy to his feet, the hunter pokes around the hideout's kitchen. I use the noise he's making to cover the sound of my footsteps. <These holes are always so shitty.>

<Stop messing around, White,> the woman orders. <I don't need Leonato reaming me out. We get in, we get out, and we collect.>

I'm a heartbeat away from the other hunter. My hands reach out. Placing them on either side of his helmet, I wrench his neck to the side. In one fluid motion, I reach down and grab his knife, letting his body fall to the floor. The woman turns around and I ram the wicked blade into her jugular. I know her armour is weakest where it's made to bend. The knife slips through and blood spurts from the wound.

<What the fuck...?> the last one exclaims.

He makes a fatal mistake when he lets go of Frenzy. My friend falls to the side, giving me full access to his captor. If the Cop were smarter, he would have used his catch as a shield. But, like any good Cop, his first instinct was to preserve the value.

I can't let him reach for a weapon. Holding his shocked gaze, I charge. The Cop fumbles and then drops his own knife to the floor. I crash into him full force, knocking him back and into the counter. He grunts in pain when my knife finds his throat. The blood gushes onto my hand; the bounty hunter wheezes his last breaths.

Half-crazed, I study the red stains on my hands.

They're dead. They're dead and I'm the one who killed them. This isn't like the patroller a few days ago. He died when I dodged a weapon. These three, like Beck, I crushed with my own hands. I quiver with ecstasy as the power saturates my being. This is who I am now.

I'm hungry for more.

"Copper," Wulff calls, "look at me."

I turn around. My hand, still holding the dripping blade, is still. Jules has already retrieved the keys for her cuffs and unlocked them. Kneeling by Wulff, she does the same for him. Frenzy waits patiently for his turn; Jules wisely gives me a wide berth. But Wulff and I are staring at each other. His gaze let's me know I'm dangerous.

This was too close; they nearly went to the Prison. You can't allow that. Not ever. Better they die instead. Better they know release instead of horror.

"Copper," Wulff calls again, "drop the knife."

I look down at it and icily contemplate the power that I hold. It's no mystery what I might do with this blade. I see my friends, throats cut and gasping for life, writhing on the floor. I could do it. I could save them from the possibility of misery. Wouldn't that be merciful? It's the *right* thing to do. My hand tightens around the hilt.

Jules dies first.

"This is the second time you've saved me," Frenzy mutters from the floor.

His words make me hesitate. Jules has already unlocked his cuffs and he's rubbing his tender flesh. Staring at the other side of the room, Frenzy fights to control his erratic breathing.

"What do you mean?" I ask.

"The second time you've saved me," he repeats. Slowly getting to his feet, he holds my questioning gaze. "I remembered a long time ago, Copper. You were the one who let me out of Cremin's cage and delivered me my revenge. There was no way to thank you, so I didn't say anything. It's okay. We aren't going to the Prison. We don't need to die."

"Those words," I rasp. "They're in my head. You can't hear them."

"We hear you, Copper," he assures. He steps towards me, holding out his hand for the knife. "You won't ever allow us to go into the Prison. Thank you."

"We hear you..." I echo.

"I won't let anything happen to you, either. I'll take care of you," he promises. "It was my fuck up that put you in the Prison. If you hadn't led them away, we'd all have gone in. Understand that, Copper. Understand that you saved us all. And now we're going to save you."

Gently, he pries the knife out of my hand. Once it's gone, I snap back into lucidity. "We're getting out of here. Grab what you need."

They don't move. I'm covered in blood and I just threatened to kill them all. Why should they listen?

"*Now!*"

Jumping into action, they all rush to gather their things. This hideout is dead space. We have to get out as soon as possible. The woman mentioned a fourth person, someone named Leonato. It's possible he or she is waiting for them to return. If they don't contact the hunter soon there's no telling what will happen.

The three of them, carrying bags stuffed with their belongings, return to the common room. Nodding my approval, I lead them to Wulff's escape hatch. Frenzy scrambles in, followed closely by Jules. Although he wants me to go first, I motion Wulff through. Shaking his head, my friend pulls himself on to his top bunk.

That's when I feel the fourth bounty hunter coming through the steel door.

He's quiet. Wulff doesn't know he's here. And he's quick. Following his sensors, he heads straight for Wulff's door. I won't have time to escape. With an anguished cry, I jump onto the top bunk and push Wulff's legs through the hatch. Slamming it shut, I place my head against the cool surface of the wall. My heart beats wildly in my chest.

"What the...?" Wulff isn't happy that I'm not with him.

Desperate for him to escape, I hit the ceiling. "Get out of here!"

<Get down off the bunk.>

Turning around, I note the slicing shell in the bounty hunters hand. If he throws it, the metal ball will attach to my ankle and slash my tendon. Cops only use them in desperate circumstances. It severely damages the value of their catch.

<What the shit...> the bounty hunter swears when he sees my face.

There's a huge dent in his helmet. Moments of recognition are often disorienting. By the time I realize that the fourth bounty hunter is Selim, he's already recovered from his own shock. Now I just have to claw my way out of my own.

<Get the fuck down!> he orders.

Reaching out with my psychic talent I see Wulff, Frenzy and Jules scrambling through the escape route. They're safe. That's all I can ask for.

As I jump down to the floor, I catch my reflection in Selim's visor. Covered in blood and stony faced, I look superior and defiant, a far cry from the nervous wreck that I am.

<Turn around, hands behind your head, on your knees.>

Slipping into despair, I watch him pull a small metal box from one of his side packs. I'm fucked. Selim hasn't underestimated me; the motion inhibitor will make sure he gets me back to the Perimeter and into an interrogation room. Swallowing hard, I do as he ordered.

<Good night.>

He steps into striking range but he's faster than me. Before I have a chance to react, he places the box on the side of my head. I fall to the ground, completely limp, and blink uselessly. Selim releases the lock on his helmet and takes it off. Staring down at me with a confused expression, he carefully examines my face.

"Chen," he says into a microphone sewn into his sleeve.

<Go ahead Leonato,> a feminine voice replies.

"I have one of the Criminals."

Selim leaves my field of vision and I know he's checking on his fallen comrades. The intense waves bombarding my brain are making me ill. Before I pass out, I hear Selim curse—his friends are dead.

26

Waking from a technologically induced coma isn't pleasant. My whole body spasms before I regain control of my muscles; my stomach churns violently. Gasping, I try to lean forward but a thick leather strap, buckled tightly over my chest, prevents me from moving. I try to wriggle my fingers, but they've been taped together. My hands are swaddled in thick fabric. The bandages around my arms have been removed, revealing dozens of fresh cuts and tiny scars. My wrists and ankles are manacled to the arms and legs of my chair. Even my head is being held in place by two thick metal plates locked around my neck.

With no other options available, I open my mouth and puke all over myself. The acidic vomit burns my throat and mouth, leaving a vile taste that makes me gag. Any attempt at dignity will now be severely hindered.

"The nausea will pass soon," Selim assures as my eyes adjust to the light. His voice is gentle, almost concerned.

A cup is placed against my dry lips. Cool water slides down my throat, neutralizing the terrible burn in my esophagus. I enjoy the sensation while I can; this will be the last kindness that my captor will offer me.

Swishing what's left of the water around in my mouth, I spit it out. It runs down my chin and drips onto my chest, but I don't care. I'm in an interrogation room—this is the place of no return. Out of the corner of my eye, I see the black chest. It's waiting patiently for Selim to get all the information he wants before it takes me for the last ride. I won't be released until I'm back in the Prison, and then there won't be anything left of me. But, oddly enough, determination overrules my fear. I'm not in the black chest yet. There might be some way to get out of this.

Ignoring the pain in my eyes, I concentrate on the man sitting in front of me. He's close, hardly half a meter away, and looking at me with intense curiosity. Little by little, his features come into focus.

I can't help but smirk. "We meet again."

"Do you know where you are?" Selim asks.

He gently wipes my face with a soft cloth but he does not look happy. That's strange considering he's just made the catch of a lifetime. I've been caught next to the bodies of three murdered bounty hunters. He can retire with the credits he makes off of me. Not to mention there are probably dozens of Cops waiting for a chance to get their hands on me. The only thing holding them back is the fact that I'm Selim's catch. He decides what happens to me. I'm completely at his mercy.

"Do you know where you are?" he repeats.

"The Perimeter," I answer.

"What's your name?"

Even if I were thinking clearly I wouldn't know what answer to give him. The last time I was in this position I just told them my alias. The Cop didn't ask questions. But that was a straight up catch, my captor just wanted to get his credits and get out. Selim, however, saw me walk straight through a gate and into Cop Sector. He won't be fooled. If I'm caught without a real name, if the system thinks I'm a ghost, it will send me straight to incineration. If I can't get out of here, that's exactly what I want.

"Your name," Selim repeats, growing impatient.

My name isn't the issue here. What he really wants to know is burning in his eyes: *how did you get into A Sector?*

But he doesn't have the courage to ask it; there are too many consequences if I answer honestly. It's a scary notion, Criminals being able to infiltrate A Sector. It would be the end of the world that he feels entirely secure in. Studying my captor's handsome face, it suddenly dawns on me how Luck has blessed me. Out of all the bounty hunters Selim was the one who brought me in. I can avoid hours of agonizing torture. With a little creativity, I might even find a way out of this chair.

Glancing around the small room, I'm glad to see that he's decided to interrogate me alone. He's not a fool—he knows what's at stake if I start talking about our little encounter yesterday..

"Your *name*," he demands once more. "You have no identity card. Yesterday, a woman from E Sector, Yulie Thorp, entered the Perimeter but never officially exited. About ten minutes later, Daryl Rhys went through a gate and a moment later I stepped through the same one. Now, what's your name?"

I use the name that will fuck up his world the most. "Daryl Rhys."

"Bullshit," Selim shoots back, "Daryl Rhys was a Cop."

"And an orphan," I reply.

"And she's dead," Selim states.

"Is she...?" I muse. "I should be listed as *missing* on the system, not *dead*."

"Patrick Meir killed her when she tried to escape his custody. Her body was delivered along with her brother over ten years ago." Selim is confident that he's caught me in a lie. "Want to try again?"

"Funny guy, that Meir," I say as I piece the mystery together. "He must have found another orphan, about my age. Maybe she was dead already, maybe he killed her himself, it doesn't much matter. Dead orphans are common enough and you can't read a corpses biorhythm. The detectives wouldn't have looked too close and a dead body is still worth half the credits. Clever guy... It's too bad I snapped his neck."

Selim's hand flies to a silver square he has clipped to his belt. "Patrick Meir, status." There's a short pause as he listens to the answer. "He hasn't been reported as dead. He opened his door two days ago."

"I remember. That was when I killed him." I shrug nonchalantly. "You can check it out later."

"What's your name," Selim demands again.

"Daryl Rhys."

"I won't play this game," he says. "You don't want to give me your name but you can give me the names of the people that you work with. We were told four Criminals. There's no way you killed all those Cops yourself."

"Didn't I? Haven't you reviewed their helmet recordings? I'll be the only one holding a knife."

"Their names and where I can find them," Selim repeats, a subtle hint of pleading in his voice. "It's the only way you're going to get out of this undamaged."

"I can't give you any names except my own."

"Then what's your name?"

"Daryl Rhys."

Selim shakes his head. "Remember...this was your choice."

He gets to his feet and heads for the door. I already know what he's going to do; it's exactly what happened the first time I was caught. Refuse to cooperate and an *expert*, someone skilled in torture, joins the conversation. They'll get a fifth of the credits. The last time I was here, the interrogator wanted my crew, as well. It's amazing how love can make you endure the worst kind of pain. I might have talked if I hadn't cared much for the others. But I'm never going to be in an expert's hands ever again.

I learned a little something from Lily a couple days ago. It's time to prove to my captor that I can take care of myself.

"I'll tell you everything," I promise as he puts his hand on the door-knob. My words make him hesitate, "just like I'll tell the expert everything."

Selim turns around to look at me, "expert?"

"That's right," I say. "I know what an expert is. I think he'll be very interested to know that a bounty hunter helped me gain access to A Sector, don't you?"

Selim eyes me suspiciously. "What are you talking about?"

"I assume you didn't tell anyone about how you know me," I continue. "Having a connection like me could damage your career, couldn't it?"

Selim steps away from the door. I've definitely made him cautious. "What are you getting at?"

"I infiltrated A Sector and you were right there beside me. *You* gave me a ride to 3rd block. I guess it doesn't really matter whether or not you helped me get in, what's important is that we had a conversation. Your buddy, Ellis, can confirm that. Imagine what will happen to you when a politician finds out that you didn't prevent a Criminal from getting into A. You might find yourself on the boring side of the Cop world, clerking it up with all the people you usually ignore." I pause for a second to let my threat sink in. "I know the Cop world, Selim, I understand how it works. An expert could get a real boost for proving that a bounty hunter didn't do his job. He'll check my accusation. Maybe you can get to Ellis first, maybe you can't. Maybe Ellis isn't as good a friend as you might want him to be. Maybe Ellis will go in with the expert to prove that you're a fuck-up.

"And then where will someone like you be? I know your type, Selim, I might have been you. Everything you are is wrapped up in the hunt. Not only do you need the rush, you need the adulation. All those people fawning all over you, hoping you'll recommend their child or their sibling's child for the academy, everybody fighting to be your friend. That'll be gone. A few people might keep in touch, but not for long, you don't have anything to give them anymore.

"How long before the loneliness creeps in? How long before you start counting the days until you can ask a Guide to put you out of your misery? You're what…twenty-eight, twenty-nine? That's eleven years before you can even put in an application for suicide. You'll probably just get depressed. Once the detectives find out, it's a one-way ticket into the Prison. The end."

"How do you know so much…?"

I introduce myself again. "Daryl Rhys. Don't believe everything the system tells you."

"You were a Cop," Selim finally acknowledges. Astonished, he sits back down in his chair. "This doesn't make any sense."

"Get ready for another shock. I'm also a repeat offender."

"There's no such thing," Selim blurts out. "They only exist in theory."

"Not anymore. Check the name Rose Odin then check my thumbprint."

Selim can't fight his morbid curiosity. He repeats the name into his microphone and unclips the silver square from his belt. Cautiously, he removes the fabric from my left hand, opens the square, and removes the tape around my fingers. Pressing my thumb firmly on a black rectangle at its base, he requests a match. It's a pricy request, but he needs to know. A moment later the system proves my claim.

Features contorted with anger, he swears at the silver square. "Why are you telling me this?"

"I have my reasons," I answer.

I smile up at him as I quietly slip my unbound hand out of its shackle; I've always had small hands. Selim doesn't notice my slight movement. Even with my threat he can still throw me into the Prison. If he doesn't call in an expert I can't tell anyone what I know. All he has to do is lock me in the black chest and collect the bounty. It's his only option and Selim knows it. Everything else is too risky.

There's a small button he has to push on the back of my chair. Once it's activated, it will place me in the chest. Selim won't have to touch me. But all I need is for him to get close enough for one accurate strike.

My captor sits for a few minutes, mulling over everything that I've told him. In his mind, the good part about my being a former Cop is that I should be the only one who can get in and out of A Sector. He doesn't know that I created a line, but that doesn't matter. The secret will be locked up with me.

Shit! I should have at least told Wulff where to look.

I eagerly await Selim's next move. The assumption when these chairs were designed was no one could escape them. They should have put the button on the floor, or on the interrogators chair, but they didn't. Instead, it's on the back of the chair. And it's my captor's fault he didn't rebind me when he checked my thumbprint.

Selim looks me over one last time before moving to my left side. I don't hesitate. I punch him squarely in the throat. It doesn't have much power behind it, but it doesn't need to. Selim falls backward, gasping for breath. Understanding that I don't have much time, I anxiously get to work.

I use my left hand to unbind my right. Slipping it out of its manacle, I pull a pin out of the flesh of my wrist and insert it into the lock around my throat. When I close my eyes I see exactly where I have to twist. Within moments, I've pushed the metal plates away from my head. Unbuckling the leather strap around my chest I watch Selim try to push himself to his feet, but he's still struggling for air—I have another few seconds.

I psychically examine the manacles around my ankles and realize that they have a flaw in their design. One solid hit in the right place and the locking mechanisms pop right open. Jumping to my feet, I head straight for Selim, intent on knocking him unconscious with a well placed kick.

Selim has already recovered. I just wanted to stun him so I didn't crush his windpipe. I should know by now that mercy only fucks you over, but I never considered the possibility of killing him.

He sweeps my legs out from under me and I crash to the floor. This guy is bloody fast. Even short on oxygen he manages to pin me face down. Wrapping his arm around my neck, he squeezes my airway closed. I struggle frantically against the hold, terrified that he's going to win. On my feet I can get out of something like this, but pinned to the floor I writhe around uselessly. His knees press on my wrists, making it impossible for me to move my arms. I'm not strong enough to push him off. Worst of all, the more I struggle, the faster I use the little air that's getting into my body.

Just before I pass out the bounty hunter drags me over to the chest. Once I'm placed in the coffin-like box chains automatically lock around my ankles, wrists and chest. The release for the locks is outside. There's no way I'm going to pick them.

Moaning in anguish, I start knocking my head against the sides of the box. This can't be happening. I can't go back there!

"You have any other surprises?" Selim rasps, laying a hand on his bruised throat.

"You don't know Selim. . .that place. Please. Don't put me back in there. I can't go back. Please. . . ." Whimpering, I struggle pathetically against my restraints. My voice sounds distant. I barely understand that I'm begging for mercy.

"Then you shouldn't have gone back to being a Criminal," he says. But his coldness doesn't reach his eyes. He's staring down at me, wondering if my despair is genuine. "There's nothing I can do for you."

"Tell the system I don't have an identity!"

"What?" He stares down at me angrily. He knows I'll be incinerated. "I'm not a murderer."

"Please."

He presses a button on the side of the box with his foot. "Leonato Selim, bounty hunter, incarcerating Yulie Thorp from E Sector for bounty hunter triple murder in B Sector."

<Incarceration confirmed,> the system's calm voice replies.

Selim pins me with a regretful, mystified gaze. I whimper pathetically as the lid of the box slides shut.

The locks whir into place with morbid finality.

27

The lid and walls of the chest fall away. I could struggle against the chains, but they're flawless. But this place needn't bother with the restraints. I've already given up.

The room, my cell, is dark, and I can hear the machines whirring.

I'm scared of them. I'm scared of the syringes that take blood and inject strange fluids; I'm scared of the tubes forced down my throat, into my ears and up my nose; I'm scared of the claws that hold my eyes open and the series of flashing lights that send waves of pain through my brain; I'm scared of the cold, metal room that will serve as my cell for who knows how long; I'm scared of the door, the gateway to horror; and, worst of all, I'm scared of my frailty.

Stretched out on a metal table, choking on the tubes in my throat, I stare wretchedly into the darkness. I don't have the energy to fight. Best to drift away and leave this reality behind, best to forget where I am. The machines will finish their work no matter what I do. I learned that the hard way last time.

And then they're done, and they're gone, and it's deathly silent, and it's just like before; it's just like always. But I'm not fooled. Because they're watching. Even in this darkness, they're watching. Involuntarily, I feel the other people in their cells. Sometimes, I hear them in my head. And they're talking—talking, talking, talking. Their thoughts are louder than my own; and I can't find me. But I can beat them, I've done it before.

I lie still. I lie still and focus on one person, on her scattered sanity. She's remembering what strawberries taste like and how the sun glitters on crystals.

When the Prison spit me out I could still hear them. I couldn't turn them off. The *voices* were everywhere, picking at my brain. They wouldn't shut up, they wouldn't stop. Picking, picking, picking. Pleading, pleading, pleading. Shouting, shouting, shouting!

You can't save them! Ignore them.

But this voice isn't asking for help. She knows I'm in here with her. She's empathetic and she's soothing. Tears stream down my cheeks.

Don't try to help me, I beg. And her voice disappears.

The air is chilly; the floor is cold. I'm so tired. I want to lie down and fall asleep, but I know better—I don't sleep until the buzzing begins. If I close my eyes before then, the machines will come back.

The machines. They're familiar. I was in here for over two years. Even if I hate the rules I already know part of the game.

That counts for something.

That realization flips a switch inside my brain. It's dark and cold, but I've been here before. There's no mystery for me. I sit up and slowly slide backwards towards the wall. This cell will be like the last one. Carefully, I examine it with my psychic talent and see I'm right. The familiar square room is comforting. My courage slowly returns, bringing my sanity with it. As I sit against the wall, I allow myself to remember.

Time doesn't exist in here. There's no way to tell one day from another. When you're let out in the courtyard—if you're let out into the court-yard—nobody can tell you how long they've been inside. The sun is like a glittering jewel in the bright blue sky. Some cry when they see that it still exists.

But the courtyard is the last place that I want to be. Only their cells keep prisoners safe from each other. My first day outside, it might have been weeks since I'd seen another human face. I had to fight off a whirlwind of sexual advances. I was lucky that I can take care of myself but others aren't as capable as me.

The screaming was deafening, but it was the ones who just bent over without a fight that disturbed me the most. By the end of my first visit, I never wanted to go outside again. On the inside, at least, I only endure my own suffering.

My first time here, I was drenched in cold water every time I touched the walls; something in the floor electrocuted me when I made a sound; sometimes my food was laced with poisons that left me sick and miserable. And the rules always changed. I never knew what would happen next. After a while, though, my psychic talent started giving me a small edge. I felt it in the walls: that thing, it was watching. Then I knew something would happen. The pain would slice through my heart and the torture would start over again.

But my cell was always better than the chair. The door would open and the chair would rise out of the floor. No telling where it would take me, no telling if I would survive. Every time something new, something horrible, something ugly.

But I can't think about it. I'll clear my mind and drift away. I'll go where the other voices are and disappear.

Making myself as comfortable as possible, I concentrate on the sound of my heart beating. The blood pumps serenely through my body. It's strange how easily I fall back into this behaviour, how simple it seems while I'm trapped inside this metal cell.

Before long I am gone, I forget where and who and why: I have descended into a profound and unfathomable trance. I will sit this way—unmoving, barely breathing—until I have a reason to return.

28

There's nothing random in what this place does. There's a link the others can't see, but I can feel it.

And it's here—it's fucking here.

I can't stay in my trance; the Prison has other plans for me. Before long I notice a near unbearable heat. Sweat is pouring down my face and body, and it's difficult to breathe. Looking around, I can see the ceiling and walls turning red: my cell has turned into an oven.

Wretched and exhausted, I whisper for the Prison to go fuck itself.

But no one is listening. There aren't any free people in this place. I would have sensed them long ago if there were. This entire place is auto-mated. Maybe it's run from somewhere else in A Sector, or maybe it's just a giant computer with no people commanding it whatsoever. Either way, it doesn't matter right now. I'm still being broiled alive.

Actually, Luck is shining on me this time: the floor isn't being heated.

Wiping the sweat from my face, I stare at my hands and try to ignore the terrible thumping pain in my skull. I'm losing too much water. The air is burning my lungs, my skin is turning red, and my lips are dry and cracking. Any moment now and my skin will start blistering. But this time it doesn't faze me. I've done this before.

The last time I passed out. It got so hot I thought my skin was going to melt. By then my boots were gone, a gang of people in the courtyard had held me down and stolen them off my feet. My tattered socks didn't provide much insulation from the super-heated floor. Losing consciousness was the most sensible thing for me to do.

I woke up swaddled in a strange plastic covering with tubes stuck down my throat. Some interminable amount of time later, I was unwrapped and delivered back to my cell. Except for the old burn scar on the right side of my stomach, and my sanity, I was completely undamaged. There weren't any marks on my body to suggest I had been cooked alive.

Another tim, I was strapped down to the floor. The lights went up and the machines came out of the walls. They cut off my hands and feet then let me go. I howled and writhed, screaming at the top of my lungs, but then the lights went out. At some point, I fell asleep, and when I woke up my hands and feet were exactly where they were supposed to be. I had full mobility, there wasn't any scarring, but then the machines came back for my limbs. They cut my arms off at the elbows, my legs off at the knee, and turned off the lights. Yet again, when I opened my eyes, I was intact. I began to doubt that anything was happening to me at all.

But I can still remember the pain. It's the only thing that *is* real in here.

The temperature in my cell continues to rise. Doubling over, I heave the contents of my stomach onto the floor. There isn't much in there. It feels like my body is being torn in two, so I curl into the fetal position. I'm so tired—I just want to give up. Dehydration isn't the prettiest way to go but dying doesn't look particularly attractive on anyone.

I wonder, is it possible to will your own death? Could I just close my eyes and push myself out of this body and never come back? The people in the Prison always ask themselves that question before they disappear entirely. Some manage to hold on. They won't be beaten, they won't let go, so they retreat inside. That was Radcliff when he got out; that was me face down in the alley three months ago. We found a place deep down that the Prison couldn't touch and just waited it out; finding our way back, that was the real test.

Only I won't go there anymore.

I'm so thirsty my head feels like it's going to fall off. I'm fading in and out of consciousness. At some point the temperature stops rising and metal arms reach into my cell, clamping around my wrists and ankles. Pulling me onto my back, they firmly secure me to the floor as the machines appear from the walls. Once again, tubes are forced down my throat and then pulled out, wires are attached to my head and body. The whirring and beeping continues and then a needle half the length of my forearm, filled with a yellow-tinged liquid, is inserted into my stomach. The pain is excruciating and, before I can stop myself, I start laughing.

The sound is a mixture of lunacy and despair. When I hear it, I barely understand that it's coming from me. My face is contorting into strange and unknowable expressions and I'm counting how many I can make.

"42!" I yell into my cell. "42 you freak!"

I'm laughing again, heartily throwing my voice at the machines as they click and whir and beep. The injection cures my dehydration. I don't feel ill, the headache is gone and my energy is restored. Yet again the tubes are forced down my throat, effectively shutting me up, and this time I deliberately choke on them. I bite down, *hard*, but they're made of stiff materials; my jaw is no match for them. A few minutes later they retreat from my stomach and I'm left gagging.

"That doesn't look comfortable," Wulff mentions from behind me. Always happy to see him, I crane my neck and smile. His gaze is always reassuring.

"You should try it out," I shoot back. "It's way better than getting laid. I promise."

"You almost fooled me last time, Copper!" He chuckles at my ludicrous situation. "Why don't you get up out of there? Frenzy and Jules are waiting. We don't want to go without you."

"I'll be there soon," I answer, playing the game. "You just have to wait."

"You always say that."

"She doesn't want you bugging her," Frenzy pipes in. Standing at my feet, he shoots Wulff a chastising look. "Can't you see she's in the middle of something?"

"It's okay! You guys can visit anytime. Where's Jack?"

"You know him," Wulff answers, "out and about. He promises he'll be here next time."

"But you never know with Jack," Jules says. Standing to my right, she examines my chains. "Hey, those are amazing! Can I borrow them sometime?"

"They're not mine," I explain. "I've never seen *you* here before. Are you coming to stay?"

"Just passing through," she replies. "Lily sends her love."

"I love her too." I sigh heavily. "She doesn't come around as often as she used to."

"She and Hyde are getting ready for the breeding house."

"That's right! I forgot."

"Do we have to talk about Lily?" Frenzy is trying not to pout and failing miserably. "I'm not going to the farewell party."

"You're going," Wulff assures him. "You're going to kiss her on the cheek and wish her the best. After everything she and Lenny have done for you, it's the least you can do."

"I don't wanna go without Copper," he insists.

"She's all tied up right now!" Wulff argues. "You don't mind if he goes without you, do you?"

"Not at all. Tell Lily I wish her the best."

"She knows," Frenzy says, rolling his eyes at Wulff.

"I'll be waiting for you." Wulff fixes Frenzy with a brotherly stare before he leaves. "Don't make me tie you up and drag you there."

"Bully!" Frenzy yells after him.

"He loves you," I say, laughing at Frenzy's frustration.

"I know. Hey! Remember that dream you had?"

"Dream...?"

"The Oasis. Do you remember the Oasis?"

"Maybe... It's a little fuzzy."

"You'll need to remember, Copper. It's important."

"I'll try," I promise.

The section of floor that I've been secured to begins to rise. Once it reaches a certain height, it folds twice. I am now sitting in the chair. Looking around the cell, I search for my friends, but they're already gone. I hate their brief visits. They make it impossible to give up.

The chair starts moving. I might be going to the courtyard or the place I call *the tearoom*. It's where prisoners are allowed to talk but they're still strapped to chairs. Being there reminded me of the afternoons that my mom would take me to visit her sister. They would sit around drinking tea, sitting for hours and hours while they talked—hence my nickname for that room. Of course, in *the tearoom* you get an electric shock if you stop talking. You'll even get a shock if you aren't talking at a certain volume. I met an elderly woman there who recognized me from B Sector. She asked how Jack was doing. Other than my horribly sore throat, that was a comparatively good experience.

But my guess is that the Prison isn't going to go easy on me. To my horror, I feel the familiar slice of pain in my heart.

I'd slit my own wrists right now if I had a razor; I'd use my own nails to rip my arteries out of my arms. The chair is taking me down a long, straight corridor. Pictures of the place I nicknamed *the field* flash in my brain. I can already see the people in my head, lined up on metal tables like slabs of meat; drugged if they're lucky, crying if they're not, waiting to be harvested.

It was in *the field* that I was impregnated and gave birth. I used to wake up from a drug-induced sleep and my belly would be that much bigger. The people lying next to me, a small boy to my left and a middle-aged man to my right, were being taken apart one organ at a time. One day I looked over at the boy and his eyes were missing. Another day I watched as the machines opened up the man's chest and took out his heart. And then it was my turn. I went into labour and the Prison cut the baby out. She was squalling at the top of her lungs. The machines swaddled her, placed her in a metal box and took her away. The next time I opened my eyes I was back in my cell, hoping beyond hope that I would never go there again.

The chair moves drearily on. Struggling against my restraints, desperately wriggling and squirming, I scream in frustration. On instinct, I use my psychic talent to look inside the locking mechanism. I see how it all fits together but there aren't any keyholes. There's no way to unlock these bastards from the outside. Panicked and miserable I focus on the small, metal parts, willing them to unfasten.

All at once, something fantastically strange happens—the band around my left wrist pops open.

Astonished, I raise my hand to my face and stare at it. How the *hell*? Warily I stare at the band around my right wrist. Concentrating, I look inside and examine how it works. It's the same mechanism, the same metal parts. And when I concentrate, giving one of them a small push, my right wrist is suddenly free.

It isn't a mistake—I'm opening them with my mind.

But there isn't time to think about what I've done. My ankles are still locked in.

"C'mon, c'mon, c'mon, c'mon, c'mon," I plead anxiously under my breath. Sitting back, I close my eyes and take a tour through the bands around my ankles. The left one pops off first and then the right.

It's time to get the hell out of here.

Opening my eyes, I curse under my breath when I realize I'm already inside *the field*. It's a giant warehouse, maybe three stories high. The chair is moving along a catwalk near the ceiling. Below us, rows upon rows of people are lying, unmoving, on metal slabs. Their low moans and agonized whimpering tear me to pieces. My heart rends. I can block out the torture, I can take my own pain, but I can't watch what happens to the others. I can't watch them break; I can't watch how their bodies hold on to life long after their spirit has vanished. Lost in anguish, I uselessly fall out of the chair. It continues along its way; down a long ramp, along another catwalk, down another ramp. It doesn't realize that it no longer has a passenger.

Overwhelmed with my own helplessness, I shakily get to my feet. I can't block out the quiet crying. The people know better than to make any loud sounds. The machines aren't far away and they don't like unnecessary noise.

I remember being amongst the bodies. Waiting. That's all you can do when you're down there. You go crazy being so close to people but not being allowed to talk. Then you hear that familiar whirring noise. You lie as still as you possibly can, even though you haven't moved for ages, and hope they aren't coming for you. They tear the others to pieces and you're thankful.

You're a worthless coward.

Looking down I realize that the tips of my boots are hanging over the edge of the catwalk. There's no railing. I could just fall away and disappear. I feel light as a feather right now, as though I could step off and just float down. How *beautiful* that would be. The mere thought calms me, cradles me... frees me.

"You're not going to jump, are you?" a desperately calm and familiar voice asks.

I don't turn around. It's just another hallucination. "Jack... Why would I do a silly thing like that?"

"Then step away, Copper. Reach out behind you so I can take your hand."

"Reach out behind me so that you can take my hand... What good would that do?" I serenely rock back and forth, keeping my hands at my sides. His voice is making my chest ache. How is that possible? "I used to fantasize about you guys coming to rescue me. It was impossible, but I thought you might find a way."

"Reach back, Copper."

"One day I knew you weren't coming. I couldn't even find a way out of my cell or out of my chains. How were you supposed to find your way inside?"

"Just reach back." He's growing tense now. "What have you got to lose?"

"Nothing, I suppose." So why am I leaning forward instead of reaching back?

"Don't you fucking dare!" he yells.

His words echo down the warehouse and the machines whir to life. They *heard* him; the machines bloody heard him.

Or is this a trick? This place...nothing is as it seems. He's not behind me. How could he be?

But hope is flickering painfully in my chest. Hesitantly, my body curling around the small flame that his fear kindled, I reach out behind me. His warm hand grabs mine and pulls me roughly away from the edge of the catwalk. Jerked back to reality, I stare into Jack's relieved face.

I manage a half-crazed grin. "What took you so long?"

He doesn't answer. Concern flashes over his face as he straps a harness around my torso. Tying a rope through a metal ring, he secures my body to his. Risking a glance around the warehouse, his body suddenly tenses.

"Fuck me."

"Not what you were expecting?" I ask. I examine his care-worn face, terrified that he isn't real. "Please, get me the hell out of here."

"I've got her," he says into the microphone pinned inside his jacket, "standby for signal three."

Jack presses a button on a small black box. The rope pulls us up towards a hole that's been punched through the ceiling. Placing a protective hand on my head, Jack continues to stare down at the people, grimacing at a machine surgically removing a young woman's kidneys.

We're whisked to the floor above *the field*, into an empty metal corridor. Jack puts his feet on the solid ground. Untying us both from the winch that pulled us up, he grabs the small engine. He shoves it into a bag and slings the rope like a bandolier around his torso.

"Through there," he orders, pointing at an open duct.

I don't ask any questions but I'm not sure this is real. I might be strapped to a metal slab and hallucinating, for all I know. After all, who can open chains with their mind? None of this makes any sense, but I'm not going to fight. It's better than reality. I'm going to enjoy it while I can.

Jack moves in and starts climbing. My boots slip for a second but I manage to keep my footing. Shimmying up this small, narrow space is wonderful. It feels like the old days and I savour it for as long as my mind will let me. Jack leads me through countless passages. Everywhere we go I can feel the people in their cells. I have to tune them out and order them to stop talking to me. One woman leaps at her wall, screaming. She knows we're in here.

Jack reaches the end of the duct and hops out. Turning around, he grabs my hand and pulls me out into the night. I don't want to question Jack's plans, but I'm starting to get a weird feeling. Why would my hallucination take me to the roof?

Jack pulls out two helmets, complete with small air tanks hanging down the back. I let him put one over my head. It makes a beeping noise as it fits over my neck and seals tight. The air turns on immediately and I suck it in gratefully. A little confused, I watch Jack do the same to himself. He takes out a black tarp. Hooking a metal carabiner to the metal ring on his harness, he pulls me towards him and secures me to him. Next thing I know he loops a long leather belt through our harnesses. Buckling it tightly around our chests, he straps us firmly together.

<Tuck this around my back,> he orders through our helmets' com systems.

Pushing the black tarp into my hands, he wraps me into it. I do as he says but I'm not moving as quickly as I could. Any second now this is all going to melt away. I'll find myself in *the field*, praying for death.

Jack picks me up and carries me to the edge of the roof. <Get ready.>

How many stories up are we? I don't really want to look but I can't help it. I see the public lights along the sidewalk and my stomach lurches: there's a truck parked on the side and it looks like somebody's toy.

<Signal three,> Jack says into his microphone. He waits impatiently for the response. A few moments later, all the lights for a few blocks turn off.

<Frenzy,> I whisper.

<Hold on,> Jack whispers back.

He heaves us over the side of the building.

My stomach jumps into my mouth; I manage to swallow my scream. Wrapping my body around Jack's, I cling to him for strength. The fall feels so real, is it possible that this is happening? It's so dark below us I can't see the ground. Every moment I am expecting to either wake up screaming or hear the sickening crunch of my helmet splitting open.

But then I'm immersed in a cold gel. I can't move, without the helmet I wouldn't be able to breathe. We've landed in what Criminals call the gelatin: a crazy, jell-o like substance that will break the fall of almost anything travelling at terminal velocity. The interesting thing about the gelatin is that if you're not travelling fast enough you'll bounce right off of it. It's also incredibly cold and, if your skin touches it, you eventually fall asleep.

<I know this is a dream.> I sigh softly. <There's no way anyone could get this much gelatin.>

<Go to sleep, Copper,> Jack replies. <I'll wake you when we get home.>

29

It was a trick. Nothing is real. Nobody came to rescue me. I'm lying on a metal slab, staring at *the field*'s dull ceiling, praying for death. A woman whimpers pathetically to my left. Shattered, I listen to her ragged breathing. A machine ripped out her kidneys but her body refuses to give up. I keep asking Luck to let her go, but her suffering continues. Sweet sky, why can't she die?

If I could reach out for her I would, but my hands are bolted down. Despite my parched throat, I manage to speak. "You'll be all right."

My voice causes others to shift on their slabs. Lifting their heads, they search for the source of the words. A moment later, the machines whir to life. Deep down I know I should be terrified, but I don't have the energy for fear anymore. Finally, I make the decision I should have made the first time I was here—it's time to take myself out of this equation.

"You'll be all right," I repeat, and the machines rush towards me. "Let go. Let yourself go."

"I-I-I c-c-c-can't," the woman replies, "I-I-I…"

"You can," I assert. "You're not alone. The Origins are waiting."

A hulking robotic arm hovers over me. In one fluid movement, it reaches into my throat and removes my vocal chords. Choking on blood, I feel hot tears flowing down my cheeks.

You're not alone, I repeat in my mind. Turning my head towards her I will her to look at me.

I'm here with you, she replies, her face calm. Her familiar, peaceful eyes meet mine and I freeze.

Mom...?

Jolting awake, I scream inside the gelatin. Heart in my throat, blood pumping furiously through my veins, I struggle against my cold prison.

<Get me out!> I cry. <Get me out, get me out! Fuck, get me out!>

<Copper,> Jack whispers. His steady voice fills my head. <You're all right.>

<You're not real!> I accuse. Despite my cold cell, I'm burning up. <Fuck you! Let me go, let me go.>

<You're going to use up your oxygen,> Jack says. His reassuring voice reaches inside of me. <You'll never break out of the gel. Focus on your breathing. Wulff is just outside, he's coming to get us. Breathe in... breathe out. That's right. Breathe in...breathe out. I'm sorry we took so long, Copper. We'd have come earlier if we could. Breathe in...breathe out.>

Little by little, I start to calm down. Just outside our opaque womb, a red light turns on and I realize that I'm not hallucinating. The crew came for me; Jack infiltrated the Prison.

I'm home.

I stop breathing entirely. Even if I could move, I wouldn't. I've reached a place where my reality is more difficult to believe than my hallucinations. Body still wrapped around Jack, I finally let myself hold him. I am adrift in the depths of my muddled emotions and I need him to be my anchor. My saviour's arms tighten around me. Afraid he's going to slip away, I squeeze as hard as I can.

The gelatin starts to tremble. A faint buzzing noise penetrates the stillness. You have to cut people out of this stuff with a fine laser. The process can take hours depending on whose doing the cutting. Wulff, with his steady hands, frees my head first. He pries off my helmet and I suck in cool, refreshing breaths.

"You're as close to home as we could come to it," Wulff says with tear filled eyes. Placing a calloused hand on my forehead, he welcomes me back. "We thought...we might be too late. It took me a month to get this much gelatin."

I don't know what to say. Everything is fuzzy right now. It doesn't *feel* like a month. It feels like Selim caught me yesterday, like he caught me a hundred years ago. Was I in the courtyard again? Maybe. I remember squatting in a corner, growling at anyone who came too close. Are those my fingers in someone's eye sockets? Was that this time or last time? I don't know. It's all blurred together—one big heaving mass of congealed memory.

Wulff stops waiting for me to reply. Eyes bright with concern, he gets back to work. Jack's head needs to be freed from the gelatin.

I'm having trouble connecting with my surroundings. It all feels distant even though I know it's real. We're not in the hideout but there's something familiar about this place. I can hear soft buzzing and whirring noises. In the distance, metal is clanking on metal. Kentucky Jim! We're in the old man's hideout. He's nowhere to be seen but I can feel him pacing, nervously waiting for news.

"We did it," Frenzy cries behind me. His astonishment is evident in the breathless way that he's speaking. "We fucking did it. We got Copper out!"

Wulff pulls off Jack's helmet. "Everything smooth?"

"No hitches to report, fearless leader," Wulff reports. "Just have to get you out of this stuff and I'd say the job is over."

Gazing happily into my eyes, Jack graces me with his soft smile. "I don't want to know what I saw in there, do I?"

I don't have the energy or the presence of mind to answer him.

"According to the Prison's system, Yulie Thorp is still inside," Frenzy chimes in excitedly. "It doesn't even know she's gone.

"You won't believe it, Copper! I got into the Cop security system, I made Wulff a biorhythm, I infiltrated the Prison's system—did you know it operates from a completely different power source than the rest of the City, using different codes but the same symbols? I gave the truck security clearance, I powered down four A Sector blocks." Frenzy can't stop talking. His voice is getting louder and louder. "No manipulator has ever done anything like this; *none* of them *could* if they tried! And Jules didn't have to strap me down afterwards. It took moments instead of hours; there was no adjustment period. It was insane, Copper, absolutely insane!"

"Sweet Sky! Give it a rest, Frenzy," Jules says. "You haven't stopped chattering for ten minutes!"

Is she still with the crew? What the hell are they seeing in her that I'm missing? In my mind she's a liability, but Jack is the boss, not me. Besides, I just got out of the Prison for the second time. She isn't my concern.

Wulff is working down at our feet, carefully leaving a quarter inch of gelatin around our bodies. Picking up a portable heater, Jules puts it near the remaining gelatin and it slowly evaporates.

"Doesn't anybody else realize what this means?" Frenzy continues. "Not one of you guys understands."

"I get it," Jack mutters. "I just don't like it."

"What's not to like?" Frenzy cries. He looks as though he might jump out of his skin. "The system runs the City, the system is made of code... I can control the codes! Think big, Jackson. It's what you do. I can plug into the system and not blow my brains out doing what everyone thinks is impossible. We hold the keys to this entire place!"

"I get it, Frenzy," Jack replies, "and I'm thinking even bigger than you. What you've got is power. One wrong move and our entire society will collapse. Not even the walls will be able to keep the chaos in."

"What good are the walls anyway? What do they really do? I could shut the gates down, open them wide and let the people decide!"

"Yeah, you could do that," Jack agrees, "but do you really want to see what will happen when the walls are gone? Our planet is dead. There isn't enough to go around. Take away the walls or the system and you take away how we survive. Remember: *the City born out of the ashes of a ruined world, humankind working together for survival, for the good of the people, beyond their understanding, forever, without question.* The system keeps this City alive; it keeps us alive."

"Spoken like a Scientist," Jules pipes in.

"As long as Criminals are making credits by getting around the walls they won't thank anyone for opening the gates," Jack adds. "Besides, each Sector makes its own rules."

"And if you don't like it you can pay a Criminal to get you out," Wulff says. "Or become a Criminal, if the life suits you. In the Bank, most everyone has some contact with Criminals."

"It's the same in K," Jack says.

"Almost got you out," Wulff mutters as a giant slab of gelatin falls to the floor. He brings the hand-held laser around my shoulders and down my back. "Frenzy, you might want to look to that."

Looking to my red-eyed friend, I see blood trickling from his nose and down his chin. He quickly puts a finger to his face. Half smiling, half frowning at the bright red stain on his fingertips, he shrugs.

"Maybe it was harder than I thought," he whispers. Wiping the blood onto his pants he accepts a tattered piece of cloth from Wulff.

"You should be careful how you use that brain of yours," Jules says.

Wulff lets out a little whoop of excitement. "Here goes nothing!"

Another piece of gelatin slides to the floor. Grabbing me around the waist, he gently pulls me away from Jack's embrace. My muscles have taken a vacation. Using the table for support, I let Wulff guide me toward the nearest seat. Shoulders hunched and chin on my chest, I try to keep the room from spinning. I'm not all here yet.

"You gonna be OK?" Wulff asks.

I can't answer his question; I'm too wrecked. If I open my mouth my heart will jump right out of my chest and flop uselessly around on the floor. My senses tell me that I'm home, but everything is dulled right now. My mother's face keeps flashing through my brain, torturing my already overstretched emotions. Pressing my lips firmly together, I stare at the floor.

Wulff smiles encouragingly. "You give yourself time to recuperate. When you find your voice again, you'll have to explain why Locket was so eager to get you out of there."

Locket. The mention of his name sends jolts of electricity through my muscles. Wulff gives me a significant look. I hold his gaze as I wait for an explanation.

"He's the one who told us where the line is," Jules obliges. She holds the heater over the final remains of gelatin on my back. "That's how we got Jack into A."

"Does anybody else remember him asking us not to tell her?" Jack calls from the gelatin.

"Fuck it!" Wulff brushes away Jack's protest with a wave of his hand. "I'm too curious to keep that promise. Why do you think I cut you out last? Now you can't do anything about my asking. How does Locket know so much about A, anyway? Does anybody know what Sector he's originally from? Maybe he was a Cop like our girl here."

He doesn't fight like a Cop, I think uselessly. My mouth is hanging open in bewilderment. My mind is starting to focus again. Locket could have taken the line for himself. No one would have been the wiser. What does he gain by getting me out of the Prison?

"Get over here and get me out of this stuff," Jack orders. Wulff jumps towards his boss and continues shaving off pieces of gelatin.

"Locket even told us where the Prison is," Frenzy chimes in. Putting a finger under his nose, he checks to see if the bleeding has stopped. "And he told me where to look in the system to access their security."

"He was a fountain of knowledge," Wulff says as he continues to cut around Jack.

Jumping to my feet, I grab Jules' shoulder for support. The room is spinning uncontrollably but I have to know, I have to understand, I have to find Locket. One foot in front of the other; but my legs aren't cooperating.

"You need to rest," Jules says.

"I need to figure out what the hell is going on," I rasp back. "Locket has some fucking explaining to do."

"What are you going to do, beat it out of him?" Jules frowns and fixes me with a look of condescension. "He's not going to tell you anything he doesn't want you to know."

"At any rate, it's not like you can go outside," Wulff adds.

"And why is that?" I ask.

"Madman was the one who gave the order," he explains. "He's the one who brought the Cops to our front door."

Shocked, I finally accept Jules' offer of a chair. Elbows on my knees I stare at Wulff as he continues to carve Jack out of the gelatin. "What...?"

"Lyons was desperate," he continues. "The public doesn't know about this, it was strictly a private job. According to Locket he hired some nobody to lead them straight to us."

"They *must* have been desperate." Jules offers me a drink of water that I gladly accept. "If the citizens knew about this they would rip whoever it was limb from limb."

The bounty hunters' words echo in my head: *Weren't there supposed to be four? Maybe the girl was wrong.* The girl.

Jules smiles in congratulations. "That's *exactly* what the Cops said. We don't know who *the girl* is, but Locket said he'll keep his eyes and ears open for us."

"Isn't that nice of him," I reply sarcastically. The fuzziness in my brain is finally dropping away. "Did everyone forget that Locket *works* for Madman?"

Wulff lets out a hefty guffaw. "I do keep forgetting."

"Forgetting? Are you kidding?"

"The point is that Lyons thinks you're in the Prison," Jack explains. Another piece of gelatin slides to the floor and he slowly unfolds himself. Covered in the clear, oily substance he ineffectually tries to brush it off. "He's already broken two codes to get rid of you—never disturb the sanctuaries, never involve the Cops. There's no telling what he'll do once he finds you're out."

"There's no telling what the citizens will do once they find out, either," Wulff adds. "They think you're gone, Copper. Nobody could survive the Prison twice. If they see that you got out, there might be a riot."

I roll my eyes at the thought. "I'm sure that's an exaggeration."

Cursing my physical weakness, I look up at Jack. He's carefully studying my face, searching for the warrior I used to be. Someone must have told him about my *episodes*. He wants to know if they exaggerating.

I slowly scan the crew. They're watching Jack, awaiting his decision. It's possible they broke me out of the Prison just to lock me up down here. I might be exchanging one jailer for another. Meeting Jack's probing gaze I raise an eyebrow.

After a few moments of silent contemplation, he finally speaks. "It's good to see you."

His words are genuine, but there's a note of suspicion in his voice. Gone are the days of lively admiration. He can't decide if I'm a danger to the crew. If I am, he won't hesitate. I'll be dosed and bound before I have a chance to struggle.

My mother's face flashes through my brain. She was there; she was there! She told me, she said... She said, 'I'm here with you'.

The fuzziness returns, swaddling my overstretched nerves. Retreating into the hazy fog, I decide to rest.

"Nobody goes top-side until we figure this out," Jack orders, his soft voice a stark contrast to his iron will.

I slowly nod. It's okay to let him make the decisions. I'm not in any place to make them for myself. Exhausted beyond measure, I let my head fall back and stare at the ceiling. I'll figure out what I'm doing when I feel better.

30

The people in Heidi's Restaurant go stone cold quiet when I walk through the front door. Pinned by their shocked stares, I nervously shift from one foot to the other. They've actually stopped eating Lenny's food—that's downright unnerving. As I sweep my gaze over the stunned crowd, I spot Hyde sitting in a small booth. Relieved to see a familiar face, I hurry over to him. The lethargic Criminal gets up to greet me. Smiling with contained joy, he offers me his hand in friendship.

"Nothing will surprise me after this," he says. "You're a bloody miracle worker."

I squeeze his hand warmly. "Hello *Adam Sorhab*. Everything working out for you and Lily?"

"We were already at the breeding house. Lily wanted to have a parade in your honor. When she heard you were back in the Prison..." He trails off and shrugs helplessly.

"That's the reason I'm here," I explain. "I want to make sure she's okay."

Hyde nods approvingly at my concern and offers me a seat at his booth. When I slide in, we descend into friendly silence.

The crew doesn't know I'm here. I snuck out through Kentucky's back door. Frenzy was taking well-deserved naps; Kentucky was fixing a glitch in his suit; I don't much care what Jules was up to; Jack was discussing a new hideout with Wulff. Apparently, he's already scouted a new spot. The new hideout will be in H Sector and Jack's planning on expanding. Not quite as big as Kentucky's place, but definitely multi-leveled. He and Wulff were animatedly discussing the details before I slipped behind the industrial storage unit.

I experienced a moment of deep self-loathing when I reached the surface. The sky was cloaked with threatening clouds. According to Jules, the lightning storms have been coming every few days or so, but it still hasn't rained. I wasn't thinking about the strange weather, though. I was thinking about Wulff. He asked me not to disappear again but that's exactly what I'm going to do. Locket has no reason to seek me out so I should be able to find someplace that's well out of Cop radar and far away from my old life. Before I got pulled into this mess I thought I was just going to retire. Silly me. I refuse to live in a straight jacket but I also refuse to endanger the people I love. Like my mother explained so many years ago—it's for the best.

But I still feel like shit. I can't shake the feeling that I'm betraying the crew, that I'm making a cowardly choice. It was fine when I could stand on my own two feet, when I could carry my share of the burden. Now, I *am* the burden; I don't know how to let the others carry me.

"Daryl?" Lily's hope filled eyes heighten my shame. Her shaking hands cover her mouth as tears stream down her face. "Is it really you?"

"Hey, Lily." I get to my feet. The people around us start muttering to each other. "Hyde was just telling me how much you miss me."

"It's not possible...you're gone!"

"I was gone, but now I'm back."

"H-how?"

I suddenly feel the entire restaurant lean in towards me, eyes staring and ears straining. They all want to understand. But I'm not a Whisperer; I can't tell this story. Hyde motions towards the back and I follow gratefully. Retreating through the swinging door into the kitchen, I look around for Lenny.

"He's on break," Lily says. Her soulful eyes drink me in. "He's going to have a heart attack when he sees you!"

"Sorry, I can't stay long," I apologize. The people's attention is starting to alarm me. Peeking into the sit-down portion of the restaurant, I realize a crowd has started gathering outside the building. Soon, Heidi's Restaurant will be full beyond capacity. I nervously examine the back door of the restaurant. "I just came to make sure you're doing okay."

Lily lets out a giant sigh before collapsing into a chair. "I'm fine…now! But I'm exhausted and things are going to get mighty uncomfortable when this baby really starts to grow. Do you want to know about Locket before you leave?"

Hyde chuckles. "Didn't he ask you to just say the name?"

"*Daryl* is my priority." Shooting Hyde a rebellious look Lily turns to me. "He came in three days ago. He said that if any one of your crew came in I should whisper the name in their ear."

"Name?" Intrigued, I give Lily my full attention. "What name?"

"Sonora. Apparently, that's supposed to mean something to you guys." Lily shakes her head. Looking to the ceiling, she lets out a frustrated groan. "You and Locket are absolutely maddening!"

For a moment the world drops away. All my senses have abandoned my body. I know what that name means—Locket found the girl who betrayed us to the Cops. Clarissa Tyler, the scavenger otherwise known as Sonora. It isn't surprising. Orphans don't think ahead. Life goes from meal to meal for them.

"Why did you guys break up?" Lily finally asks.

I have to resist the urge to strangle her. "Lily, we couldn't break up because we were never together."

"Oh, give over," she returns. "It's so obvious you guys had a thing. What happened, anyway? I'm *dying* from the curiosity!"

"Locket's eyes nearly fell out of his head when Lily asked him the same questions." Hyde can't control his laughter. The deep, rolling sounds are grating on my nerves. "I've never seen him look so scared."

Rolling my eyes, I quickly readjust my day's schedule. I came here to say good-bye. It was my plan to find another manipulator this afternoon, but I won't until after I find Clarissa Tyler. It's a fucking shame. She had something, real talent. She could have made a career for herself.

"Tell Lenny I'll be back later," I mutter under my breath.

"You just got here!" Lily protests, but Hyde puts a hand on her shoulder. She glares at him before standing up and giving me a hug. "I'll tell Lenny to make your favourite."

Offering Lenny's food is her way of making sure I come back. Smiling, I head straight for the back door.

Hyde whistles under his breath when he looks out into the restaurant. The crowd has grown exponentially. "It looks like they might break the window."

I open the back door and step outside. Focused completely on my task, I slip in and out of relatively empty streets. Because of the gathering crowd I have to take a non-direct route. My goal is to find a scavenger. Any one of them will lead me to Sonora for the right price. I haven't been walking long before a chill goes up my spine: someone is following me. Whoever it is, they aren't friendly.

Anxiously glancing over my shoulder, I move into another alley. I don't want to draw unnecessary attention.

I'm half way down the empty alley before I sense the danger. My hands go numb and my feet feel like lead, pain slices through my heart. I was hoping to draw my stalker out, but now I feel more than one person. Worst of all, I can't sense any citizens. Somebody wants to have a private audience with me. Everyone makes mistakes and I just made a big one. I don't have any leverage if someone wants me dead. Gathering my courage. I stop walking. It's time to meet my enemies.

I feel her before she steps out of the shadows behind me; I feel him a few seconds later. Orion Dennis and Stephen Arik.

Disgusted with my stupidity, I turn around to face them. Lyons must have already heard about my miraculous return. He's decided the politics are over. It's time to get rid of me once and for all. I have to laugh at the irony, I *was* going to disappear. Now I want to stick around just to piss Madman off.

It only took twenty minutes to walk from Kentucky's hideout to Heidi's Restaurant. Lyons works bloody fast. Turning around, I watch Orion slip her wicked blades out of their leather sheaths. It's fascinating to watch her work with knives. There's poetry to the way she balances them in her hands, the way they become a part of her body. A look of pure love spreads over her face; she trusts her blades completely. Twirling them in her fingers, she shoots me a predatory smile. She's ready to cut me down if I try to run.

Arik massages his hands calmly, steadily, before slipping on his diamond-studded brass knuckles. The former Miner studies his chosen weapons before looking me in the eye. "Nothing personal."

"Why do fuck-nuts always say that?" I ask.

Cocking my head to the side, I anxiously wait for his first move. My only remaining question is where are the other two Generals? Ishida isn't the type to miss out on violence and Locket...I don't know what to make of him anymore.

As if I had summoned him, Ishida enters the chosen arena. He steps out from behind a corner, blocking my only exit. Shit. Risking a glance his way, I note his hollow expression. A feeling of terrible dread makes my head spin. I'm not going to win.

A loud, booming noise overhead startles us all. Looking up I watch the large, dark clouds swirl chaotically. Flashes of intense lightning jump through the black, malevolent storm. Large drops of cold water careen into the streets, crashing down on our heads and making me wince. The rain has finally begun. Within seconds I'm soaked to the bone. Another intense rumble shakes the surrounding buildings. Awe-struck, I stare into the storm and thank Luck for the cool water running down my face.

There's no time to develop a strategy. Snapping back into my fighting stance, I anxiously wait for them to make the first move. Ishida ignores the wet interruption; he nods at the others and they step towards me at the same time. If I were smart I'd move towards Orion and let her slit my throat. It would be a quick death. But I've never been noted for my brains.

My first priority is to neutralize her blades: out of the three she's the real threat. Even if I manage to sneak through these guys she'll bring me down. I believe I can take her out. If I do, I can try to run.

Quick as lightning, I grab the small knife from my boot and fling it towards Orion. I'm not expecting to hit, just to distract, but the pelting rain camouflages both my actions and the metal flying through the air. The blade sinks into the flesh of her right shoulder. Gasping in pain, she drops one of her knives. Encouraged by the unexpected advantage, I move in. I smash my left fist into her stomach and prepare to bring my right elbow up under her jaw. I need her to go down quick.

But Arik moves faster than I expected. When Orion doubles over from the force of my punch, the bejewelled General steps over. Slamming a fist firmly into my right side, he prevents me from completing my attack. The brass knuckles sink into my flesh with a sickening crunch; the diamonds effortlessly rip through my shirt and flesh. In one horrifying moment, I hear my ribs cracking under the power of Arik's brutal punch. He's not as strong as Locket, but his brass knuckles give his attack enough power to take most of the fight out of me. My right side, from my head to my toes, has gone completely numb. His other fist, aimed for my face, flies through the air with deadly force.

I desperately duck under the swing. Grabbing Arik's forearm with my left hand, I twist my body and pull. If I could use my right side I'd push the back of his shoulder with my other hand, but the rain does the rest of the job for me. Not only does Arik lose his balance, he slips on the wet cement. As he crashes to the ground, I deny him the chance to regain his feet. Forcing the right side of my body to co-operate I jump onto his back, place a knee on his spine, and grab a fistful of hair. A furious and vicious energy envelops me. Through my haze of aggression and destruction, I start smashing Arik's head into the cement. A bone-chilling war cry erupts from my lungs; I don't stop until his skull caves in.

Orion grabs the hilt of the knife sticking out of her shoulder. Pulling it out, she watches in confusion as I destroy her comrade. Her right arm is hanging limply at her side but she still has full movement in her left. I sense her spring towards me, my bloodstained knife aimed for the back of my neck. Tucking my head into my right shoulder, I roll to one side. I spring to my feet and turn just as she regains her own footing.

The right side of my body is just as useless as Orion's. Circling one another, squinting to see each other's movements in the pouring rain, we search for other weaknesses.

As far as I know, Orion is right hand dominant; I have no weapons but I'm left-handed. Before I can react, Orion's blade slashes through the air, leaving a bright red line across my chest. I examine the stinging wound in horrified disbelief—Orion is ambidextrous.

Frantically dodging and ducking, I evade the flurry of attacks that follows. She's only missing me by the smallest fraction of an inch, nicking me on my forearms and shoulders. As lightning splits the sky, a gigantic boom of thunder cracks overhead. Her attacks suddenly falter. Her eyes flicker nervously to the bellowing storm and terror flashes across her face. When I jump back to avoid her next lunge, the pouring rain works against me; my feet slip. I crash down onto the pavement. Dazed from the impact, I lose precious seconds and Orion pounces.

Another flash of lightning and loud crash of thunder makes her duck her body towards me. Her deadly blade freezes for an instant. In her second of terror, I find the opportunity I need. Grabbing her wrist, I ram the knife towards her exposed throat. It's an awkward movement, a hopeless attempt at surviving, but she's stunned. She doesn't deflect the desperate strike. The razor-sharp blade sinks into her flesh, opening a gaping wound in her throat. Orion Dennis' warm, red blood gushes over my chest and the light drains from her astonished eyes. Her lean body slumps onto mine.

Covered in blood, I frantically pry the knife out of her hands and push her corpse to the side. The rain has let up some, making it easy to see Ishida standing as motionless as a statue. He was all this time watching, waiting to see what happened, knowing Orion would wear me out. Getting Arik out of the game so quickly was a fucking fluke, he and I know it, but the dead General's crushed head has made Ishida cautious.

I can't run, I can scarcely stand; Arik and Orion have seen to that. Exhausted but determined, I desperately clutch the knife in my hand.

Ishida doesn't use weapons. He thinks they're beneath him, a waste of the power he can unleash with his bare hands. I've seen them at work; I've seen them subdue and kill. Even at the top of my game, I would never face this guy in a fair fight. I'd hit him from behind, get the first attack in and pray that it was fatal. But I don't have that luxury now. I don't even have the benefit of being able to use both my hands.

"I have always wished that Luck would favour me as it does you," Ishida says. Watching my legs shake, he waits for them to give out. "This strange weather...it's as though it was sent here specifically for you. Without this storm you would already be dead."

"Shut the fuck up." I'm not in the mood for a conversation. Waves of throbbing pain are making it hard to concentrate; the effort of standing is straining the limits of my endurance and my knees are buckling. Right now, I don't care if he kills me. I just want to knock out his front teeth. I'm going to need him to attack sooner rather than later if I'm going to have the strength. "Get over here and fight."

"And you have always been Locket's greatest weakness," he continues, ignoring my challenge. "I've heard these strange rumours about you two. But of course, it's impossible. Locket might fuck you, but he'd never be your lover."

"I guess you didn't see Amber as a weakness." No emotion whatsoever flickers in his ruthless eyes. I spit blood onto the wet pavement and sneer at my executioner. "You fucked her and then you killed her. I guess Luck didn't favour her."

"She was the most amazing woman I'd ever met," he replies. Despite his claim, however, he still shows no emotion. "It was *I* that Luck did not favour when I ended her life."

My eyes roll skyward. I don't know how much longer I can stay on my feet. Ishida doesn't move towards me. He isn't afraid but he knows that I'm not down yet. That means I can still fight. Despite my annoyance, I have to applaud his good sense. Exhausted, I fall to my right knee.

Ishida shrugs as he finally walks towards me. "That's enough small talk."

I await Death with startling composure and serenity. At first I sluggishly raise my knife, but I drop it quickly again to my side. I've decided it's best to look completely helpless. I'll save my last burst of energy to ram my fist into his mouth. Then I can go out with a smile on my face.

Eyes narrowed in fury, Locket appears next to Ishida. With lightning fast movement, the last General puts an arm around the front of Ishida's neck, forcing the smaller man to bend backwards. With a monstrous flex of Locket's shoulder and arm muscles, Ishida's neck cracks. Through a haze of pain and adrenaline, I watch Locket unceremoniously drop his victim, face-first, into a puddle.

I can't help but say something sarcastic. "Shit, Locket. I'm sure he would have let you kill me if you'd just *asked*."

"How badly are you injured?" Locket demands.

"One quick jerk of my neck," I say, dropping my knife. I can't be sure if I'm joking or not. "That's all it will take."

"You and your death wish," he replies, unimpressed.

"I won't even fight."

"You mean you *can't* fight."

His intense blue gaze scans my body. Strangely self-conscious, I run a shaking hand over my hair before gasping with pain.

Locket flinches when he sees the state of my right side. It must be severely mangled for his lips to curl over his teeth like that. Lowering himself to his knees beside me, he pulls the shredded pieces of my shirt away from my battered ribs. The tattered material falls back as he reaches into his pocket. Ripping open a small, silver packet he grabs my chin and orders me to open my mouth. I shoot him a woozily unimpressed look as he pours a white powder onto my tongue.

"Swallow," he commands. I recognize the bitter taste in my mouth. Painkillers; potent ones. I swallow the meds without protest. "I'm taking you to a Doctor."

A pleasantly heavy feeling spreads through my limbs, taking all of my pain and all of my questions with it. Lifting me into his arms, Locket rushes me to an isolated emergency tube. As he fits himself into the provided compartment he struggles to keep me balanced on it's side. The lights turn on automatically once he puts his weight on the seat. A small engine roars to life. Placing me between his legs, he slides us onto our backs and shuts the compartment's door.

The calm City voice welcomes us. <Enter coordinates or wait to be delivered to the next available Doctor.> Locket pounds a series of numbers into a key pad on the compartment door. <Coordinates accepted. Doctor Samson Nyria is available.>

"Who is that?" I ask through my drug-induced haze.

"You don't know her," he answers.

The compartment beeps three times and the engine fires. We are being raced at break-neck speeds along the underground emergency tubes of the City. Next stop N Sector, otherwise known as the Hospital.

31

"What have you brought me, Jace?"

A surprised and unconsciously alluring voice penetrates the foggy haze in my brain. The combination of painkillers and physical trauma has made my muscles turn to rubber. When I hear the question, however, I manage to roll my head to the side. A delightfully beautiful woman, with long black hair pulled into a braid and glowing black eyes, is patiently waiting for an answer.

Groggy from the drugs I drool all over the left side of my face. The white powder is good stuff.

Locket pushes me into a sitting position so that he can slip out from beneath me. I attempt to clean up the spit but I can't seem to find my face. Mumbling an apology, I chortle at my lack of motor skills. It feels amazing to be so relaxed. Nothing can disturb me.

Smiling serenely, the Doctor looks to Locket. "Spinal trauma?"

"Right side is messed up," Locket says, "she got mixed up with the wrong people."

"And I suppose you need this to be off the record?"

Putting one arm under my shoulders and his other arm under my knees, Locket effortlessly lifts me out of the compartment. Even in my drugged state I notice how he's avoiding her warm gaze. The Doctor, who

I'm guessing is Nyria, studies Locket's cool expression. It doesn't seem to be hurting her feelings at all, but I can see nostalgia, maybe even regret, in her friendly gaze.

"Uh oh," I blurt out, "sexual tension!"

Doctor Nyria's eyebrows shoot up in surprise. A mischievous gleam sparkles in her eyes. "Your friend is very observant."

"Never bring a loud-mouthed, drugged psychic to an old lover's re-union," Locket mutters. "Where should I put her?"

"On the table will be fine," Nyria answers.

Locket gently sets me down. I feel as though I'm gliding even though my body is completely still. The ceiling undulates soothingly while bright lights dance across its surface. Mesmerized, I barely notice when Nyria peels the tattered fabric away from my mangled side.

"What happened to her?"

"Diamond studded knuckle dusters, I assume. Knife wounds to the arms, shoulders and chest. I didn't get there until after this happened." Locket's tone is laced with a severe self-reprimand. Concern fills his bright blue eyes as he finally meets his former lover's gaze. "Will she be all right?"

Without a word, Nyria presses a button on the side of the table. A ma-chine whirs to life. Gliding along tracks screwed into the ceiling, it bleeps towards me. I watch it suspiciously, but I'm too relaxed to care if it's going to take my kidneys. A blue light slowly scans my body.

"Shattered ribs," Nyria mutters as she studies a screen. She points at something on the scan. "Internal bleeding... She either needs surgery or a few hours in a restoration bed. I'm only trained for diagnostics, Jace. I can't perform the procedures. I assume neither of you are wealthy enough for the bed."

"My employer is," Locket replies. Reaching into his pocket, he pro-duces a shiny credit balance. "Slide it through. If someone asks you say I was injured. Don't tell them about her."

"I don't want to know, do I?" Nyria shoots him a disappointment look after she examines the card in her hands. "It's these situations that I never missed. I'll prep the bed. You bring her through in a few minutes."

Walking over to a metal door, she slides the card through a box hanging on the wall. It beeps a few times and the door unlocks. Locket watches her leave. His expression is unreadable, but I'm not really concentrating on him. The drugs are starting to wear off. The dull, aching pain pulsing down my right side slices through the fog in my brain. I know that it's going to get worse. Groaning, I close my eyes and force back my tears.

"Nice woman," I say through clenched teeth. "You want to tell me what the fuck is going on?"

"Nope."

I expected that answer. He's not going to tell me anything and my curiosity is the only thing that's keeping the pain at bay. Another dose of those painkillers will probably make me an addict and that's not a risk that I'm prepared to take. Users are the human trash of the City. You can see their pathetic carcasses huddled in alleys; no one cares about them and they couldn't care less about anything other than their next dose. I'll take agony over that any day.

Locket watches me struggle with the pain and shakes his head angrily. "You should have stayed with your crew. It's a miracle you're alive."

"Those are going around, I hear." Sucking in a painful breath, I let the air out slowly. "I had my reasons for leaving."

"Any of them include common sense?"

"I haven't been fully stocked on that for a while." I return his livid glare with a curious one. "Why didn't you kill me?"

"What does it matter?" he asks.

"Ishida said something before you showed up, I guess curiosity is getting the better of me. You've hated me from day one. You hate me so much you nearly had me sold into slavery; you even had Sherman Quentin breathing down my neck. So why am I still alive? You must need something from me and I want to know what it is."

Everything is starting to hurt; the pain grows exponentially with each passing moment. I keep hoping that my brain will give out so that I can sink into sweet nothingness. Standing thoughtfully at my side, Locket watches me grow pale from agony. He slowly leans over me.

"Let's just get one thing straight," he breathes. "I have never hated you."

The pain ebbs for a blissful second. Ensnared by his intense gaze, I respond before thinking. "I've always hated you."

"And you say you don't have any common sense."

Nyria's voice over the intercom breaks our bizarrely intimate moment. <I'm ready for her.>

Pulling away, Locket lifts me into his arms again. The pain returns with ruthless cruelty. I try to block it out, but my body is insisting that I pay attention. Clutching at Locket's shirt, I bury my head in his chest. His warmth is comforting. It's all that stands between me and giving up.

A restoration bed is a lidless rectangular box that restores damaged tissue back to health. It has something to do with energy and how it interacts with living cells. I'm no Doctor or Scientist, but Jack used to work with them before he became a Criminal. His family wanted to shorten the time it takes for the bed to heal life-threatening injuries. Obviously, the worse the damage to a body the longer it takes to repair. Some people lie inside of these things for days. Putting someone in one for over twenty-four hours, however, is a risky move. According to Jack, the bed can eventually take over automatic functions, such as the heartbeat. If that happens, the patient goes into cardiac arrest when you take them out. There's no way to reverse that side effect.

Locket carries me through the door into a small room. The restoration bed is calmly awaiting my arrival. Placing me in its warm interior, Locket flashes me a reassuring glance before stepping away. Nyria fastens small plastic loops around my forehead, wrists and ankles. She cuts the ruined portion of my shirt in half and tapes a warm, spicy smelling compound on my shattered ribs.

"You're going to feel sick at first, but it won't last. If you experience more intense pain than what you've already felt, press this button." She slips something plastic into my hand and I feel the button under the tip of my thumb. "Otherwise, you just have to wait. You can fall asleep if you want to—I encourage it—but if you can't we'll be right here to keep you company. Ready?"

I love the way her voice wraps warmly around my frazzled nerves. If she would just keep talking I think I could fall asleep. I nod my head and my stomach suddenly flips. Grimacing, I wait for the nausea to pass; she wasn't kidding about feeling sick. Beyond exhausted, I let my eyes drift closed. I don't realize I've fallen asleep until voices penetrate my heavy slumber.

"Thanks for this," I hear Locket say to Nyria.

She's still too attracted to him not to sound awkward. "It's not a problem."

"I didn't know what was going on until it was too late," Locket continues. "If I'd been quicker I wouldn't be bothering you for this kind of help."

"For three years I kept hoping you'd *make up* a reason to come and see me. But even in the years we were together your mind was always somewhere else. I don't know why I expected it to be any different when we were apart." Her voice never rises but I can sense her bitterness. "You're only here because you had no other choice, aren't you?"

Locket doesn't offer her any comfort. "Our worlds can't mix. We knew that from the beginning."

"Yes," she agrees, deliberately calm, "we always knew that we couldn't last. But you didn't have to completely disappear when I was ordered to procreate."

"I didn't want to complicate your life. But that doesn't mean I didn't want to see you. And I did…more than I thought I would."

The dense pause in their conversation makes me fidget. My right side doesn't hurt anymore. When I look down at my body I notice that the blood has dried onto my clothes; the wounds from Orion's knives have healed. A little embarrassed by my eavesdropping, I peek over the side of the box. The Doctor is leaning on the wall, staring at the floor. Locket gazes at her apologetically.

"Remember the time you told me that you were looking for the woman that you would move the stars for?" Nyria finally asks with a note of fear. "Will you move the stars for her?"

"I said that a long time ago," Locket admits with a sheepish expression, "and I was trying to get laid."

"People say things like that all the time. And then, one day, they meet *the one*. My brother told me that just before he moved to V Sector to be with Yvonne."

"He sounds like a born romantic."

"Not really," Nyria returns. "My first born looks so much like him I almost feel like I have him back."

"You should let me smuggle him here for a day," Locket suggests. "That's something I've always wanted to do for you."

"And I tell you again and again that I won't accept those kinds of gifts."

He offers her a teasing smile. "You and your law abiding ways."

I don't want to interrupt but I can't watch their little drama all day. "Um, how long have I been in here?"

Locket saunters over and peers down at me. "She turned it off about a half an hour ago. You should be good as new."

I slowly sit up and look around the bare room. Locket's right, there's no pain and I feel energized. He offers me his hand but I ignore it as I crawl out of the bed. Tentatively touching my ribs I discover strange ridges on my skin.

"*'Good as new'* never applies to any major injury," Nyria says. "Your right side will always be more delicate now. You'll see the scars when you find a mirror. That's the price we pay for quicker healing."

"I'm not going to complain," I mutter, mystified by how good I feel.

"Jace will have to apply a compress to your ribs for the next month," she continues. She hands bandages and a large jar of cream to Locket. "Your cells have been super-charged and most patients experience burning or itchiness, even scaling over the traumatized area. The compress will reduce the side-effects."

I wave off the Locket suggestion. "I can do it on my own."

"No, I'm afraid you can't," she insists. "Jace will have two hands to apply the compress, and he has the necessary training to identify complications. Otherwise you'd have to come back and see me every three or four days. From what I've gathered about your lifestyle you won't have time for that."

It's hard for me to argue with Doctors. They always sound like they know way more than I do. But I have a good feeling about Nyria. She's not lying to me about what's going on. I glance unhappily at my unlikely hero.

"We should get out of here," he says.

He hands me the bandages and jar. Next thing I know he's pressed a small gadget to my neck. My body goes limp. He's hit me with some kind of paralysis drug. Shocked, I fall unceremoniously into his waiting arms.

"Jace, what are you doing?" Nyria rushes to my side and checks my vitals.

"Trust me, it's as much for her health as mine," Locket says. I'm as floppy as a rag doll. My head rolls back and forth as he picks me up. "She doesn't trust me. This is the only way I can get her where she'll be safe without either of us getting hurt."

I'd like to kick Locket's ass, but all I can seem to do right now is blink menacingly. After a few seconds I can't even do that anymore. Frustrated and angry I can only watch as Locket's deadly serious expression silences Nyria's protest. She picks the bandages and jar off the floor, puts them in a sack, and hands them to Locket.

"Luck," she blesses.

Putting a hand on her heart and then touching mine she performs an old ritual to invoke inner power. As a small kindness she closes my eyes so that they won't dry out.

I am now blind and paralyzed—completely at Locket's mercy.

32

We're in the dilapidated basement of an abandoned building. That fucking bastard has tied me to a fucking chair and he ties a wicked fucking knot.

Tucking the bottom of my shirt into my bra, he shoots me a wary look. "Just hold still. This will take longer than either of us wants if you keep struggling."

I had no idea I could swallow this much fury. Staring daggers at my kidnapper, I do as he instructs. He opens the jar of medication and scoops out a liberal amount of yellow cream onto his fingers. Gently, but still watching me with one eye, he rubs it into the affected area of my skin. His blue gaze flickers over the burn scars on the left side of my stomach. A moment later his fingers brush over my stretch marks, my only external proof that I gave birth. His eyes narrow thoughtfully before he continues his ministrations.

"You're a scaler," he mutters under his breath, "but it's better than surgery and weeks of recuperation."

Pulling a bandage tight around my side he smoothes it over the cream and tapes it down. Amazed at his gentle but firm touch, I do my best not to enjoy his warmth. Healing hands—that's what everyone would say he has if he wasn't a killer.

He puts the jar and bandages into a bag. Hanging the beat-up leather over his shoulders, he disappears around a corner. Anxious about his plans I quickly get to work on the ropes.

These knots are amazing! I can hardly move my wrists. When I struggle the rope just gets tighter. Soon I'm going to lose all feeling in my fingers. If I wasn't gagged I'd scream in frustration. As it is, all I can manage is a pathetic groan.

Locket returns with a towel slung around his neck. He wipes his face a few times and throws it to the side. Grabbing a worn out chair and placing it right in front of me, he sits down.

"We need to talk," he says. I manage a huff of indignation through my gag. "Fine, I need to talk. You need to listen.

"You underestimated what Madman was willing to do to get you out of the way. I thought you were smarter than this; I thought you'd at least know to stay underground."

He has no right to criticize me! Livid, I continue to struggle against the ropes. They're biting into my flesh but I'm ignoring the pain. I want to tell him to fuck off, I want to smash a fist into his face and feel bones crunch under my knuckles.

"Jack should have dosed you like I suggested," Locket continues, "but he didn't want to betray your trust. He was skeptical even when Wulff explained about your little *episodes*. I should have told him that Madman is willing to cut off his right arm if it means taking you out. I made a mistake. Pay attention when I tell you this! He only ordered your termination; your crew is still safe. But if you're seen within a block of Kentucky's hideout, he'll take them all out without a second thought. They won't have a chance to run for cover."

His words give me pause. Confident he has my attention, Locket removes my gag. I don't struggle, I don't scream, but I have to ask. "Why is Lyons so obsessed with me?"

"People are talking about you. They believe in you."

"They're fucking crazy," I return.

Locket shrugs solemnly, "... the essence of faith. You're a living Legend now and you only have yourself to blame."

My eyes flash angrily; I hate it when my enemies are wiser than me. Made wretched from the truth I fight back my tears. "What am I going to do?"

"Leave that to me," he answers. Producing a small knife from his boot, Locket leans over and cuts the ropes. He offers a hand to help me up. "I can get you back to your crew."

Looking up at my unlikely champion, I finally surrender. My fingers slide into his strong, welcoming hand. He grips my palm firmly and one side of his mouth lifts up. Warmth creeps into his cool gaze and his sincere smile of assurance captivates me. Trusting Locket is making me feel safe. It's a painful reminder that I'm the one who can't be trusted.

"I'm a liability *not* a Legend."

"That might be true," Locket replies.

"Why are you helping me?"

He hesitates with his answer. Stepping closer, he studies my baffled expression. "Because I'm just as crazy as the rest of them. Follow me."

Follow him? I'm not ready to go back. After what happened with the bounty hunters I can't feel secure in a hideout. Before I return I need to guarantee that no one will ever lead the Cops to our door ever again. I'm going to keep the crew safe no matter what the cost.

"I saw Lily today," I say

Locket's expression hardens. He already knows what I'm going to do. "Sonora."

"You know where she is. I'll need a knife."

"Only let the scavengers see you," he charges under his breath. Reaching behind his back, he produces his blade. "She's made a small home for herself in 12th block. It isn't hard to find. I'll be waiting."

My hand wraps around the hilt of his knife. A surge of power rushes through my body as I envision Clarissa's hair knotted around my fingers as I tear her head from her neck. She made a bad fucking mistake and now she's going to pay for it.

33

12th block—I lived here with Ivana.

Scanning my old haunt, I note the same run-down buildings, the same monolithic slabs of cement that no one will ever bother to remove, the same twisted rebar sticking out of crumbling walls. This type of place is a haven for scavengers. It's where they perpetuate the purest hierarchy. The stronger ones take whatever they want and live wherever they want. The weaker ones hoard what they can. When they die their bodies will be flung into collection bins. If anyone survives they graduate into street gangs. Only the strongest become Criminals.

Ivana and I were strong. We slept under the remains of a mechanics shop. It was cool in the heat and easy to defend. Those were interesting days, living moment to moment. I was happy if I had a full stomach. But Ivana was a victim of her own greed. I didn't realize it back then, but her eye for all that glitters was a death sentence. It was only a matter of time.

Wrapped in a cloak, I listen to the rain run down the stiff leather. The City wasn't designed for this kind of weather and water is gathering in the streets. Orphans race through the large pools, laughing and splashing, their voices rising happily. Today, they are children instead of scavengers. There's room for everyone. Content to watch, I enjoy their antics.

Sonora is playfully wrestling with another orphan. Shouting and hollering, they drag each other into the water. The boy breaks free of Sonora's hold but she tackles him once again. Screaming with excitement, they play a wild game that has no rules. Soaked through, they collapse happily into the water.

Their laughter wraps warmly around my heart. I think about Ivana, about the games we used to play when we had full stomachs, those times when we could find a small piece of happiness. It rips out my guts to know what I have to do. I am disgusted with Clarissa Tyler... Sonora. Watching her play with her friend makes it difficult to see her as little more than a child. She had a future; she could have gotten off the streets. But she destroyed her chances when she crossed me.

Hardening my heart, I step towards her.

The scavengers bristle at my intrusion; my presence reminds them of their grim reality, but they move out of my way. They know better than to take me on. Sonora isn't aware of me yet. She's still laughing, still shouting and playing. It isn't until I put my arm around her neck that she stops smiling.

"We have an appointment," I whisper into her ear.

Lifting her struggling form off the ground, I haul her into an abandoned building. Sick children snarl angrily before dragging themselves out of their makeshift beds. They'll wait impatiently outside until it's safe for them to return. To them, Sonora is already dead and they're better off if she is—one less person to fight for food and shelter.

"I warned you I wasn't a novice." Throwing her against the crumbling wal,l I produce Locket's knife. "You've sealed your own fate."

"Daryl...I. Please—*don't.*"

It's hard not to see the girl standing in front of me, the ten year old with the innocent grey-green eyes. I've never killed anyone so much smaller than me and I can feel how wrong it is in every bone in my body. But I remember the crew lying wretchedly on the floor. I remember the bounty hunters preparing to haul them off to the Prison. I think about Wulff and Frenzy disappearing into that unspeakable place.

My fury takes over. Shaking with anger, I grab her hair and force her head back. The pulse in her throat throbs; her eyes are wide with fear. It reminds me of Ivana all those years ago. Locket's hands around her head, the light going out of her eyes.

Sonora is too frightened to struggle. She's so scared she's making strange mewling sounds. The pathetic noise makes me hesitate with the killing blow. But then I remember the Prison—she's the one who sent me back there.

That thought banishes my uncertainty. I place the knife against her throat. The sharp blade makes it too easy. I never noticed until now, what little effort is required to slice through flesh. Sonora's life spills out of the wound, coating my hand and her chest with dark red blood. Thick with misery, I watch the life drain from her eyes. My own close involuntarily and tears spill down my cheeks.

Her body slumps to the floor and I tumble after it. Turning onto my back, I examine the cracks in the ceiling, the cement threatening to crash down. It will give soon. When it does it will take everyone with it.

34

There's a veil between reality and me; I'm watching everything from under water. I don't know how long I've been here but the tears are gone and I'm empty. Staring at Sonora's corpse, the white face and unblinking eyes, I realize it's over. She's returned to the Origins and I've crossed a line I didn't know existed.

The first time is never easy. It's always a shock to the system, a sucker punch to the solar plexus. Everything goes white for a moment and you know that you've changed indefinitely. There's no moving backwards; there's no getting back to the way you were. I already know that I couldn't let her live. Not in this lifetime, not in this world. This was about survival. You can't let anybody cross you without making them pay. The moment Sonora helped Madman, she invited Death in the form of me and I curse her for it. I curse Lyons for involving a child.

I curse myself for being able to kill her.

"She went to Lyons with the proposal." I don't respond. No matter what Locket says I still a I'm a child-killer. "It was her idea. She bargained for complete access to the Madman lines, a false identity card, and a monthly allowance."

"A new life," I murmur. The information penetrates the dullness of my brain. "What was she still doing here?"

"It was her home," Locket answers. "She didn't know what to do with her new found wealth."

"She suffered from a lack of imagination," I diagnose woodenly. She was too young to understand the possibilities. "Locket, why are you working for Lyons?"

At first, he steels himself against my sorrow; the coldness returns to his gaze. But then, just as quickly, he softens. "He has something I need."

I nod quietly at his vague explanation. There's no need to delve. It's enough to know that Locket is still an independent at heart. Slowly rising to my feet, I hold out his bloodstained knife.

"Keep it," he says. "You took it off of me after you beat me to a bloody pulp—it's a trophy. Ishida turned on Madman, I had to kill him, and you took me down from behind. I don't know where you are, I don't know if you're going to go public."

"You think Lyons is going to buy that?"

Locket shrugs. "It's none of your business if he doesn't."

"So, we aren't friends yet," I realize, "even after all of this."

"No," he confirms. But his gentle gaze helps me understand that we aren't enemies. "I can't always make up reasons not to kill you. Stay out of my way. Don't even entertain the thought of coming near. I'll find you when your bandages need to be changed."

Despite my disappointment, I agree. "Don't forget."

"I'll take you back."

He pulls a cloak over his head, hiding his face, and I follow him into the streets. I don't give myself the luxury of looking back. What's done is done and I can't change it.

Locket leads me back to the building where he tied me to the chair. Striding towards what looks like a destroyed table, he pulls on one if its legs. Something pops then releases and a piece of the wall springs open.

My curiosity brings me back to life. Excited at the prospect of a hidden door, I resist the urge to clap my hands like a child.

Locket guides me through a maze of cramped, dirty passages. It doesn't occur to me until a few minutes into the adventure that this musty path is somehow familiar. My mind is screaming at me to remember. All the clues are here but I can't put them together.

"Don't make any sudden movements," Locket instructs.

Staring at what looks like a dead end, he searches for something on the wall. An ominous click sets my teeth on edge—traps are engaging. We're in the foyer of someone's hideout. A camera slides out of the wall, examines Locket's face and returns to its small home. The traps neutralize and a hidden door to our left pops open.

"After you," Locket says.

I have no more doubts about where I am. Rows upon rows of tables, piled high with the City's technological trash, spread out for a quarter mile or so. Little robots of all shapes zip around the underground room, sorting through the crap with speedy efficiency. Before I can turn around and fix Locket with a quizzical look, I hear the hydraulics of Kentucky Jim's metal legs clanking towards us. Confused, I look back at the hidden passage. I didn't know that entrance existed.

"Considering you've come through the back door I already know this isn't a social call," Kentucky says.

"Ran into a little trouble with Madman," Locket answers. He pulls the door closed behind him. "Where are the others?"

"Went out looking for this one." He sneers as he jabs a finger at me. "They're afraid."

Kentucky and Locket continue talking as though they've known each other for years. Sweet Sky! I always knew the old man had an errand boy, I just never guessed it was Locket.

Kentucky shoots me a disapproving look. "I knew you were trouble from the moment you crawled in through the rat hole. I should have sealed it shut the day we met."

"You really think that would have kept me out?" I gratefully fall in to our old pattern. "It only would have made getting into your place more of a challenge."

"The great living Legend speaks!" Despite the deep frown on his face I see a twinkle of humour shining in Kentucky's eyes. He notes the blood on my hands and cringes. "You know where the shower is."

"Yeah, I know where it is."

I turn around to thank Locket but he has already slipped out. My heart sinks with disappointment. It would have been nice to say good-bye. But I'm a hardened Criminal, his disappearance shouldn't bother me so much.

Besides, I should know better than to fall for someone like him.

35

The shower washes the blood away but not the grief. I don't want to think about it, but I can still feel the knife slicing through Sonora's throat; I can still see the life draining from her eyes. Disturbed by the dark intensity of the memory, I try to banish the images with scalding water.

Stop thinking. Let it be. For now, just let it be.

But my mind refuses to cooperate. Every time I push one memory away another one takes its place. Frustrated, I turn off the water and step out of the shower. The large, fluffy towel envelops me completely as I sit on the floor.

Stop it, stop it, stop it.

Voices are creeping back into my head. Whispering at first, they intrude on my sanity.

Are you coming back…? A woman asks. *Can you come back…? I don't know how much longer I can last in here.*

You're a coward, another woman screams.

Wretched with guilt I answer her. "I already know that."

I saw you in the courtyard. I saw how you quaked and sobbed. A man taunts. *You're nothing, like everyone in here. You don't exist. Nothing exists if it's outside of this place.*

"Jealous!"

Yet another man asks for my help. *Give my sister a message. Tell her I need her to find my children.*

"Why the fuck should I?"

My anguish drives a hole through my heart. I can't help them. The Prisoners are begging but I'm powerless. I bury my head in the towel and put my hands over my ears. The voices become louder and more demanding. Rocking back and forth I plead with them to leave me alone. I can't do anything!

A sharp knock at the door brings me back to reality.

"There are other things you can do around here," Kentucky shouts. "You're not my guest."

Pulling myself together, I try to clear my thoughts. I'm standing but I don't remember getting to my feet. Confused, I stare at my finger on the fogged mirror—I've used a code to write something in the steam.

SAVE US.

Shocked I put my back against the solid wall. I don't know what it means, but I have my suspicions. There's only one reply I can make. "Fuck you."

It took Jack's crew a month to organize a plan to get me out. Imagine the time it would take for a full-scale siege. Even knowing a way in, I can't start plucking them out one by one. The prisoners are dreaming. But, in that place, there's nothing else for them to do.

Frantically pulling on my clothes I retreat from the bathroom. Eventually, the steam will fade, taking their message with it.

36

*D*raw *a new* *line*.

A new line. It isn't that simple: every time I find a new one I discover that I'm capable of crossing it. I can't see the purpose of pretending that I won't do whatever it takes to survive. That includes putting Sonora down. I know, without question, that I would do it again. I also know, the second time round, killing an orphan will be much easier. Oddly enough, this realization doesn't disturb me. It gives me a new found sense of peace.

I'm finally coming to terms with myself.

"You need to earn your keep," Kentucky says, interrupting my thoughts. He points towards a mop and bucket. "While you're here, you work."

"Why don't you have a machine for that?"

"Machine…? Ha!" He laughs heartily. "Don't clean yourself into a corner. Get on your hands and knees if you have to."

"How long have you known Locket?" I ask, knowing he won't answer. "How long has he been your errand boy?"

"*Errand boy*… Never did like how that sounds. Sweet mother of Christ, he doesn't run any damn errands."

"Sweet mother of who…?"

"Get to work. I've known him longer than I've known you. That's all you're getting."

"Known him longer than you've known me." Crossing my arms over my chest I fix his retreating form with an evil stare. "That's absolutely no help."

"Get to work!"

I don't grab the mop and bucket. Kentucky's metallic body disappears around a pile of junk and I head for his kitchen. The floors can wait: I need caffeine. Filling a mug with hot coffee I sit down at the scarred, wobbling kitchen table. Everything in this place needs a fresh coat of paint. I'm sure that will be my next job if I ever get around to following Kentucky's commands.

As I wait for the hot drink to cool I reach for the sugar. The old tin box sits just out of reach on the other end of the table. I could shift to grab it, but I remember my first and only conversation with Sonora. She thought I'd used a magic trick to move the box; Wulff claimed I was telekinetic; in the Prison, I told my chains to open and they did.

Tense with curiosity, I examine my scarred hand. There's no harm in trying.

Staring at the sugar tin I place my hand, palm facing the old box, on the table. All it takes is a moment of concentration—the box slides quickly across the scarred wood. Bewildered, I catch it and study its dented surface. There's no explaining it away this time, I am able to move objects with my mind. The discovery sends a chill down my spine. There are too many questions surrounding my newfound power. Only one thing is for certain, no one else can do what I just did. That gives me an edge.

"That's a new one," someone comments from behind me.

My stomach jumps into my throat. Dropping the tin, I whirl around to find Jack standing a few inches away from me. Relieved, I put a hand on my chest and will my heart to slow down. Every time with him! One of these days he's going to sneak up on me and I really will have a heart attack.

"*Jack!* you have to find a new hobby."

Eyes gleaming with impish fun, Jack studies me with calm curiosity; my telekinesis interests him. But we both know he isn't going to ask. He'll wait for me to come to him. That's always been his style.

"It occurs to me that I should have asked you this sooner," he finally says. "Are you still with us?"

"Still... with you? I don't understand the question."

"A part of the crew," he qualifies. "I assumed you were, that was my fault. Leaving us like that, when it was safer to stay put, making us worry, making us think the worst... that was the action of a loner. You don't trust us."

"No," I disagree, pleading with him to understand. "I don't trust myself. I almost killed the crew when you were gone. I was going to. It's a miracle I didn't. Knowing that, we'd have to keep me dosed when you aren't around. I couldn't exchange one jail for another."

His thoughtful silence draws me into a fit of self-loathing. Standing there, waiting for his response, I think about the crew. They broke into the Prison to save me and I repaid them with nothing but fear. Something sick and miserable opens inside of me. I'm more of a coward than I want to admit.

"You don't have any faith in us," Jack finally states.

"There's that word again," I return, biting back bitter tears. Too ashamed to meet Jack's steadfast gaze I stare at his chest. "*Faith...* I don't even know what it means. Does it mean dragging your friends into a deep, dark hole with you? Forcing them to cope with what they can't understand? Turning them into jailers? Making them hate what they used to love?"

"Not at all," Jack replies. "It just means trusting them to do what they can. Everything else you leave to Luck."

"Those questions were rhetorical." Wiping at my eyes, I finally meet his searching gaze. "I don't know what to do, Jack."

"I'd start small," he advises. "We're going to finalize the plans for the new hideout when everyone gets back. If you're not here, we won't make a space for you."

"Lyons will tear the City apart looking for me."

"I know," he replies, unmoved. "I saw what you did to Orion, Arik and Ishida. He probably already has three more lined up. The Madman choosing the Generals... it's never been done before."

"We need to take him out! He'll rip through you to get to me."

"You already know that's not an option," Jack asserts. "Lyons is still too powerful and too cautious. Thanks to you, there are still places in the City he can't reach. If you stay, we lay low."

"What about my *episodes*?"

"If you give us the chance we'll take care of you," Jack says. Putting a friendly hand on my shoulder, he gives it a warm squeeze. "We'll find a way to keep everyone safe. But you're either all the way in or all the way out. There's no in between here."

That is his final decision. Staying means I must respect it. Even the independents have a power system, unless you're a loner. I could make a life for myself without the crew. The line to A is enough to keep me in jobs and credits for the rest of my life. But, even knowing the crew was here I let Locket bring me back. That wasn't the action of a loner.

Sensing that I'm making a decision, Jack disappears behind a pile of junk and I'm left to my tumultuous thoughts. Before long, however, I hear footsteps and voices. The rest of the crew has returned.

"Heath," Wulff calls, "other than that pile of corpses there's no sign of her. The City is flooded with water *and* supposed Daryl sightings. There aren't any good leads. At least the sky is clearing. We'll go back out in a few hours."

"That's fine," Jack returns. "Leave it up to her."

"But what if she's hurt?" Frenzy protests. "She might be unconscious and slowly bleeding to death in a back alley. No way she killed three Generals and came out without a scratch."

"It was her choice to leave in the first place," Jack gently reminds him. "There was never any guarantee that she was going to come back. You know it, I know it."

"But...we can't just *leave* her," Frenzy pleads. "Not with Madman's goons out for blood. Give us another couple of days. I need this, Jackson."

"We all need it," Wulff corrects.

Stretching my psychic talent I see Jack leaning against an old, steel table as he considers their request. He knows I'm listening to every word.

"I won't stop you," he finally says. "But, for now, we need to get to work. Kentucky can't let us stay here forever."

Torn, I listen to their excited voices. The flooded streets, the new hideout, the chance to find me... they all love a good challenge. Frenzy pulls out Marietta's rectangle. As he studies the strange markings he hums one of my favourite tunes and I tap my foot to the familiar beat. Wulff and Jules break off to one side of the piles of junk. Jules hasn't said anything for finding me but she hasn't said anything against finding me either. If I stay, we'll have a few things to sort out. Maybe I can toughen her up.

Kentucky gave the crew full access to everything he isn't already using. Sorting through a few piles, Wulff shouts excitedly when he finds something. Jules holds the rusted metal in her hands and shrugs.

"I'm guessing it's something useful?"

Wulff laughs at Jules' confused expression. Frenzy continues to hum and Jack places his equipment on the steel table. He's going to clean it while he waits for my decision. He may have given the crew a few days but he knows it doesn't matter. If I choose to leave they won't find me. The only way they see me again is if I stay.

I pull out Jace Locket's knife. Ignoring the wicked blade, I study the beautifully carved hilt and remember what I used to assume about him. He was cold and violent, with no merit or depth. People can surprise you if you let them.

I suddenly realize that the crew is my family, my oasis in this fucked up life. It's time to start believing in them.

My decision brings a surge of strength with it. Walking into the open, I take a seat across from Jack. He gently dusts off his equipment and shoots me a proud smile. Neither of us alerts the others, they'll see me soon enough. The earthy smell of Jack's leather softener wafts through the air, reminding me of happy years spent in a cramped hideout.

This is a leap of faith that I do not want to regret.

Made in the USA
Lexington, KY
16 August 2019